THE CHILDREN OF THE NEW FOREST

THE CHILDREN OF THE NEW FOREST

by

CAPTAIN MARRYAT

ABRIDGED

A BANCROFT

CLASSIC

BANCROFT BOOKS

LONDON

BANCROFT BOOKS
49–50 Poland Street
London W. 1

First published in the "Bancroft Classics" 1967
This impression 1971

430 00091 X

CHAPTER 1

THE CIRCUMSTANCES which I am about to relate to my juvenile readers took place in the year 1647. By referring to the history of England of that date, they will find that England had rebelled; after a civil war of nearly five years King Charles had been defeated, and was a prisoner at Hampton Court. The Cavaliers, or the party who fought for King Charles, had all been dispersed, and the Parliamentary army under Cromwell were beginning to control the Commons.

It was in the month of November in this year that King Charles, accompanied by Sir John Berkely, Ashburnham, and Legg, made his escape from Hampton Court, and rode as fast as the horses could carry them towards that part of Hampshire which led to the New Forest. The king expected that his friends had provided a vessel in which he might escape to France; but in this he was disappointed. There was no vessel ready, and he resolved to go to Titchfield, a seat belonging to the Earl of Southampton. After a long consultation with those who attended him, he yielded to their advice, which was to trust to Colonel Hammond, governor of the Isle of Wight for the Parliament, but who was supposed to be friendly to the king. Whatever might be the feelings of commiseration of Colonel Hammond towards a king so unfortunately situated, he was firm in his duties towards his employers, and the consequence was that King Charles found himself again a prisoner in Carisbrook Castle.

A short distance from the town of Lymington, which is not far from Titchfield, where the king took shelter, but on the other side of Southampton Water, and south of the New Forest to which it adjoins, was a property called Arnwood, which belonged to a Cavalier of the name of Beverley. It was a property of considerable value, being very extensive; it abutted on the New Forest, and might have been supposed to have been a continuation of it. This Colonel Beverley, as we must call him, for he rose to that rank in the king's army, was a valued friend and companion of Prince Rupert's and at last fell in his arms at the battle of Naseby. Colonel Beverley had married into the family of the Villiers, and the issue of his marriage was two sons and two daughters; but his zeal and sense of duty had induced him, at the commencement of the war, to leave his wife and family at Arnwood, and he was fated never to meet them again. The news of his death had such an effect upon Mrs. Beverley that a few months afterwards she followed him to an early tomb, leaving the four children under the charge of an elderly relative till such time as the family of the Villiers could protect them; but this was not at that period possible. The life of a king and many other lives were in jeopardy, and the orphans remained at Arnwood, still under the care of their elderly relation, at the time that our history commences.

The New Forest was first enclosed by William the Conqueror as a royal forest for his own amusement. Since that time to the present day, it has continued a royal domain. At the period of which we are writing, it had an establishment of verderers and keepers, paid by the Crown, amounting to some forty or fifty men. At the commencement of the civil war they remained at their posts, but soon found that their wages were no longer to be obtained; and then, when the king had decided upon raising an army, Beverley, who held a superior office in the forest, enrolled all the young and athletic men who were employed in the forest, and marched them away with him to join the king's army. Some few remained, their age not rendering their services of value, and among them was an old and attached servant of Beverley's, a man above sixty years of age, whose name was Jacob Armitage, and who had obtained the situation through Colonel Beverley's interest. Those who remained in the forest lived in cottages many miles asunder, and indemnified themselves for the nonpayment of their salaries by killing the deer for sale and for their own subsistence.

The cottage of Jacob Armitage was situated on the skirts of the New Forest, about a mile and a half from the mansion of Arnwood; and when Colonel Beverley went to join the king's troops he requested the old man, by his attachment to the family, not to lose sight of Arnwood, but to call there as often as possible to see if he could be of service to Mrs. Beverley. The colonel would have persuaded Jacob to have altogether taken up his residence at the mansion, but to this the old man objected. He had been all his life under the greenwood tree, and could not bear to leave the forest. He promised the colonel that he would watch over his family, and ever be at hand when required; and he kept his word. The death of Colonel Beverley was a heavy blow to the old forester, and he watched over Mrs. Beverley and the orphans with the greatest solicitude; but when Mrs. Beverley followed her husband to the tomb he then redoubled his attentions, and was seldom more than a few hours at a time away from the mansion. The two boys were his inseparable companions, and he instructed them in all the secrets of his own calling. Such was the state of affairs at the time that King Charles made his escape from Hampton Court.

As soon as the escape of Charles I was made known to Cromwell and the Parliament, troops of horses were despatched in every direction to the southward, towards which the prints of the horses' hoofs proved that he had gone. As they found that he had proceeded in the direction of the New Forest, the troops were ordered to scour the forest, in parties of twelve to twenty, while others hastened down to Southampton, Lymington, and every other part of the coast from which the king might be likely to embark. Old Jacob had been at Arnwood on the day before, but on this day he had made up his mind to procure some venison, that he might not go there again empty-handed; for Miss Judith Villiers was very partial to venison. Jacob had gone out accordingly; he had gained his leeward position of a fine buck, and was gradually nearing him by stealth when on a sudden the animal, which had been quietly feeding, bounded away and disappeared in the thicket. At the same time Jacob perceived a small body of horse galloping through the glen in which the buck had been feeding. Jacob had never yet seen the Parliamentary troops, for they had not during the war been sent in that part of the country; but their iron skullcaps, their buff accoutrements, and dark habiliments, assured him that such these must be; so very different were they from the gaily-equipped Cavalier cavalry commanded by Prince Rupert. At the time that they advanced, Jacob had been lying down in the fern near to some low blackthorn bushes; not wishing to be perceived by them, he drew back between the bushes, intending to remain concealed until they should gallop out of sight. But Jacob was disappointed in his expectations of the troops riding past him; on the contrary, as soon as they arrived at an oak tree within twenty yards of where he was concealed, the order was given to halt and dismount, and the old man expected to be immediately discovered; but one of the thorn-bushes was directly between him and the troopers, and effectually concealed him. At last Jacob ventured to raise his head and peep through the bush; and he perceived that the men were loosening the girths of their black horses, or wiping away the perspiration from their sides with handfuls of fern.

A powerfully framed man, who appeared to command the others, was standing with his hand upon the arched neck of his steed. "Spare not to rub down, my men," said he, "for we have tried the mettle of our horses, and have now but one half-hour's breathing time. We must be on, for the work of the Lord must be done."

"They say that this forest is many miles in length and breadth," observed another of the men, "but here is James Southwold, who once was living in it as a verderer; nay, I think that he said he was born and bred in these woods. Was it not so, James Southwold?"

"It is even as you say," replied an active-looking young man; "I was born and bred in this forest, and my father was a verderer before me."

Jacob Armitage immediately recognized the young man in question. He had joined the king's army with the other verderers and keepers. It pained him much to perceive that one who had always been considered a frank, true-hearted young man, and who left the forest to fight in defence of his king, was now turned traitor, and had joined the ranks of the enemy; and Jacob thought how much better it had been for James Southwold if he had never quitted the New Forest, and had not been corrupted by evil company. "He was a good lad," thought Jacob, "and now he is a traitor and a hypocrite."

"If born and bred in this forest, James Southwold," said the leader of the troop, "you must fain know all its mazes and paths. Now, call to mind, are there no secret hiding-places in which people may remain concealed? Peradventure thou mayest point out the very spot where this man Charles may be hidden."

"I do know one dell, within a mile of Arnwood," replied James South-wold, "which might cover double our troop from the eyes of the most wary."

"We will ride there, then," replied the leader. "Arnwood, sayest thou? is not that the property of the Malignant, Cavalier Beverley, who was shot down at Naseby?"

"Even so," replied Southwold; "and many is the day of revelry that I have passed there; many the cup of good ale that I have quaffed."

"And thou shalt quaff it again," replied the leader. "Good ale was not intended only for Malignants, but for those who serve diligently. After we have examined the dell which thou speakest of, we will direct our horses' heads towards Arnwood."

"Who knows but what the man Charles may be concealed in the Malignant's house?" observed another.

"In the day, I should say no," replied the leader; "but in the night the Cavaliers like to have a roof over their heads; and therefore at night, and not before, will we proceed thither."

"I have searched many of their abodes," observed another; "but search is almost in vain. What with their spring panels and secret doors, their false ceilings and double walls, one may ferret for ever and find nothing."

"Yes," replied the leader, "their abodes are full of these Popish abominations; but there is one way which is sure, and if the man Charles be concealed in any house, I venture to say that I will find him. Fire and smoke will bring him forth; and to every Malignant's house within twenty miles will I apply the torch; but it must be at night, for we are not sure of his being housed during the day. James Southwold, thou knowest well the mansion of Arnwood?"

"I know well my way to the offices below—the buttery, the cellar, and the kitchen; but I cannot say that I have ever been into the apartments of the upper house."

"That it needeth not; if thou canst direct us to the lower entrance, it will be sufficient."

"That can I, Master Ingram," replied Southwold.

"Enough, Southwold, enough. Now, my men, we will just ride to the dell: if it conceals not whom we seek, it shall conceal us till tonight, and then the country shall be lighted up with the flames of Arnwood, while we surround the house and prevent escape. Levellers, to horse!"

The troopers sprang upon their saddles, and went off at a hard trot. Southwold leading the way. Jacob remained until they were out of sight, and then rose up. He looked for a short time in the direction in which the troopers had gone, stooped down again to take up his gun, and then said, "There's providence in this; yes, and there's providence in my not having my dog with me, for he would not have remained quiet for so long a time. Who would ever have thought that James Southwold would have turned a traitor! This is a bad world, and I thank Heaven that I have lived in the woods. But there is no time to lose;" and the old forester threw his gun over his shoulder and hastened away in the direction of his own cottage.

"And so the king has escaped," thought Jacob, as he went along, "and he may be in the forest! Who knows but he may be at Arnwood, for he must hardly know where to go for shelter? I must haste, and see Miss Judith immediately. 'Levellers, to horse!' the fellow said. What's a leveller?" thought Jacob.

A large proportion of the Parliamentary army had at this time assumed the name of Levellers, in consequence of having taken up the opinion that every man should be on an equality and property should be equally divided. The hatred of these people to anyone above them in rank or property, especially towards those of the king's party, which mostly consisted of men of rank and property, was unbounded, and they were merciless and cruel to the highest degree. Cromwell had great difficulty in eventually putting them down, which he did at last accomplish by hanging and slaughtering many. Of this Jacob knew nothing; all he knew was, that Arnwood was to be burnt down that night, and that it would be necessary to remove the family. As for obtaining assistance to oppose the troopers, that he knew to be impossible. He had been about eight miles from Arnwood when he had concealed himself in the fern. Jacob first went to his cottage to deposit his gun, saddled his forest pony, and set off for Arnwood. In less than two hours the old man was at the door of the mansion; it was then about three o'clock in the afternoon, and, being in the month of November, there was not so much as two hours of daylight remaining. "I shall have a difficult job with the stiff old lady," thought Jacob, as he rang the bell; "I don't believe that she would rise out of her high chair for old Noll and his whole army at his back. But we shall see."

CHAPTER 2

Before Jacob is admitted to the presence of Miss Judith Villiers we must give some account of the establishment at Arnwood. With the exception of one male servant, who officiated in the house and stable as his services might be required, every man of the household of Colonel Beverley had followed the fortunes of their master, and as none had returned they, in all probability, had shared his fate. Three female servants, with the man above mentioned, composed the whole household. Miss Judith Villiers, therefore, found it difficult to maintain the present household; and although she did not tell Jacob Armitage that such was the case, the fact was, that very often the venison which he brought to the mansion was all the meat that was in the larder. The three female servants held the offices

9

of cook, attendant upon Miss Villiers, and housemaid, the children being under the care of no particular servant, and left much to themselves.

As we have before said, the orphans were four in number; the two eldest were boys, and the youngest were girls. Edward, the eldest boy, was between thirteen and fourteen years old; Humphrey, the second, was twelve; Alice, eleven; and Edith, eight. As it is the history of these young persons which we are about to narrate, we shall say little about them at present, except that for many months they had been under little or no restraint, and less attended to. Their companions were Benjamin, the man who remained in the house, and old Jacob Armitage, who passed all the time he could spare with them. Benjamin was rather weak in intellect, and was a source of amusement rather than otherwise. As for the female servants, one was wholly occupied with her attendance on Miss Judith, who was very exacting, and had a high notion of her own consequence.

"Benjamin," said Jacob, as the other came to the door, "I must speak with the old lady."

"Have you brought any venison, Jacob?" said Benjamin grinning, "else, I reckon, you'll not be over welcome."

"No, I have not; but it is an important business, so send Agatha to her directly."

"I will; and I'll not say anything about the venison."

In a few minutes, Jacob was ushered up by Agatha into Miss Judith Villiers' apartment. The old lady was about fifty years of age, very prim and starched, sitting in a high-backed chair, with her feet upon a stool, and her hands crossed before her, her black mittens reposing upon her snow-white apron.

The old forester made his obeisance.

"You have important business with us, I am told," observed Miss Judith.

"Most important, madam," replied Jacob. "In the first place, it is right that you should be informed that His Majesty King Charles has escaped from Hampton Court."

"His Majesty escaped!" replied the lady.

Jacob then entered into the details of what he had overheard that morning, when he fell in with the troopers, concluding with the information that the mansion would be burned down that very night. He then pointed out the necessity of immediately abandoning the house, as it would be impossible to oppose the troopers.

"And where am I to go to, Jacob?" said Miss Judith calmly.

"I hardly know, madam; there is my cottage, it is but a poor place, and not fit for one like you."

"So I should presume, Jacob Armitage; neither shall I accept your offer. It would ill befit the dignity of a Villiers to be frightened out of her abode by a party of rude soldiers. Happen what will I shall not stir from this—no, not even from this chair. Neither do I consider the danger so great as you suppose. Let Benjamin saddle, and be prepared to ride over to Lymington immediately. I will give him a letter to the magistrate there, who will send us protection."

"But, madam, the children cannot remain here. I will not leave them here. I promised the colonel——"

"Will the children be in more danger than I shall be, Jacob Armitage?" replied the old lady stiffly. "They dare not illtreat me—they may force the buttery and drink the ale—they may make merry with that and the venison which you have brought with you, I presume; but they will hardly venture to insult a lady of the house of Villiers."

"I fear they will venture anything, madam. At all events, they will frighten the children, and for one night they will be better in my cottage."

"Well, then, be it so; take them to your cottage, and take Martha to attend upon the Miss Beverleys. Go down now, and desire Agatha to come to me, and Benjamin to saddle as fast as he can."

"They'll all leave her," thought Jacob; "well, my duty is plain; I'll not leave the children in the house." Jacob then went in search of them, and found them playing in the garden. He called the two boys to him, and told them to follow him. "Now Mr. Edward," said he, "you must prove yourself your father's own son. We must leave this house immediately; come up with me to your rooms, and help me to pack up yours and your sisters' clothes, for we must go to my cottage this night. There is no time to be lost."

"But why, Jacob; I must know why?"

"Because the Parliamentary troopers will burn it down this night."

"But we will fight them, Jacob; we can bolt and bar; I can fire a gun, and hit too, as you know; then there's Benjamin and you."

"And what can you and two men do against a troop of horse, my dear boy? If we could defend the place against them Jacob Armitage would be the first; but it is impossible, my dear boy. Recollect your sisters. Would you have them burnt to death, or shot by these wretches? No, no, Mr. Edward; you must do as I say, and lose no time. Let us pack up what will be most useful and load White Billy with the bundles; then you must all come to the cottage with me, and we will make it out how we can."

"That will be jolly!" said Humphrey. "Come, Edward."

But Edward Beverley required more persuasion to abandon the house. At last old Jacob prevailed, and the clothes were put up in bundles as fast as they could collect them.

"Your aunt said Martha was to go with your sisters, but I doubt if she will," observed Jacob, "and I think we shall have no room for her, for the cottage is small enough."

"Oh no, we don't want her," said Humphrey. "Alice always dresses Edith and herself too, ever since mamma died."

"Now we will carry down the bundles, and you make them fast on the pony while I go for your sisters."

"But where does Aunt Judith go?" enquired Edward.

"She will not leave the house, Master Edward; she intends to stay and speak to the troopers."

"And so an old woman like her remains to face the enemy, while I run away from them!" replied Edward. "I will not go."

"Well, Master Edward," replied Jacob, "you must do as you please; but it will be cruel to leave your sisters here; they and Humphrey must come with me, and I cannot manage to get them to the cottage without you go with us; it is not far and you can return in a very short time."

To this Edward consented. The pony was soon loaded, and the little girls, who were still playing in the garden, were called in by Humphrey. They were told that they were going to pass the night in the cottage, and were delighted at the idea.

"Now, Master Edward," said Jacob, "will you take your sisters by the hand and lead them to the cottage? Here is the key of the door; Master Humphrey can lead the pony; and, Master Edward," continued Jacob, taking him aside, "I'll tell you one thing which I will not mention before your brother and sisters: the troopers are all about the New Forest, for King Charles has escaped, and they are seeking for him. You must not, therefore, leave your brother and sisters till I return. Lock the cottage door as soon as it is dark. You know where to get a light, over the cupboard; and my gun is loaded, and hangs above the mantelpiece. You must do your best, if they attempt to force an entrance; but, above all, promise me not to leave them till I return. I will remain here to see what I can do with your aunt; and when I come back we can then decide how to act."

This latter ruse of Jacob's succeeded. Edward promised that he would not leave his sisters, and it wanted but a few minutes of twilight when the little party quitted the mansion of Arnwood. As they went out of the gates they were passed by Benjamin, who was trotting away with Martha behind him on a pillion, holding a bundle as large as herself.

"Why, where can Martha be going?" said Alice. "Will she be back when we come home tomorrow?"

Edward made no reply, but Humphrey said, "Well, she has taken plenty of clothes in that huge bundle, for one night, at least."

Jacob, as soon as he had seen the children on their way, returned to the kitchen, where he found Agatha and the cook collecting their property, evidently bent upon a hasty retreat.

"Have you seen Miss Judith, Agatha?"

"Yes, and she told me that she should remain, and that I should stand behind her chair, that she might receive the troopers with dignity; but I don't admire the plan."

"When did Benjamin say he would be back?"

"He don't intend coming back. He said he would not, at all events, till tomorrow morning, and then he would ride out this way, to ascertain if the report was false or true. But Martha has gone with him."

"I wish I could persuade the old lady to leave the house," said Jacob thoughtfully. "I fear they will not pay her the respect that she calculates upon. Go up, Agatha, and say I wish to speak with her."

"No, not I; I must be off, for it is dark already."

"And where are you going, then?"

"To Gossip Allwood's. It's a good mile, and I have to carry my things."

"Well, Agatha, if you'll take me up to the old lady, I'll carry your things for you."

Agatha consented, and as soon as she had taken up the lamp, for it was now quite dark, Jacob was once more introduced.

"I wish, madam," said Jacob, "you would be persuaded to leave the house for this night."

"Jacob Armitage, leave this house I will not, if it were filled with troopers; I have said so."

"But, madam—"

"Leave my presence, Jacob Armitage, and never appear again. Quit the room, and send Agatha here."

"She has left, madam, and so has the cook, and Martha went away behind Benjamin; when I leave, you will be alone."

"They have dared to leave?"

"They dared not stay, madam."

"Leave me, Jacob Armitage, and shut the door when you go out." Jacob still hesitated. "Obey me instantly," said the old lady. And the forester, finding all remonstrance useless, went out, and obeyed her last commands by shutting the door after him.

Jacob found Agatha and the other maid in the courtyard; he took up their packages, and, as he promised, accompanied them to Gossip Allwood, who kept a small alehouse about a mile distant.

"But, mercy on us! what will become of the children?" said Agatha, as they walked along, her fears for herself having, up to this time, made her utterly forgetful of them. "Poor things! and Martha has left them."

Now Jacob, knowing that the children of such a Malignant as Colonel Beverley would have sorry treatment if discovered, and knowing also that women were not always to be trusted, determined not to tell them how they were disposed of. He therefore replied:

"Who would hurt such young children as those? No, no, they are safe enough; even the troopers would protect them."

The conversation here ended, and in due time they arrived at the inn. Jacob had just put the bundles down on the table when the clattering of horses' hoofs was heard. Shortly afterwards, the troopers pulled their horses up at the door, and dismounted. Jacob recognized the party he had met in the forest, and among them Southwold. Jacob would have retreated quietly, but he found a sentinel posted at the door to prevent the egress of any person. He reseated himself, and while he was listening to the conversation of the troopers he was recognized by Southwold, who accosted him. Jacob did not pretend not to know him, as it would have been useless; and Southwold put many questions to him as to who were resident at Arnwood. Jacob replied that the children were there, and a few servants, and he was about to mention Miss Judith Villiers, when a thought struck him—he might save the old lady.

"You are going to Arnwood, I know," said Jacob, "and I have heard who you are in search of. Well, Southwold, I'll give you a hint. I may be wrong; but if you should fall in with an old lady or something like one when you go to Arnwood, mount her on your crupper, and away with her to Lymington as fast as you can ride. You understand me?" Southwold nodded significantly, and squeezed Jacob's hand.

"One word, Jacob Armitage; if I succeed in the capture by your means, it is but fair that you should have something for your hint. Where can I find you the day after tomorrow?"

"I am leaving the country this night, and go I must. I am in trouble, that's the fact; when all is blown over I will find you out. Don't speak to me any more just now." Southwold again squeezed Jacob's hand, and left him. Shortly afterwards the order was given to mount, and the troopers set off.

Armitage followed slowly and unobserved. They arrived at the mansion and surrounded it. Shortly afterwards he perceived the glare of torches, and in a quarter of an hour more thick smoke rose up in the dark but clear sky. At last the flames burst forth from the lower windows of the mansion, and soon afterwards they lighted up the country round to some distance.

"It is done," thought Jacob, and he turned to bend his hasty steps towards his own cottage, when he heard the galloping of a horse and violent screams. A minute afterwards James Southwold passed him with the old lady tied behind him, kicking and struggling as hard as she could. Jacob smiled, as he thought that he had by his little stratagem saved the old woman's life, for that Southwold imagined that she was King Charles dressed up as an old woman was evident; and he then returned as fast as he could to the cottage.

In half an hour Jacob had passed through the thick woods which were between the mansion and his own cottage. He knocked at the cottage door. Smoker, a large dog, cross-bred between the fox and bloodhound, growled till Jacob spoke to him, and then Edward opened the door.

"My sisters are in bed and fast asleep, Jacob," said Edward, "and Humphrey has been nodding this half-hour; had he not better go to bed before we go back?"

"Come out, Master Edward," replied Jacob, "and look." Edward beheld the flames and fierce light between the trees, and was silent.

"I told you that it would be so, and you would all have been burnt in your beds, for they did not enter the house to see who was in it, but fired it as soon as they had surrounded it."

"And my aunt!" exclaimed Edward, clasping his hands.

"Is safe, Master Edward, and by this time at Lymington."

"We will go to her tomorrow."

"I fear not; you must not risk so much, Master Edward. These Levellers spare nobody, and you had better let it be supposed that you are all burnt in the house."

"But my aunt knows the contrary, Jacob."

"Very true; I quite forgot that," and so Jacob had. He expected that the old woman would have been burnt, and then nobody would have known of the existence of the children. He forgot, when he planned to save her, that she knew where the children were.

"Well, Master Edward, I will go to Lymington tomorrow and see the old lady; but you must remain here, and take charge of your sisters till I come back, and then we will consider what is to be done. The flames are not so bright as they were."

"No. It is my house that these Roundheads have burned down," said Edward, shaking his fist.

"It was your house, Master Edward, and it was your property; but how long it will be so remains to be seen. I fear it will be forfeited."

CHAPTER 3

THE NEXT morning, Jacob set off towards Arnwood. He knew that Benjamin had stated his intention to return with the horse and see what had taken place, and he knew him well enough to feel sure that he would do so. He thought it better to see him, if possible, and ascertain the fate of Miss Judith. Jacob arrived at the still-smoking ruins of the mansion, and found several people there, mostly residents within a few miles, some attracted by curiosity, others busy in collecting the heavy masses of lead which had been melted from the roof, and appropriating them to their own benefit. At last Jacob perceived Benjamin on horseback riding leisurely towards him, and immediately went up to him.

"Well, Benjamin, this is a woeful sight. What is the news from Lymington?"

"Lymington is full of troopers, and they are not over civil," replied Benjamin.

"And the old lady— where is she?"

"Ah, that's a sad business," replied Benjamin, "and the poor children, too. Poor Master Edward! he would have made a brave gentleman."

"But the old lady is safe," rejoined Jacob. "Did you see her?"

"Yes, I saw her; they thought she was King Charles—poor old soul."

"But they have found out their mistake by this time?"

"Yes, and James Southwold has found it out too," replied Benjamin. "To think of the lady breaking his neck!"

"Breaking his neck? You don't say so! How was it?"

"Why, it seems that Southwold thought that she was King Charles dressed up as an old woman, so he seized her and strapped her fast behind him, and galloped away with her to Lymington but she struggled and kicked so manfully that he could not hold on, and off they went together, and he broke his neck."

"Indeed!—a judgment—a judgment upon a traitor," said Jacob. "Well, and where is the old lady, then? Did you see and speak to her?"

"I saw her, Jacob, but I did not speak to her. I forgot to say that when she broke Southwold's neck, she broke her own too."

"Then the old lady is dead?"

"Yes, that she is," replied Benjamin; "but who cares about her? it's the poor children that I pity. Martha has been crying ever since."

"I don't wonder."

"I was at the Cavalier, and the troopers were there, and they were boasting of what they had done, and called it a righteous work. I could not stand that, and I asked one of them if it were a righteous work to burn poor children in their beds? So he turned round, and struck his sword upon the floor, and asked me whether I was one of them,—'Who are you, then?' and I—all my courage went away, and I answered, I was a poor rat-catcher. 'A rat-catcher, are you?—Well, then, Mr. Rat-catcher, when you are killing rats, if you find a nest of young ones, don't you kill them too? or do you leave them to grow, and become mischievous, eh?' 'I kill the young ones, of course,' replied I. 'Well, so do we Malignants whenever we find them.' I didn't say a word more, but went out of the house as fast as I could."

"Have you heard anything about the king?" enquired Jacob.

"No, nothing; but the troopers are all out again, and, I hear, are gone to the forest."

"Well, Benjamin, good-bye; I shall be off from this part of the country—it's no use my staying here. Where's Agatha and cook?"

"They came to Lymington early this morning."

"Wish them good-bye for me, Benjamin."

"Where are you going then?"

"I can't exactly say, but I think London way. I only stayed here to watch over the children; and now that they are gone, I shall leave Arnwood for ever."

With such thoughts running in his head, Jacob arrived at the cottage, and found the children outside the door, watching for him, They all hastened to him, and the dog rushed before them, to welcome his master. "Down, Smoker, good dog! Well, Mr. Edward, I have been as quick as I can. How have Mr. Humphrey and your sisters behaved? But we must not remain outside today, for the troopers are scouring the forest, and may see you. Let us come in directly; for it would not do that they should come here."

They all entered the cottage, which consisted of one large room in front, and two back rooms for bedrooms. There was also a third bedroom, which was behind the other two, but which had not any furniture in it.

"Now let's see what we can have for dinner—there's venison left, I know," said Jacob. "Come, we must all be useful. Who will be cook?"

"I will be cook," said Alice, "if you will show me how."

"So you shall, my dear," said Jacob, "and I will show you how. There's some potatoes in the basket in the corner, and some onions hanging on the string; we must have some water—who will fetch it?"

"I will," said Edward, who took up a pail, and went out to the spring.

The potatoes were peeled and washed by the children; Jacob and Edward cut the venison into pieces; the iron pot was cleaned, and then the meat and potatoes put with water into the pot and placed on the fire.

"Now I'll cut up the onions, for they will make your eyes water."

"I don't care," said Humphrey. "I'll cut and cry at the same time."

And Humphrey took up a knife, and cut away most manfully, although he was obliged to wipe his eyes with his sleeve very often.

"You are a fine fellow, Humphrey," said Jacob. "Now we'll put the onions in, and let it all boil up together. Now, you see you have cooked your own dinner; ain't that pleasant?"

"Yes!" cried they all; "and we will eat our own dinner as soon as it is ready."

"Then, Humphrey, you must get some of the platters down which are on the dresser; and, Alice, you will find some knives in the drawer. And let me see, what can little Edith do? Oh, she can go to the cupboard and find the salt-cellar. Edward, just look out, and if you see anybody coming or passing, let me know. We must put you on guard till the troopers leave the forest."

The children set about their tasks, and Humphrey cried out, as he very often did, "Now, this is jolly!"

But just before dinner was ready, Edward came in and said, "Here are troopers galloping in the forest!" Jacob went out, and observed that they were coming in a direction that would lead near to the cottage.

He walked in, and after a moment's thought he said, "My dear children, those men may come and search the cottage; you must do as I tell you, and mind that you are very quiet. Humphrey, you and your sisters must go to bed, and pretend to be very ill. Edward, take off your coat and put on this old hunting-frock of mine. You must be in the bedroom attending your sick brother and sisters. Come, Edith, dear, you must play at going to bed, and have your dinner afterwards."

Jacob took the children into the bedroom, and removing the upper dress which would have betrayed that they were not the children of poor parents, put them in bed, and covered them up to the chins with the clothes. Edward had put on the old hunting-shirt, which came below his knees, and stood with a mug of water in his hand by the bedside of the two girls. Jacob went to the outer room to remove the platters laid out for dinner; and he had hardly done so when he heard the noise of the troopers, and soon afterwards a knock at the cottage door.

"Come in," said Jacob.

"Who are you, my friend?" said the leader of the troop, entering the door.

"A poor forester, sir," replied Jacob, "under great trouble."

"What trouble, my man?"

"I have the children all in bed with the smallpox."

"Nevertheless, we must search your cottage."

"You are welcome," replied Jacob; "only don't frighten the children if you can help it."

The man, who was now joined by others, commenced his search. Jacob opened all the doors of the rooms, and they passed through. Little Edith shrieked when she saw them; but Edward patted her, and told her not to be frightened. The troopers, however, took no notice of the children; they searched thoroughly, and then came back to the front room.

"It's no use remaining here," said one of the troopers. "Shall we be off? I'm tired and hungry with the ride."

"So am I; and there's something that smells well," said another. "What's this, my good man?" continued he, taking off the lid of the pot.

"My dinner for a week," replied Jacob. "I have no one to cook for me now, and can't light a fire every day."

"Well, you appear to live well, if you have such a mess as that every day in the week. I should like to try a spoonful or two."

"And welcome, sir," replied Jacob; "I will cook some more for myself."

The troopers took him at his word. They sat down to the table, and very soon the whole contents of the kettle had disappeared. Having satisfied themselves, they got up, told him that his rations were so good that they hoped to call again; and, laughing heartily, they mounted their horses, and rode away.

"Well," said Jacob, "I little thought to get off so cheap."

As soon as they were out of sight, Jacob called to Edward and the children to get up again, which they soon did. Alice put on Edith's frock, Humphrey put on his jacket, and Edward pulled off the hunting-shirt.

"They're gone now," said Jacob, coming in from the door.

"And our dinners are gone," said Humphrey, looking at the empty pot and dirty platters.

"Yes, but we can cook another; and that will be more play, you know," said Jacob.

"Nasty men eat our dinner," said Edith. "Shan't have any more. Eat this ourselves."

And so they did as soon as it was cooked; but they were very hungry before they sat down.

"This is jolly!" said Humphrey, with his mouth full.

"Yes, Master Humphrey. I doubt if King Charles eats so good a dinner this day. Mr. Edward, you are very grave and silent."

"Yes, I am, Jacob. Have I not cause? Oh, if I could but have mauled those troopers!"

"But you could not; so you must make the best of it. They say that

18

every dog has his day, and who knows but King Charles may be on the throne again!"

There were no more visits to the cottage that day, and they all went to bed and slept soundly.

The next morning, Jacob, who was most anxious to learn the news, saddled the pony, having first given his injunctions to Edward how to behave in case any troopers should come to the cottage. He told him to pretend that the children were in bed with the smallpox, as they had done the day before. Jacob then travelled to Gossip Allwood's, and he there learnt that King Charles had been taken prisoner, and was at the Isle of Wight, and that the troopers were all going back to London as fast as they came. Feeling that there was now no more danger to be apprehended from them, Jacob set off as fast as he could for Lymington. He went to one shop and purchased two peasant dresses which he thought would fit the two boys, and at another he bought similar apparel for the two girls. Then, with several other ready-made articles, and some other things which were required for the household, he made a large package, which he put upon the pony, and, taking the bridle, set off home.

"Now, recollect, you are all my grandchildren," said Jacob; "for I shall no longer call you Miss and Master—that we never do in a cottage. You understand me, Edward, of course?" added Jacob.

We must now describe the cottage of Jacob Armitage, in which the children have in future to dwell. As we have said before, it contained a large sitting-room, or kitchen, in which were a spacious hearth and chimney, table, stools, cupboards, and dressers; the two bedrooms which adjoined it were now appropriated, one for Jacob, and the other for the two boys; the third, or inner bedroom, was arranged for the two girls, as being more retired and secure. But there were outhouses belonging to it; a stall in which White Billy, the pony, lived during the winter; a shed and pig-sty rudely constructed, with an enclosed yard attached to them; and it had, moreover, a piece of ground of more than an acre, well fenced in to keep out the deer and game, the largest portion of which was cultivated as a garden and potato-ground, and the other, which remained in grass, contained some fine old apple and pear trees. Such was the domicile. The pony, a few fowls, a sow and two young pigs, and the dog Smoker, were the animals of the establishment. Here Jacob Armitage had been born—for the cottage had been built by his grandfather—but he had not always remained at the cottage. When young he had for several years served in the army. His father and brother had lived in the establishment at Arnwood, and he was constantly there as a boy. The chaplain of Arnwood had taken a fancy to him, and taught him to read—writing he had not acquired. As soon as he grew up, he served in the troop commanded by Colonel Beverley's father; and after his death, Colonel Beverley had procured him the situation of forest ranger which had been held by his father, who was then alive, but too aged to do the duty. Jacob

Armitage married a good and devout young woman, with whom he lived several years, when she died; after which, his father being also dead, Jacob Armitage had lived alone till the period at which we have commenced this history.

CHAPTER 4

THE OLD forester lay awake the whole of this night, reflecting how he should act relative to the children; he felt the great responsibility that he had incurred, and was alarmed when he considered what might be the consequences if his days were shortened. He had no fear, if his life was spared, that they would do well; but if he should be called away before they had grown up and were able to help themselves they might perish. Edward was not fourteen years old. It was true that he was an active, brave boy, and thoughtful for his years; but he had not yet strength or skill sufficient for what would be required. Humphrey, the second, also promised well; but still they were all children. "I must bring them up to be useful—to depend upon themselves. There is not a moment to be lost, and not a moment shall be lost. I will do my best, and trust to God. I ask but two or three years, and by that time I trust that they will be able to do without me. They must commence tomorrow the life of foresters' children."

Acting upon this resolution, Jacob, as soon as the children were dressed, and in the sitting-room, opened his Bible, which he had put on the table, and said:

"My dear children, you know that you must remain in this cottage, that the wicked troopers may not find you out. They killed your father, and if I had not taken you away they would have burnt you in your beds. You must therefore live here as my children, and you must call yourselves by the name of Armitage, and not that of Beverley; and you must dress like children of the forest, as you do now, and you must do as the children of the forest do: that is, you must do everything for yourselves, for you can have no servants to wait upon you. Now, Edward is the oldest, and he must go out with me in the forest, and I must teach him to kill deer and other game for our support; and when he knows how, then Humphrey shall come out and learn how to shoot."

"Yes," said Humphrey, "I'll soon learn."

"But not yet, Humphrey, for you must do some work in the meantime. You must look after the pony and the pigs, and you must learn to dig in the garden with Edward and me when we do not go out to hunt; and sometimes I shall go by myself, and leave Edward to work with you when there is work to be done. Alice, dear, you must, with Humphrey, light the fire and clean the house in the morning. Humphrey will go to the spring for water, and do all the hard work; and you must learn to wash, my dear Alice—I will show you how; and you must learn to get dinner ready with Humphrey, who will assist you, and to make the beds. And little Edith shall take care of the fowls, and feed them every morning, and look for the eggs—will you, Edith?"

"Yes," replied Edith, "and feed all the little chickens when they are hatched, as I did at Arnwood."

"Now, Edward, we are going after a fine stag, if we can find him—which I doubt not—but the difficulty is to get within shot of him. Recollect that you must always be hid, for his sight is very quick; never be heard, for his ear is sharp; and never come down to him with the wind, for his scent is very fine. Then you must hunt according to the hour of the day. At this time he is feeding; two hours hence he will be lying down in the high fern. The dog is of no use unless the stag is badly wounded, when the dog will take him. Smoker knows his duty well, and will hide himself as close as we do. We are now going into the thick wood ahead of us, as there are many little spots of cleared ground in it where we may find the deer; but we must keep more to the left, for the wind is to the eastward, and we must walk up against it. And now that we are coming into the wood, recollect, not a word must be said, and you must walk as quietly as possible, keeping behind me. Smoker, to heel!"

They proceeded through the wood for more than a mile, when Jacob made a sign to Edward, and dropped down into the fern, crawling along to an open spot, where, at some distance, were a stag and three deer grazing. The deer grazed quietly, but the stag was ever and anon raising up his head and snuffing the air as he looked round, evidently acting as a sentinel for the females.

The stag was perhaps a long quarter of a mile from where they had crouched down in the fern. Jacob remained immovable till the animal began to feed again, and then he advanced, crawling through the fern, followed by Edward and the dog, who dragged himself on his stomach after Edward. This tedious approach was continued for some time, and they had neared the stag to within half the original distance, when the animal again lifted up his head and appeared uneasy. Jacob stopped and remained without motion. After a time the stag walked away, followed by the does, to the opposite side of the clear spot on which they had been feeding, and, to Edward's annoyance, the animal was now half a mile from them. Jacob turned round and crawled into the wood, and when he knew that they were concealed he rose on his feet and said:

"You see, Edward, that it requires patience to stalk a deer. What a princely fellow! But he has probably been alarmed this morning, and is very uneasy. Now we must go through the woods till we come to the lee of him on the other side of the dell. You see he has led the does close to the thicket, and we shall have a better chance when we get there, if we are only quiet and cautious."

"What startled him, do you think?" said Edward.

"I think, when you were crawling through the fern after me, you broke a piece of rotten stick that was under you, did you not?"

"Yes, but that made but little noise."

"Quite enough to startle a red deer, Edward, as you will find out before you have been long a forester. Now, then, to make the circuit—we had better not say a word. If we get safe now to the other side, we are sure of him."

In half an hour they had gained the side where the deer were feeding. When about three hundred yards from the game, Jacob again sank down on his hands and knees, crawling from bush to bush, stopping whenever the stag raised his head, and advancing again when it resumed feeding; at last they came to the fern at the side of the wood, and crawled through it as before, but still more cautiously as they approached the stag. In this manner they arrived at last to within eighty yards of the animal, and then Jacob advanced his gun ready to put it to his shoulder, and, as he cocked the lock, raised himself to fire. The click occasioned by the cocking of the lock roused up the stag instantly, and he turned his head in the direction from whence the noise proceeded; as he did so, Jacob fired, aiming behind the animal's shoulder; the stag made a bound, came down again, dropped to his knees, attempted to run, and fell dead, while the does fled away with the rapidity of the wind.

Edward started up on his legs with a shout of exultation. Jacob commenced re-loading his gun, and stopped Edward as he was about to run up to where the animal lay.

"Edward, you must learn your craft," said Jacob; "never do that again; never shout in that way—on the contrary, you should have remained still in the fern."

"Why so? the stag is dead."

"Yes, my dear boy, that stag is dead; but how do you know but what there may be another lying down in the fern close to us, or at some distance from us, which you have alarmed by your shout? Suppose that we both had guns, and that the report of mine had startled another stag lying in the fern within shot, you would have been able to shoot it."

"I see," replied Edward, "I was wrong; but I shall know better another time."

"That's why I tell you, my boy," replied Jacob. "Now let us go to our quarry. Ay, Edward, this is a noble beast. I thought that he was a hart royal, and so he is."

"What is a hart royal, Jacob?"

"Why, a stag is called a brocket until he is three years old; at four years he is a staggart; at five years a warrantable stag; and after five years he becomes a hart royal."

"And how do you know his age?"

"By his antlers. You see that this stag has nine antlers. Now, a brocket has but two antlers, a staggart three, and a warrantable stag but four; at six years old, the antlers increase in number until they sometimes have twenty or thirty. This is a fine beast, and the venison is now getting very good. Now you must see me do the work of my craft."

Jacob then cut the throat of the animal, and afterwards cut off its head, and took out its bowels.

"Are you tired, Edward?" said Jacob, as he wiped his hunting-knife on the coat of the stag.

"No, not the least."

"Well, then, we are now, I should think, about four or five miles from the cottage. Could you find your way home? But that is of no consequence; Smoker will lead you home by the shortest path. I will stay here, and you can saddle White Billy and come back with him, for he must carry the venison back. It's more than we can manage—indeed, as much as we can manage with White Billy to help us."

Edward immediately assented, and Jacob, desiring Smoker to go home, set about flaying and cutting up the animal for its more convenient transportation. In an hour and a half, Edward, attended by Smoker, returned with the pony, on whose back the chief portion of the venison was packed.

As soon as they arrived at the cottage the venison was hung up, the pony put in the stable, and then they sat down to dinner with an excellent appetite after their long morning's walk. Alice and Humphrey had cooked the dinner themselves, and it was in the pot smoking hot, when they returned; and Jacob declared he never ate a better mess in his life. Alice was not a little proud of this, and of the praises she received from Edward and the old forester. The next day Jacob stated his intention of going to Lymington to dispose of a large portion of the venison, and bring back a sack of oatmeal for their cakes. Edward asked to accompany him, but Jacob replied:

"Edward, you must not think of showing yourself at Lymington, or anywhere else, for a long while, until you are grown out of memory. It would be folly, and you would risk your sisters' and brother's lives, perhaps, as well as your own. Never mention it again: the time will come when it will be necessary perhaps; if so, it cannot be helped. At present you would be known immediately. No, Edward, I tell you what I mean to do: I have a little money left, and I intend to buy you a gun, that you may learn to stalk deer yourself without me; for recollect, if any accident should happen to me, who is there but you to provide for your brother and sisters? At Lymington I am known to many; but, out of all who know me, there is not one who knows where my cottage is; they know that I live in the New Forest and that I supply them with venison, and purchase other articles in return. That is all they know; and I may therefore go without fear. I shall sell the venison tomorrow, and bring you back a good gun; and Humphrey shall have the carpenter's tools which he wishes for—for I think, by what he does with his knife, that he has a turn that way, and it may be useful. I must also get some threads and needles for Alice, for she can sew a little, and practice will make her more perfect."

Jacob went off to Lymington as he had proposed, and returned late at night with White Billy well loaded. He had a sack of oatmeal, some spades and hoes, a saw and chisels, and other tools; two scythes and two three-pronged forks; and when Edward came to meet him he put into his hand a gun, with a very long barrel.

"I believe, Edward, that you will find that a good one, for I know where it came from. It belonged to one of the rangers, who was reckoned the best shot in the forest. I know the gun, for I have seen it on his arm, and have taken it in my hand to examine it more than once. He was killed at Naseby, with your father, poor fellow! and his widow sold the gun to meet her wants."

"Well!" replied Edward. "I thank you much, Jacob, and I will try if I cannot kill as much venison as will pay back the purchase-money—I will, I assure you."

"I shall be glad if you do, Edward; not because I want the money back, but because then I shall be more easy in my mind about you all, if anything happens to me. Tomorrow we will not go out; we have meat enough for three weeks or more, and now the frost has set in, it will keep well. You shall practise at a mark with your gun, that you may be accustomed to it; for all guns, even the best, require a little humouring."

Edward, who had often fired a gun before, proved the next morning that he had a very good eye; and after two or three hours' practice, hit the mark at a hundred yards almost every time.

The winter now set in with great severity, and they remained almost altogether within doors. Jacob and the boys went out to get firewood, and dragged it home through the snow.

"I wish, Jacob," said Humphrey, "that I were able to build a cart, for it would be very useful, and White Billy would then have something to do; but I can't make the wheels, and there is no harness."

"That's not a bad idea of yours, Humphrey," replied Jacob; "we will think about it. If you can't build a cart, perhaps I can buy one. It would be useful, if it were only to take the dung out of the yard on the potato-ground; for I have hitherto carried it out in baskets, and it's hard work."

"Yes, and we might saw the wood into billets, and carry it home in the cart instead of dragging it this way: my shoulder is quite sore with the rope, it cuts me so."

"Well, when the weather breaks up, I will see what I can do, Humphrey; but just now the roads are so blocked up, that I do not think we could get a cart from Lymington to the cottage, although we can a horse, perhaps."

But if they remained indoors during the inclement weather they were not idle. Jacob took this opportunity to instruct the children in everything. Alice learnt how to wash and how to cook. It is true that sometimes she scalded herself a little, sometimes burnt her fingers; and other accidents did occur, from the articles employed being too heavy for them to lift by themselves; but practice and dexterity compensated for want of strength, and fewer accidents happened every day. Humphrey had his carpenter's tools; and although at first he had many failures, and wasted nails and wood, by degrees he learnt to use his tools with more dexterity, and made several little useful articles. Little Edith could now do something, for she made and baked all the oatmeal cakes, which saved Alice a good deal of time and trouble in watching them. In the evening Alice sat down with her needle and thread to mend the clothes. At first they were not very well done; but she improved every day. Edith and Humphrey learnt to read while Alice worked, and then Alice learnt; and thus passed the winter away so rapidly that, although they had been five months at the cottage, it did not appear as if they had been there as many weeks. All were happy and contented, with the exception, perhaps, of Edward, who had fits of gloominess, and occasionally showed signs of impatience as to what was passing in the world, of which he remained in ignorance.

CHAPTER 5

As we have before said, time passed rapidly. With the exception of one or two excursions after venison, they remained in the cottage, and Jacob never went to Lymington. The frost had broken up, the snow had long disappeared, and the trees began to bud. The sun became powerful, and in the month of May the forest began again to look green.

"And now, Edward," said Jacob Armitage, one day at breakfast, "we will try for venison again to sell at Lymington, for I must purchase Humphrey's cart and harness; so let us get our guns, and go out this fine morning. The stags are mostly by themselves at this season, for the does are with their young calves. We must find the slot of a deer, and track him to his lair, and you shall have the first shot if you like, but that, however, depends more upon the deer than upon me."

They had walked four or five miles when they came upon the slot or track of a deer, which Jacob declared to be that of a warrantable stag— that is, one old enough to kill and to be good venison.

"We must now track him to his lair, Edward."

This took them about a mile farther, when they arrived at a small thicket of thorns about an acre in extent.

"Here he is, you see, Edward; let me now see if he is harboured."

They walked round the ticket, and could not find any slot or track by which the stag had left the covert, and Jacob pronounced that the animal must be hid in it.

"Now, Edward, do you stay here while I go back to the lee side of the covert: I will enter it with Smoker, and the stag will, in all probability, when he is roused, come out to breast the wind. You will then have a good shot at him; recollect to fire so as to hit him behind the shoulder: if he is moving quick, fire a little before the shoulders; if slow, take aim accurately."

Jacob then left Edward, and went down to the lee side of the covert, where he entered it with Smoker. Edward was stationed behind a thorn bush, which grew a few yards clear of the covert, and he soon heard the creaking of the branches.

A short time elapsed, and a fine stag came out at a trot; he turned his head, and was just bounding away when Edward fired and the animal fell. Remembering the advice of Jacob, Edward remained where he was, in silence, reloading his piece, and was soon afterwards joined by Jacob and the dog.

"Well done, Edward!" said the forester in a low voice, and covering his forehead to keep off the glare of the sun, he looked earnestly at a high brake between some thorn trees, about half a mile to windward. "I think I see something there—look, Edward, your eyes are younger than mine. Is that the branch of a tree in the fern, or is it not?"

"I see what you mean," replied Edward. "It is not; it moves."

"I thought so, but my eyes are not so good as they once were. It's another stag, depend upon it; but how to get near him? we never can get across this patch of clear grass without being seen."

"No, we cannot get at him from this spot," replied Edward; "but if we were to fall back to leeward and gain the forest again I think that there are thorns sufficient from the forest to where he lies to creep from behind one to the other, so as to get a shot at him; don't you?"

"It will require care and patience to manage that; but I think it might be done. I will try; it is my turn now, you know. You had better stay here with the dog, for only one can hide from thorn to thorn."

Jacob, ordering Smoker to remain, then set off. He had to make a circuit of three miles to get to the spot where the thorns extended from the forest, and Edward saw no more of him, although he strained his eyes, until the stag sprung out, and the gun was discharged. Edward perceived that the stag was not killed, but severely wounded, running towards the covert near which he was hid. "Down, Smoker," said he, as he cocked his gun. The stag came within shot, and was coming nearer, when, seeing Edward, it turned. Edward fired, and then cheered on the dog, who sprang after the wounded animal, giving tongue, as he followed him. Edward, perceiving Jacob hastening towards him, waited for him.

They both caught up their guns and ran as fast as they could, when, as they entered the wood, they heard the dog at bay.

"We shan't have far to go, Edward; the animal is done up; Smoker has him at bay."

They hastened on another quarter of a mile, when they found that the stag had fallen on his knees, and had been seized by the throat by Smoker.

"Mind, Edward, now, how I go up to him, for the wound from the horn of the deer is very dangerous."

Jacob advanced from behind the stag, and cut his throat with his hunting-knife. "He is a fine beast, and we have done well today; but we shall have two journeys to make to get all this venison home. I could not get a fair shot at him—and see, I have hit him here in the flank."

"And here is my ball in his throat," said Edward.

It was late in the evening before they had made their two trips and taken all the venison home, and very tired were they before it was all safely housed. Edward was delighted with his success. The next morning Jacob set off for Lymington, with the pony loaded with venison, which he sold, as well as two more loads which he promised to bring the next day and the day after. He then looked out for a cart, and was fortunate in finding a small one just fitted to the size of the pony, who was not tall, but very strong, as all New Forest ponies are. He also procured harness, and then put Billy in the cart to draw him home; but Billy did not admire being put in a cart, and for some time was very restive, and backed and reared, and went every way but the right; but by dint of coaxing and leading he at last submitted, and went straight on, and at last arrived safe at the cottage. Humphrey was delighted at the sight of the cart, and said that now they should get on well. The next day Jacob contrived to put all the remainder of the venison in the cart, and White Billy made no more difficulty; he dragged it all to Lymington, and returned with the cart as quietly and cleverly as if he had been in harness all his life.

"Well, Edward, the venison paid for the cart, at all events," said Jacob; "and now, I will tell you all the news I collected while I was at Lymington. Captain Burly, who attempted to incite the people to rescue the king, has been hung, drawn and quartered, as a traitor."

"They are traitors who condemned him," replied Edward, in wrath.

"Yes, so they are; but there is better news, which is, that the Duke of York has escaped to Holland."

"Yes, that is good news; and the king?"

"He is still a prisoner in Carisbrook Castle."

Edward remained very grave for some time.

"I trust in Heaven, we all shall have our rights yet, Jacob," said he at last. "I wish I was a man!"

"I tell you what we want," said Humphrey, who took the command altogether over the farm; "we want a cow."

"Whose cows are those which I see in the forest sometimes?" said Humphrey to Jacob.

"If they belong to anybody, they belong to the king," replied Jacob; "but they are cattle which have strayed and found their way to the forest, and have remained here ever since. They are rather wild and savage, and you must be careful how you go too near them, as the bulls will run at you. They increase very fast; there were but six a few years ago, and now there are at least fifty in the herd."

"Well, I'll try and get one if I can," said Humphrey.

"You will be puzzled to do that, boy," replied Jacob; "and as I said before, beware of the bulls."

"I don't want a bull," replied Humphrey; "but a cow would give us milk, and then we should have more manure for the garden. My garden will then grow more potatoes."

"Well, Humphrey, if you can catch a cow no one will interfere; but I think you will not find it very easy, and you may find it very dangerous."

"I'll look out for one," replied Humphrey, "anyhow. Alice, if we only had a cow wouldn't that be jolly?"

The crops were now all up, and as the days began to be long, the work became comparatively light and easy. Humphrey was busy making a little wheelbarrow for Edith, that she might barrow away the weeds as he hoed them up; and at last this great performance was completed, much to the admiration of all, and much to his own satisfaction. Indeed, when it is recollected that Humphrey had only the handsaw and axe, and that he had to cut down the tree, and then to saw it into planks, it must be acknowledged that it required great patience and perseverance even to make a wheelbarrow; but Humphrey was not only persevering, but was full of invention. He had built up a henhouse with fir poles, and made the nest for the hens to lay and hatch in, and they now had between forty and fifty chickens running about. He had also divided the pig-sty, so that the sow might be kept apart from the other pigs; and they expected very soon to have a litter of young pigs. He had transplanted the wild strawberries from the forest, and had, by manure, made them large and good. Now Humphrey was very busy cutting down some poles in the forest to make a cowhouse, for he declared that he would have a cow somehow or other. June arrived, and it was time to mow down grass to make into hay for the winter, and Jacob had two scythes. He showed the boys how to use them, and they soon became expert; and as there was plenty of long grass at this time of the year, and they could mow when they pleased, they soon had White Billy in full employment carrying the hay home. Jacob thought that there was hay enough made, but Humphrey said that there was enough for the pony, but not enough for the cow.

"But where is the cow to come from, Humphrey?"

"Where the venison comes from," replied he—"out of the forest."

After all the hay was made and stacked, Humphrey found out a method of thatching with fern, which Jacob had never thought of; and when that was done, they commenced cutting down fern for fodder. Here again Humphrey would have twice as much as Jacob had ever cut before, because he wanted litter for the cow. At last it became quite a joke between him and Edward, who, when he brought home more venison than would keep in the hot weather, told Humphrey that the remainder was for the cow. Still Humphrey would not give up the point, and every morning and evening he would be certain to be absent for an hour or two, and it was found out he was watching the herd of wild cattle who were feeding; sometimes they were very near, at others a long way off. He used to get up into the trees, and examine them as they passed under him, without perceiving him. One night Humphrey returned very late, and the next morning he was off before daylight. Breakfast was over, and Humphrey did not make his appearance, and they could not tell what was the matter. Jacob felt uneasy, but Edward laughed, and said:

"Oh, depend upon it, he'll come back and bring the cow with him."

Hardly had Edward said these words when in came Humphrey red with perspiration.

"Now then, Jacob and Edward, come with me; we must put Billy in the cart, and take Smoker and a rope with us. Take your guns too, for fear of accident."

Humphrey disappeared, and Jacob said to Edward:

"What can it be?"

"It can be nothing but the cow he is so mad about," replied Edward. "However, when he comes with the pony we shall know; let us take our guns, and the dog Smoker, as he wishes."

Humphrey now drove up the pony and cart, and they set off.

"Well, I suppose you'll tell us now what we are going for?" said Edward.

"Yes, I will. You know I've been watching the cattle for a long while, because I wanted a cow. I have been in a tree when they have passed under me several times, and I observed that one or two of the helfers were very near calving. Yesterday evening I thought one could not help calving very soon indeed, and as I was watching I saw that she was uneasy, and that she at last left the herd and went into a little copse of wood. I remained three hours to see if she came out again, and she did not. It was dark when I came home, as you know. This morning I went before daylight and found the herd. She is very remarkable, being black and white spotted; and after close examination I found that she was not with the herd, so I am sure that she went into the copse to calve, and that she has calved before this."

"Well, that may be," replied Jacob; "but now I do not understand what we are to do."

"Well, then, I'll tell you what I hope to do. I have got the pony and cart to take the calf home with us, if we can get it—which I think we can. I have got Smoker to worry the heifer and keep her employed, while we put the calf in the cart; a rope that we may tie the cow, if we can; and you with your guns must keep off the herd if they come to her assistance. Now do you understand my plan?"

"Yes, and I think it very likely to succeed, Humphrey," replied Jacob; "and I give you credit for the scheme. We will help you all we can. Where is the copse?"

"Not half a mile farther," replied Humphrey.

On their arrival they found that the herd were feeding at a considerable distance from the copse, which was perhaps as well.

"Now," said Jacob, "I and Edward will enter into the copse with Smoker, and you follow us, Humphrey. I will make Smoker seize the heifer if necessary; at all events he will keep her at bay—that is, if she is here. First let us walk round the copse and find her *slot*, as we call the track of a deer. See, here is her footing. Now let us go in."

They advanced cautiously into the thicket, following the track of the heifer, and at last came upon her. Apparently she had not calved more than an hour, and was licking the calf, which was not yet on its legs. As soon as the animal perceived Jacob and Edward she shook her head, and was about to run at them; but Jacob told Smoker to seize her, and the dog flew at her immediately. The attack of the dog drove back the heifer quite into the thicket, and as the dog bounded round her, springing this way and that way to escape her horns, the heifer was soon separated from the calf.

"Now then, Edward and Humphrey," said Jacob, advancing between the heifer and the calf, "lift up the calf between you and put it in the cart. Leave Smoker and me to manage the mother."

The boys put their arms under the stomach of the calf, and carried it away. The heifer was at first too busy defending herself against the dog to perceive that the calf was gone; when she did, Jacob called Smoker to him, so as to bring him between the heifer and where the boys were going out of the thicket. At last the heifer gave a loud bellow, and rushed out of the thicket in pursuit of her calf, checked by Smoker, who held on to her ear, and sometimes stopped her from advancing.

"Hold her, Smoker," said Jacob, who now went back to help the boys. "Hold her, boy. Is the calf in the cart?"

"Yes, and tied fast," replied Edward; "and we are in the cart too."

"That's right," replied Jacob. "Now I'll get in too, and let us drive off. She'll follow us, depend upon it. Here, Smoker! Smoker! let her alone."

Smoker, at this command, came bounding out of the copse, followed by the heifer, lowing most anxiously. Her lowing was responded to by the calf in the cart, and she ran wildly up to it.

Humphrey, who had the reins, drove off; the heifer followed, at one time running at the dog, at another putting her head almost into the hind part of the cart; but the lowing of the heifer was now answered by deeper tones, and Jacob said:

"Edward, get your gun ready, for I think the herd is following. Do not fire, however, till I tell you. We must be governed by circumstances. It won't do to lose the pony, or to run any serious risk, for the sake of the heifer and calf. Drive fast, Humphrey."

A few minutes afterwards they perceived at about a quarter of a mile behind them, not the whole herd but a single bull, who was coming up at a fast trot, with his tail in the air, and tossing his head, lowing deeply in answer to the heifer.

"Now, Edward, do you fire first—aim for his shoulder. Humphrey, pull up."

Humphrey stopped the pony, and the bull continued to advance, but seemed puzzled who to attack, unless it was the dog. As soon as the bull was within sixty yards, Edward fired, and the animal fell down on its knees, tearing the ground with its horns.

"That will do," said Jacob; "drive on again, Humphrey; we will have a look at the fellow by and by. At present we had better get home, as others may come. He's up again, but he is at a standstill. I have an idea that he is hit hard."

The cart drove on, followed by the heifer; but no more of the wild herd made their appearance, and they very soon gained the cottage.

"Now, then, what shall we do?" said Jacob. "Come, Humphrey, you have had all the ordering of this, and have done it well."

"Well, Jacob, we must now drive the cart into the yard, and shut the gate upon the cow, till I am ready."

"That's easy done, by setting Smoker at her," replied Jacob; "but, mercy on us, there's Alice and Edith running out!—the heifer may kill them. Go back, Alice, run quickly into the cottage, and shut the door till we come."

Alice and Edith hearing this, and Edward also crying out to them, made a hasty retreat to the cottage. Humphrey then backed the cart against the paling of the yard so as to enable Edward to get on the other side of it, ready to open the gate. Smoker was set at the heifer, and, as before, soon engaged her attention; so that the gate was opened and the cart drove in, and the gate closed again, before the heifer could follow.

"Well, Humphrey, what next?"

"Why, now lift the calf out and put it into the cowhouse. I will go into the cowhouse with a rope and a slip-knot at the end of it, get upon the beam above and drop it over her horns as she's busy with the calf, which she will be as soon as you let her in. I shall pass the end of the rope outside, for you to haul up when I am ready, and then we shall have her fast, till we can secure her properly. When I call out 'ready,' do you open the gate and let her in. You can do that and jump into the cart afterwards, for fear she may run at you; but I don't think she will, for it's the calf the wants, and not either of you."

As soon as Humphrey was ready with the rope he gave the word, and the gate was opened; the cow ran in immediately, and hearing her calf bleat went into the cowhouse, the door of which was shut upon her. A minute afterwards Humphrey cried out to them to haul upon the rope, which they did.

"That will do," said Humphrey from the inside; "now make the rope fast, and then you may come in."

They went in, and found the heifer drawn close to the side of the cowhouse by the rope which was round her horns, and unable to move her head.

"Well, Humphrey, that's very clever; but now what's to be done?"

"First I'll saw off the tips of her horns, and then if she does run at us she won't hurt us much."

As soon as the ends of her horns were sawed off, Humphrey took another piece of rope, which he fastened securely round her horns, and then made the other end fast to the side of the building, so that the animal could move about a little and eat out of the crib.

Then they went out shutting the cowhouse door.

"Well, Humphrey, you've beat us, after all, and have the laugh on your side now," said Jacob. "I assure you, that when you were making so much hay, and gathering so much litter, and building a cowhouse, I had no more idea that we should have a cow than that we should have an elephant; and I will say that you deserve great credit for your way of obtaining it."

"That he certainly does," replied Edward. "You have more genius than I have, brother. But dinner must be ready, if Alice has done her duty. What think you, Jacob, shall we after dinner go and look after that bull?"

"Yes, by all means. He will not be bad eating, and I can sell all I can carry in the cart at Lymington. Besides the skin is worth money."

CHAPTER 6

ALICE AND Edith were very anxious to see the cow, and especially to see the calf; but Humphrey told them that they must not go near till he went with them, and then they should see it. After dinner was over, Jacob and Edward took their guns, and Humphrey put Billy in the cart, and followed them. They found the bull where they left him, standing quite still; he tossed his head when they approached him, which they did carefully, but he did not attempt to run at them.

"It's my idea that he has nearly bled to death," said Jacob; "but there's nothing like making sure. Edward, put a bullet just three inches behind his shoulder, and that will make all safe."

Edward did so, and the animal fell dead. They went up to the carcass, which they estimated to weigh at least fifty stone.

The skinning and quartering took up the whole afternoon, and Billy was heavily laden when he drew his cart home. The next day Jacob went to Lymington to sell the bull and skin, and returned home well satisfied with the profit he had made. He had procured, as Humphrey requested, some milk-pans, a small churn, and a milkpail, out of the proceeds, and still money left. Humphrey told them that he had not been to see the heifer yet, as he thought it better not.

"She will be tame tomorrow morning, depend upon it," said he.

"But if you give her nothing to eat, will not the calf die?"

"Oh, no! I should think not. I shall not starve her; but I will make her thankful for her food before she gets it. I shall cut her some grass tomorrow morning."

We may as well here say, that the next morning Humphrey went in to the heifer. At first she tossed about and was very unruly. He gave her some grass, and patted her and coaxed her for a long while, till at last she allowed him to touch her gently. Every day for a fortnight he brought her her food, and she became quieter every day, till at last, if he went up to her, she never pushed with her horns. The calf became quite tame, and as the heifer perceived that the calf was quiet, she became more quiet herself. After the fortnight, Humphrey would not allow the heifer to receive anything except from the hand of Alice, that the animal might know her well; and when the calf was a month old Humphrey made the first attempt to milk her. This was resisted at first by kicking, but in the course of ten days she gave down her milk. Humphrey then let her loose for a few days to run about the yard, still keeping the calf in the cow-house, and putting the heifer in to her at night, milking her before the calf was allowed to suck. After this, he adventured upon the last experiment, which was to turn her out of the yard to graze into the forest. She went away to some distance, and he was fearful that she would join the herd, but in the evening she came back again to her calf. After this he was satisfied, and turned her out every day, and they had no further trouble with her. He would not, however, wean the calf till the winter time, when she was shut up in the yard and fed on hay. He then weaned the calf, which was a cow-calf, and they had no more trouble with the mother. Alice soon learned to milk her, and she became very tractable and good-tempered.

"Jacob," said Humphrey, "I wish I could have a dog."

"And I a kitten," said Alice.

"Well, I ought to look out for another dog; although Smoker is not old, yet one ought to have two dogs to one's gun, in case of accident. And a kitten should be easy to get."

"I think so too," replied Edward. "See if you can get two puppies, one for Humphrey, and one for myself."

"Well, I must not go to Lymington for them. I must cross the forest to see some friends of mine whom I have not seen for a long while, and I may get some of the right sort of puppies there, just like Smoker. I'll do that at once, as I may have to wait for them, even if I do have the promise."

It was arranged that Edward should stay at home to assist in collecting acorns for the pigs, and that Jacob should cross the forest alone to see after the puppies; and he set off the next morning. He was away two days, and then returned; said that he had a promise of two puppies, and that he had chosen them; they were of the same breed as Smoker, but they were only a fortnight old, and could not be taken from the mother yet awhile, so that he had arranged to call again when they were three or four months old, and able to follow him across the forest. Jacob also said that he was very near being hurt by a stag that had made at him—for at that season of the year the stags were very dangerous and fierce—but that he had fired, and struck off one of the animal's horns, which made it turn.

"Tomorrow," said Jacob, "I will help with the acorns, and the day afterwards, if I am spared, I will take Alice's poultry to Lymington for her."

"Yes, and when you come back you will help me to churn, for then I shall have a good deal of cream."

"And don't forget to buy the kitten, Jacob," said Edith.

"My coat is a little the worse for wear, and so is yours, Edward. We must try if we cannot find means to pay for another."

"Humphrey," said Jacob, "I'll buy all you want, and trust to you for paying me again as soon as you can."

"That's just what I want," replied Humphrey. "Then you must buy me a gun and a new suit of clothes first; when I've paid for them I shall want some more tools, and some nails and screws, and two or three other things; but I will say nothing about them just now. Get me my gun, and I'll try what the forest will do for me—especially after I have my dog."

"Well, we shall see; perhaps you'll like to come out with me sometimes and learn woodcraft, for Edward knows as much as I do now, and can go out by himself."

"Of course I will, Jacob; I want to learn everything."

"Well, there's a little money left in the bag yet, and I will go to Lymington tomorrow."

Jacob put into the cart the next day about forty of the chickens which Alice had reared; the others were kept to increase the number in the poultry yard. They had cost little or nothing bringing up; for when quite young they only had a little oatmeal cake, and afterwards, with the potatoes which were left, they found for themselves, as fowls can always do when they have a great range of ground to go over.

Jacob came back at sunset with all the articles. He brought a new suit for Alice and Edith, with some needles, and thread, and worsted and gave her some money which was left from the sale of the chickens, after he had made the purchases. He also bought a new suit for Edward and Humphrey, and a gun, which was much approved of by Humphrey, as it had a larger bore and carried a heavier bullet than either Jacob's or Edward's; and there was a white kitten for Alice and Edith. There was no news, only that the Levellers had opposed Cromwell, and he had put them down with the other troops.

Time passed; the month of November came on, without anything to disturb the daily employments of the family in the forest: when one evening Jacob, who had returned from hunting with Edward, told Alice that she must do all she could to give them a dinner the next day, as it was to be a feast.

"Why so, Jacob?"

"If you cannot guess I won't tell you till the time comes," replied Jacob.

Alice made all the preparations, and had for dinner the next day a piece of baked venison, a venison stew, a pair of roast chickens, and an apple pie—which, for them, was a very grand dinner indeed. And it was very well dressed, for Jacob had taught her to cook, and by degrees she improved upon Jacob's instruction.

"And now I'll tell you," said Jacob, after saying grace, "why I asked you for a feast this day. It is because exactly on this day twelvemonth I brought you all to the cottage. Now you know."

"I did not know it certainly, but I dare say you are right," replied Edward.

"And now, children, tell me," said Jacob, "has not this year passed very quickly and very happily—quite as quickly and quite as happily as if you had been staying at Arnwood?"

The second winter now came on. Jacob and Edward went out hunting usually about twice a week; for the old forester complained of stiffness and rheumatism, and not feeling so active as he used to be. Humphrey now accompanied Edward perhaps one day in the week, but not more, and they seldom returned without having procured venison, for Edward knew his business well, and no longer needed the advice of Jacob. As the winter advanced Jacob gave up going out altogether. He went to Lymington to sell the venison and procure what was necessary for the household; but even these journeys fatigued him, and it was evident that the old man's constitution was breaking fast. Humphrey was always busy. One evening he was making something which puzzled them all. They asked him what it was for, but he would not tell them.

"It's an experiment that I am trying," said he, as he was bending a hazel stick. "If it answers, you shall know: if it does not, I've only had a little trouble for nothing. Jacob, I hope you will not forget the salt tomorrow when you go to Lymington, for my pigs are ready for killing, and we must salt the greater part of the pork. After the legs and shoulders have lain long enough in salt, I mean to try if I cannot smoke them, and, if I do, I'll then smoke some bacon. Won't that be jolly, Alice? Won't you like to have a great piece of bacon hanging up there, and only have to get on a stool to cut off what you want, when Edward and I come home hungry, and you've nothing to give us to eat?"

"I shall be very glad to have it, and I think so will you too, by the way you talk."

"I shall, I assure you. Jacob, didn't you say the ash sticks were the best to smoke bacon with?"

"Yes, boy; when you are ready I'll tell you how to manage. My poor mother used to smoke very well in this very chimney."

"I think that will do," said Humphrey, letting his hazel stick spring up, after he had bent it down, "but tomorrow I shall find out."

"But what is it for, Humphrey?" said Edith.

"Go away, puss, and play with your kitten," replied Humphrey, putting away his tools and his materials in a corner. "I've a great deal on my hands now, but I must kill my pigs before I think of anything else."

The next day Jacob took the venison into Lymington, and brought back the salt and other articles required. The pigs were then killed, and salted down under Jacob's directions; his rheumatism did not allow him to assist, but Humphrey and Edward rubbed in the salt, and Alice took the pieces of pork away to the tub when they were finished. Humphrey had been out the day before with the unknown article he had been so long about. The next morning he went out before breakfast, and when he returned he brought a hare in his hand, which he laid on the table.

"There," said he, "my spring has answered, and this is the fruits of it. Now I'll make some more, and we will have something by way of a change for dinner."

They were much pleased with Humphrey's success, and he was not a little proud of it.

"How did you find how to make it?"

"Why, I read in the old books of travels which Jacob brought home with him last summer, of people catching rabbits and hares in some way like this; I could not make it out exactly, but it gave me the idea."

CHAPTER 7

HUMPHREY WAS now after something else. He had made several traps, and brought in rabbits and hares almost every day. He had also made some bird traps, and had caught two goldfinches for Alice and Edith, which they put in the cages he had made for them. He was out early in the morning, and in the evening, when the moon was up, he came home later, long after they had all gone to bed; but they never knew why, nor would he tell them. A heavy fall of snow took place, and Humphrey was more out than ever. At last, about a week after the snow had lain on the ground, one morning he came in with a hare and rabbit in his hand, and said:

"Edward, I have caught something larger than a hare or a rabbit, and you must come and help me, and we must take our guns. Jacob, I suppose your rheumatism is too bad to let you come too?"

"No; I think I can manage. It's the damp that hurts me so much. This frosty air will do me good, perhaps. I have been much better since the snow fell. Now, then, let us see what you have caught."

Humphrey went on till they came close to a clump of large trees, and then brought them to a pitfall which he had dug, about six feet wide and eight feet long, and nine feet deep.

"There's my large trap," said Humphrey, "and see what I have caught in it."

The looked down into the pit and perceived a young bull in it. Smoker, who was with them, began to bark furiously at it.

"But how did you catch him?" said Edward.

"I read of it in the same book I did about the traps for hares," replied Humphrey. "I dug out the pit and covered it with brambles, and then put snow on top. This is the thicket that the herd comes to chiefly in winter time; it is large and dry, and the large trees shelter it, so that is why I chose this spot. I took a large bundle of hay, put some on the snow about the pit, and then strewed some more about in small handfuls, so that the cattle must find it, and pick it up, which I knew they would be glad to do, now that the snow is on the ground. And now, you see, I have succeeded."

"Well, Humphrey, you beat us, I will say," said Edward. "Shall I shoot him?"

"Yes, now that he is looking up."

Edward shot his ball through the forehead of the animal, which fell dead; but they were then obliged to go home for the pony and cart, and ropes to get the animal out of the pit, and a hard job they had of it too; but the pony helped them, and they did get it out at last.

"I will do it easier next time," said Humphrey. "I will make a windlass as soon as I can, and we will soon hoist out another, like they turn a bucket of water up from a well."

"It's nice young meat," said Jacob, who was skinning the bull, "not above eighteen months old, I should think."

They loaded the cart with the skin and quarters of the animal, and then drove home.

"It must have taken you a long while to dig that pit, Humphrey."

"Yes, it did, and as I got deeper the work was harder, and then I had to carry away all the earth and scatter it about. I was more than a month about it from the time that I began till it was finished, and I had a ladder to go up and down by at last, and carried the baskets of earth up, for it was too deep to throw it out."

"Nothing like patience and perseverance, Humphrey. You've more than I have."

During this winter, which passed rapidly away, very few circumstances of any consequence occurred. Old Jacob was more or less confined to the cottage by the rheumatism, and Edward hunted either by himself or occasionally with Humphrey. Humphrey was fortunate enough to take a bull and cowcalf in his pitfall, both of them about a year or fifteen months old, and by a rude invention of his, by way of windlass, contrived, with the assistance of Edward, to hoist them uninjured out of the pit. They were put into the yard, and after having been starved till they were tamed, they followed the example of the heifer and calf, and became quite tame. These were an important addition to their stock, as may well be imagined. The only mishap under which they laboured was old Jacob's confinement to the cottage, which, as the winter advanced, prevented him from going to Lymington; they could not therefore sell any venison, and Humphrey, by way of experiment, smoked some venison hams, which he hung with the others. There was another point on which they felt anxiety, which was, that Jacob could not cross the forest to get the puppies which had been promised them, and the time was past, for it was now January, when he was to have called for them. Edward and Humphrey pressed the old man very hard to let one of them go; but the only answer they could obtain was, "that he'd be better soon." At last, finding that he got worse instead of better, he consented that Edward should go, and the next morning he set off, mounted upon White Billy, with a little money in his pocket, in case he should want it.

"I wish I was going with you," said Humphrey, as he walked by the side of the pony.

"I wish you were, Humphrey; for my part, I feel as if I were a slave set at liberty. I do justice to old Jacob's kindness and goodwill, and acknowledge how much we are indebted to him; but still, to be housed up here in the forest, never seeing or speaking to anyone, shut out from the world, does not suit Edward Beverley. Our father was a soldier, and a right good one, and if I were old enough I think even now I should escape and join the royal party, broken as it may be, and by all accounts is, at this moment. Deer-stalking is all very well, but I fly at higher game."

"What puzzles me," replied Humphrey, "is the fear that old Jacob has of our being seen at Lymington."

"Why, what fear is there?"

"I cannot tell more than you; in my opinion, the fear is only in his own imagination. I still think that there is no fear of either you or I going out of the forest in our present dresses and under the name of Armitage. No one would recognize us; you are grown tall and so am I, and we are so tanned and sunburnt with air and exercise, that we do look more like children of the forest than the sons of Colonel Beverley."

CHAPTER 8

EDWARD PUT the pony to a trot, and in two hours was on the other side of the New Forest. The directions given to him by Jacob were not forgotten, and before it was noon he found himself at the gate of the keeper's house. Dismounting, and hanging the bridle of the pony over the rail, he walked through a small garden, neatly kept, but, so early in the year, not over gay, except that the crocus and snowdrops were peeping. He rapped at the door with his knuckles, and a girl of about fourteen, very neatly dressed, answered the summons.

"Is Oswald Partridge at home, maiden?" said Edward.

"No, young man, he is not. He is in the forest."

"When will he return?"

"Towards the evening is his time, unless he is more than usually successful."

"I have come some distance to find him," replied Edward; "and it would vex me to return without seeing him. Has he a wife, or anyone that I could speak to?"

"He has no wife; but I am willing to deliver a message."

"I am come about some dogs which he promised to Jacob Armitage, my relation; but the old man is too unwell and has been for some time, to come himself for them, and he has sent me."

"There are dogs, young and old, large and small, in the kennels, so far I do know, and no more."

"I fear, then, I must wait till his return," replied Edward.

"I will speak to my father," replied the young girl, "if you will wait one moment."

In a minute or two the girl returned, saying that her father begged that he would walk in, and he would speak with him. Edward bowed, and followed the young girl, who led the way to a room in which was seated a man dressed after the fashion of the Roundheads of the day. His steeple-crowned hat lay on the chair, with his sword beneath it. He was sitting at a table covered with papers.

"Here is the youth, father," said the girl; and having said this, she crossed the room and took a seat by the side of the fire. The man, or we should rather say gentleman—for he had the appearance of one, notwithstanding the sombre and peculiar dress he wore, continued to read a letter which he had just opened; and Edward, who feared himself the prisoner of a Roundhead, when he only expected to meet a keeper, was further irritated by the neglect shown towards him by the party. Forgetting that he was, by his own assertion, not Edward Beverley, but the relative of one Jacob Armitage, he coloured up with anger as he stood at the door. Fortunately the time that it took the other party to read through the letter gave Edward also time for recollecting the disguise under which he appeared; the colour subsided from his cheeks, and he remained in silence, occasionally meeting the look of the little girl, who, when their eyes met, immediately withdrew her glance.

"What is your business, young man?" at last said the gentleman at the table.

"I came, sir, on private business with the keeper, Oswald Partridge, to obtain two young hounds, which he promised to my grandfather, Jacob Armitage."

"Armitage!" said the other party, referring to a list on the table; "Armitage—Jacob—yes—I see he is one of the verderers. Why has he not been here to call upon me?"

"For what reason should he call upon you, sir?" replied Edward.

"Simply, young man, because the New Forest is, by the Parliament, committed to my charge. Notice has been given for all those who were employed to come here, that they might be permitted to remain, or be discharged, as I may deem most advisable."

"Jacob Armitage has heard nothing of this, sir," replied Edward. "He was a keeper, appointed under the king; for two or three years his allowances have never been paid, and he has lived in his own cottage, which was left to him by his father, being his own property."

"And pray, may I ask, young man, do you live with Jacob Armitage?"

"I have done so for more than a year."

"And as your relation has received no pay and allowances as you state, pray, by what means has he maintained himself?"

"How have the other keepers maintained themselves?"replied Edward.

"Do not put questions to me, sir," replied the gentleman; "but be pleased to reply to mine. What has been the means of subsistence of Jacob Armitage?"

"If you think he has no means of subsistence, sir, you are mistaken," replied Edward. "We have land of our own, which we cultivate; we have our pony and our cart; we have our pigs and our cows."

"And they have been sufficient?"

"Had the patriarchs more?" replied Edward.

"You are pithy at reply, young man; but I know something of Jacob Armitage, and we know," continued he, putting his finger close to some writing opposite the name on the list, "with whom he has associated, and with whom he has served. Now allow me to put one question. You have come, you say, for two young hounds. Are their services required for your pigs and cows, or to what uses are they to be put?"

"We have as good a dog as there is in the forest," replied Edward, "but we wished to have others in case we should lose him."

"As good a dog as in the forest—good for what?"

"For hunting."

"Then acknowledge that you do hunt?"

"I shall not answer that question, sir; in the first place I am not here to criminate myself; and, in the next, I must know by what authority you have the right to enquire."

"Young man," replied the other in a severe tone, "you wish to know my authority, malapert as you are (at this remark Edward started, yet, recollecting himself, he compressed his lips and stood still)—this is my commission, appointing me the agent of Parliament to take charge and superintend the New Forest, with power to appoint and dismiss those whom I please. I presume you must take my word for it, as you cannot read and write."

Edward stepped up to the table, and very quietly took up the paper and read it. "You have stated what is correct, sir," said he, laying it down; "and that date of it is, I perceive, on the 20th of the last month of December. It is, therefore, but eighteen days old."

"And what inference would you draw from that, young man?" replied the gentleman, looking up to him with some astonishment.

"Simply this, sir—that Jacob Armitage has been laid up with rheumatism for three months, during which time he certainly has not killed any venison. Now, sir, until the Parliament took the forest into their hands, it undoubtedly belonged to his Majesty, if it may not now; therefore Jacob Armitage, for whatever slaughter he does have committed, is, up to the present, only answerable to his sovereign King Charles."

"It is easy to perceive the school in which you have been brought up, young man, even if there was not evidence on this paper that your forefather served under the cavalier Colonel Beverley, and has brought you up to his way of thinking."

"Sir, it is a base dog that bites the hand that feeds him," replied Edward with warmth. "Jacob Armitage and his father before him were retainers in the family of Colonel Beverley! they were indebted to him for the situation they now hold in the forest; indebted to him for everything; they revere his name, they uphold the cause for which he fell, as I do."

"Young man, if you do not speak advisably, at all events you speak gratefully; neither have I a word of disrespect to offer to the memory of Colonel Beverley, who was a gallant man and true to the cause which he espoused, although it was not a holy one; but in my position, I cannot, in justice to those whom I serve, give places and emolument to those who have been, and still are, as I may judge by your expressions, adverse to the present government."

"Sir," replied Edward, "your language, with respect to Colonel Beverley, has made me feel respect for you, which I confess I did not at first; what you say is very just; not that I think you harm Jacob Armitage; as, in the first place, I know that he would not serve under you; and, in the next, that he is too old and infirm to hold the situation; neither has he occasion for it, as his cottage and land are his own, and you cannot remove him."

"He has the title, I presume?" replied the gentleman.

"He has the title given to his grandfather, long before King Charles was born, and I presume the Parliament do not intend to invalidate the acts of former kings."

"May I enquire what relation you are to Jacob Armitage?"

"I believe, I have before said, his grandson."

"You live with him?"

"I do."

"And, if the old man dies, will inherit his property?"

Edward smiled, and looking at the young girl said:

"Now, I ask you, maiden, if your father does not presume upon his office?"

The young girl laughed, and said, "He is in authority."

"Not over me, certainly, and not over my grandfather, for he has dismissed him."

"Were you brought up at the cottage, young man?"

"No, sir; I was brought up at Arnwood. I was a playmate of the children of Colonel Beverley."

"Educated with them?"

"Yes, for, as far as my wilfulness would permit, the chaplain was always ready to give me instruction."

"Where were you when Arnwood was burnt down?"

"I was at the cottage at that time," replied Edward, grinding his teeth, and looking wildly.

"Nay, nay, I can forgive any expression of feeling on your part, my young man, when that dreadful and disgraceful deed is brought to your memory. It was a stain that can never be effaced—a deed most diabolical, and what we thought would call down the vengeance of Heaven. If prayers could avert, or did avert it, they were not wanting on our side."

Edward remained silent: this admission on the part of the Roundhead prevented an explosion on his part. He felt that all were not so bad as he had imagined. After a long pause, he said:

"When I came here, sir, it was to seek Oswald Partridge, and obtain the hounds which he had promised us; but I presume that my journey is now useless."

"Why so?"

"Because you have the control of the forest, and will not permit dogs for the chase to be given away to those who are not employed by the powers that now govern."

"You have judged correctly, in so far that my duty is to prevent it; but as the promise was made previous to the date of my commission, I presume," said he, smiling, "you think I have no right to interfere, as it will be an *ex post facto* case, if I do; I shall not therefore interfere, only I must point out to you that the laws are still the same relative to those who take the deer in the forest by stealth. Nor can you be surprised, if a poacher is caught, that he incurs the penalty. So now there's an end of our argument. If you go into the kitchen you will find wherewithal to refresh the inward man, and if you wish to remain till Oswald Partridge comes home you are welcome."

Edward, who felt indignant at being dismissed to the kitchen, nodded his head and smiled upon the little girl, and left the room. "Well," thought he as he went along the passage, "I came here for two puppies, and I have found a Roundhead. I don't know how it is, but I am not so angry with him as I thought I should be. That little girl had a nice smile—she was quite handsome when she smiled. Oh, this is the kitchen, to which," thought he, "the lord of Arnwood is dismissed by a Covenanter and Roundhead, probably a tradesman or outlaw, who has served the cause. Well, be it so; as Humphrey says, 'I'll bide my time.' But there is no one here, so I'll try if there is a stable for White Billy, who is tired, I presume, of being at the gate."

Edward returned by the way he came, went out of the front door, and through the garden to where the pony was made fast, and led him away in search of a stable. He found one behind the house, and filling the rack with hay, returned to the house, and seated himself at a porch which was at the door which led to the back premises, for the keeper's house was large and commodious. Edward was in deep thought when he was roused by the little girl, who said:

"I am afraid, young sir, you have had but sorry welcome in the kitchen, as there was no one to receive you. I was not aware that Phœbe had gone out. If you will come with me, I may, perhaps, find you refreshment."

"Thanks, maiden, you are kind and considerate to an avowed poacher," replied Edward.

"Oh, but you will not poach, I'm sure; and if you do I'll beg you off if I can," replied the girl, laughing.

Edward followed her into the kitchen, and she soon produced a cold fowl and a venison pasty, which she placed on the table.

"There," said she, "that is all that I can find."

"Your father's name is Heatherstone, I believe? It was so on the warrant."

"Yes, it is."

"And yours?"

"The same as my father's, I should presume."

"Yes, but your baptismal name?"

"You ask strange questions, young sir; but still I will answer you that; my baptismal name is Patience."

"That's a nice little girl," thought Edward, "although she is the daughter of a Roundhead; and she calls me 'sir.' I cannot, therefore, look like Jacob's grandson, and must be careful." Edward then set to with a good appetite at the viands which had been placed before him, and had just finished a hearty meal when Patience Heatherstone again came in and said:

"Oswald Partridge is now coming home."

"I thank you, maiden," replied Edward. "May I ask a question of you? Where is the king now?"

"I have heard that he resides at Hurst Castle," replied the girl; "but," added she in a low tone, "all attempts to see him would be useless, and only hurt him and those who made the attempt." Having said this, she left the room.

CHAPTER 9

EDWARD, HAVING finished his meal, rose from the table and went out of the back door and found there Oswald Partridge. He accosted him, stating the reason for his coming over to him. "I did not know that Jacob had a grandson; indeed I never knew that he had a son. Have you been living with him long?"

"More than a year," replied Edward; "before that I was in the household at Arnwood."

"Then you are of the king's side, I presume?" replied Oswald.

"To death," replied Edward, "when the time comes."

"And I am also; that you may suppose, for never would I give a hound to anyone that was not. But we had better go to the kennels; dogs may hear, but they can't repeat."

"I little thought to have met anyone but you here when I came," said Edward; "and I will now tell you all that passed between me and the new intendant." Edward then related the conversation.

"You have been bold," said Oswald—"but perhaps it is all the better—I am to retain my situation, and so are two others; but there are many new hands coming in as rangers. I know nothing of them but that they are little fitted for their places; and rail against the king all day long, which I suppose is their chief merit in the eyes of those who appoint them. However, one thing is certain, that if those fellows cannot stalk a deer themselves they will do all they can to prevent others; so you must be on the alert, for the punishment is severe."

"I fear them not; the only difficulty is, that we shall not be able to find a sale for the venison now," replied Edward.

"Oh, never fear that; I will give you the names of those who will take all your venison off your hands without any risk on your part, expect in the killing of it. They will meet you in the park, lay down ready money, and take it away. I don't know, but I have an idea that this new intendant, or what you call him, is not so severe as he pretends to be. Indeed, his permitting you to say what he did, and his own words relative to the colonel, convince me that I am right in the opinion that I formed.

"If you come here," continued Oswald, "do not carry your gun, and see that you are not watched home. There are the dogs for your grandfather. We must go out together; and besides, I must know where the old man's cottage is (for I do not exactly); in the first place because I may want to come to you, and in the next, that I may put others on a false scent. Do you know the clump of large oaks which they call the Clump Royal?"

"Yes, I do."

"Will you meet me there the day after tomorrow, at early dawn?"

"If I live and do well."

"That's enough. Take the dogs in the leashes, and go away now."

The keeper nodded adieu to Edward, who left him to go to the stable for the pony. Edward saddled White Billy, and rode away across the forest with the dogs trotting at the pony's heels.

The next morning Edward went to Jacob, who for the last ten days had altogether kept his bed, and gave him the detail of what had happened at the keeper's lodge.

"You have been more bold than prudent, Edward," replied Jacob; "but I could not expect you to have spoken otherwise. You are too proud and too manly to tell a lie, and I am glad that it is so. As for your upholding the king, although he is now a prisoner in their hands, they cannot blame you or punish you for that, as long as you have not weapons in your hands; but now that they have taken the forest under their jurisdiction you must be careful, for they are the ruling powers at present, and must be obeyed, or the forfeit must be paid. Still I do not ask you to promise me this or that; I only point out to you that your sisters will suffer by any imprudence on your part; and for their sakes be careful. I say this, Edward, because I feel that my days are numbered, and that in a short time I shall be called away. You will then have all the load on your shoulders which has been latterly on mine. If I might advise, let your hunting in the forest be confined to the wild cattle; they are not game, and the forest laws do not extend to them, and the meat is as valuable as venison; that is to say, it does not sell so dear, but there is more of it. But stick to the farm as much as you can; for you see, Edward, you do not look like a low-born forester, nor ought you to do so; and the more quiet you keep the better. As for Oswald Partridge, you may trust him; I know him well, and he will prove your friend for my sake, as soon as he hears that I am dead. Send Alice to me, my dear boy."

Edward was much distressed to perceive the change which had taken place in old Jacob. He was evidently much worse; but Edward had no idea how much worse he was. Edward assisted Humphrey in the farm, and in the evening again went to Jacob, and then told him of the arrangement he had made to meet Oswald Partridge on the following morning.

"Go, my boy," said Jacob; "be as intimate with him as you can, and make a friend of him—nay, if it should be necessary you may tell him who you are; I did think of telling him myself, as it might be important to you one day as evidence. I think you had better bring him here tomorrow night, Edward; tell him I am dying, and wish to speak to him before I go."

Early the next morning Edward set off to the appointed rendezvous with Oswald Partridge. The Clump Royal, as it was called, from the peculiar size and beauty of the oaks, was about seven miles from the cottage; and at the hour and time indicated Edward, with his gun in his hand, and Smoker lying beside him, was leaning against one of those monarchs of the forest. He did not wait long. Oswald Partridge, similarly provided, made his appearance, and Edward advanced to meet him.

"Welcome, Oswald," said Edward.

"And welcome to you also, my fine lad," replied Oswald. "I have been hard questioned about you since we parted; first, by the Roundhead Heatherstone, who plied me in all manner of ways to find out whether you are what you assert, the grandson of Jacob, or some other person. I really believe that he fancies you are the Duke of York; but he could not get any more from me than what I knew. But the pretty little daughter was more curious still. She cross-questioned me in every way when her father was not present, and at last begged me as a favour to tell you not to take the deer, as her father was very strict in his duty, and, if caught, you would be imprisoned."

"Many thanks to her for her caution, but I hope to take one today, nevertheless," replied Edward; "a hart royal is not meat for Roundheads, although the king's servants may feast on them."

"That's truly said. Well, now I must see your woodcraft. You shall be the leader of the chase."

"Think you we can harbour a stag about here?"

"Yes, in this month, no doubt."

"Let us walk on," said Edward. "The wind is fresh from the eastern quarter; we will face it, if you please—or rather, keep it blowing on our right cheek for the present."

"'Tis well," replied Oswald; and they walked for about half an hour.

"This is the slot of a doe," said Edward in a low voice, pointing to the marks; "yonder thicket is a likely harbour for the stag." They proceeded, and Edward pointed out to Oswald the slot of the stag into the thicket. They then walked round, and found no marks of the animal having left his lair.

"He is here," whispered Edward; and Oswald made a sign for Edward to enter the thicket, while he walked to the other side. Edward entered the thicket cautiously. In the centre he perceived, through the trees, a small cleared spot, covered with high fern, and felt certain that the stag was lying there. He forced his way on his knees till he had a better view of the place, and then cocked his gun. The noise induced the stag to move his antlers, and discover his lair. Edward could just perceive the eyes of the animal through the heath; he waited till the beast settled again, took steady aim, and fired. At the report of the gun another stag sprung up and burst away. Oswald fired, and wounded it, but the animal made off, followed by the dogs. Edward, who hardly knew whether he had missed or not, but felt almost certain that he had not, hastened out of the thicket to join in the chase, and, as he passed through the fern patch, perceived that his quarry lay dead. He then followed the chase, and, being very fleet of foot, soon came up with Oswald, and passed him without speaking. The stag made for a swampy ground, and finally took to the water beyond it, and stood at bay. Edward then waited for Oswald, who came up with him.

"He has soiled," said Edward, "and now you may go in and kill him."

Oswald, eager in the chase, hastened up to where the dogs and stag were in the water, and put a bullet through the animal's head.

"How did you happen to miss him?" said Oswald, "for these are my shots."

"Because I never fired at him," said Edward; "my quarry lies dead in the fern—and a fine fellow he is."

As soon as Oswald had done his work, he hung the quarters of the animal on an oak tree, and went back with Edward.

On their arrival at the spot Oswald found that Edward had put the ball right into the eye of the stag.

"Well," said he, "you made me suppose that you knew something of our craft, but I did not believe that you were so apt as you thought yourself to be. I now confess that you are a master, as far as I can see, in all branches of the craft. This is, indeed, a hart royal. Twenty-five antlers, as I live! Come, out with your knife, and let us finish; for if we are to go to the cottage we have no time to lose. It will be dark in half an hour."

They hung all the quarters of the stag as before, and then set off for Jacobs cottage; Edward proposing that Oswald should take the cart and pony to carry the meat home the next morning, and that he would accompany him to bring it back.

Their dinner was ready for them; and Oswald praised the cooking. He was much surprised to find that Jacob had four grandchildren. After dinner he went into Jacob's room, and remained with him more than an hour. During this conference Jacob confided to Oswald that the four children were the sons and daughters of Colonel Beverley, supposed to have been burnt in the firing of Arnwood. Oswald came out, much surprised as well as pleased with the information, and with the confidence reposed in him. He saluted Edward and Humphrey respectfully, and said, "I was not aware with whom I was in company, sir, as you may well imagine; but the knowledge of it has made my heart glad."

They then entered into a long conversation, during which Oswald expressed his opinion that the old man was sinking fast, and would not last more than three or four days. Oswald had a bed made up for him on the floor of the room where Edward and Humphrey slept, and the next morning they set off, at an early hour, with the pony and cart, loaded it with the venison, and took it across the forest to the keeper's lodge. It was so late when they arrived that Edward consented to pass the night there, and return home on the following morning. Oswald went into the sitting-room to speak with the intendant of the forest, leaving Edward in the kitchen with Phœbe, the maidservant. He told the intendant that he had brought home some fine venison, and wished his orders about it. He also stated that he had been assisted by Edward Armitage, who had brought the venison home for him in his cart, and who was now in the kitchen, as he would be obliged to pass the night there; and, on being questioned, he was lavish in his praises of Edward's skill and knowledge of woodcraft, which he declared to be superior to his own.

"It proves that the young man has had much practice, at all events," replied Mr. Heatherstone, smiling. "He has been living at the king's expense, but he must not follow it up at the cost of the Parliament. It would be well to take this young man as a ranger if we could; for, although he is opposed to us, yet, if he once took our service, he would be faithful, I am sure. You can propose it to him, Oswald. The haunches of that hart royal must be sent up to General Cromwell tomorrow; the remainder we will give directions for, as soon as I have made up my mind how to dispose of it."

Oswald left the room and came back to Edward. "General Cromwell is to have the haunches of your stag," said he to Edward, smiling; "and the intendant proposes that you should take service as one of the rangers."

"I thank you," replied Edward; "but I've no fancy to find venison for General Cromwell and his Roundheads; and so you may tell the intendant, with many thanks for his goodwill towards me, nevertheless."

"I thought as much; but the man meant kindly, that I really think. Now, Phœbe, what can you give us to eat, for we are hungry?"

"You shall be served directly," replied Phœbe. "I have some steaks on the fire."

"And you must find a bed for my young friend here."

"I have none in the house, but there is plenty of good straw over the stables."

Oswald was about to remonstrate, but Edward held up his finger, and no more was said.

As soon as they had finished their supper, Phœbe proposed that they should go to bed. It was late, and she would sit up no longer. Edward rose and went out, followed by Oswald, who had given up the keeper's house to the intendant and his daughter, and slept in the cottage of one of the rangers, about a quarter of a mile off. After some conversation they shook hands and parted, as Edward intended returning very early the next morning, being anxious about old Jacob.

Edward went up the ladder into the loft. There was no door to shut out the wind, which blew piercingly cold, and after a time he found himself so chilled that he could not sleep. He rose to see if he could not find some protection from the wind by getting more into a corner; for although Phœbe had told him that there was plenty of straw, it proved that there was very little indeed in the loft, barely enough to lie down upon. Edward, after a time, descended the ladder to walk in the yard, that by exercise he might recover the use of his limbs. At last, turning to and fro, he cast his eyes up to the window of the bedroom above the kitchen, where he perceived a light was still burning. He thought it was Phœbe, the maid, going to bed; and with no very gracious feelings towards her for having deprived him of his own night's rest, he was wishing that she might have the toothache or something else to keep her awake, when suddenly through the white window curtain he perceived a broad light in the room—it increased every moment—and he saw the figure of a female rush past it, and attempt to open the window—the drawing of the curtains showed him that the room was on fire. A moment's thought, and he ran for the ladder by which he had ascended to the loft, and placed it against the window. The flames were less bright, and he could not see the female who had been at the window when he went for the ladder. He ascended quickly, and burst open the casement—the smoke poured out in such volumes that it nearly suffocated him, but he went in; and as soon as he was inside he stumbled against the body of the person who had attempted to open the window, but who had fallen down senseless. As he raised the body, the fire, which had been smothered from want of air when all the windows and doors were closed, now burst out, and he was scorched before he could get on the ladder again with the body in his arms; but he succeeded in getting it down safe. Perceiving that the clothes were on fire, he held them till they were extinguished, and then, for the first time, discovered that he had brought down the daughter of the intendant of the forest. There was no time to be lost, so Edward carried her into the stable and left her there, still insensible, upon the straw, in a spare stall, while he hastened to alarm the house. The watering butt for the horses was outside the stable; Edward caught up the pail, filled it, and hastening up the ladder, threw it into the room, and then descended for more.

By this time, Edward's continual calls of "Fire! fire!" had aroused the people of the house, and also of the cottages adjacent. Mr. Heatherstone came out half dressed, and with horror on his countenance. Phœbe followed screaming, and the other people now hastened from their cottages.

"Save her! my daughter is in the room!" exclaimed Mr. Heatherstone. "Oh, save her, or let me do so!" cried the poor man, in agony; but the fire burst out of the window in such force that any attempt would have been in vain.

Oswald set the men to work, and Edward was now supplied with water so fast that the fire began to diminish. The window was now approachable, and a few more buckets enabled him to put one foot into the room, and then every moment the flames and smoke decreased.

Meanwhile it would be impossible to describe the agony of the intendant, who would have rushed up the ladder into the flames, had he not been held by some of the men. "My daughter! my child!—burnt—burnt to death!" exclaimed he, clasping his hands.

At that moment a voice in the crowd called out, "There were four burnt at Arnwood!"

"God of heaven!" exclaimed Mr. Heatherstone, falling down into a swoon, in which state he was carried to a neighbouring cottage.

"She is safe and well," replied Edward; "I think so, at least. I brought her down the ladder, and put her in the stable, before I attempted to put out the fire. See, there she is; she has not recovered yet from her swoon. Bring some water. She breathes! thank God! There, that will do, Oswald, she is recovering! Now let us cover her up in your cloak, and carry her to your cottage. We will recover her there."

Oswald folded up the still unconscious girl in his cloak, and carried her away in his arms, followed by Edward.

"Where is my father?" cried Patience, as soon as she was sufficiently recovered.

"He is safe and well, miss," replied Oswald.

Patience attempted to stand, but found that she was too much exhausted, and she fell back again on the bed. "I can't stand," said she. "Bring my father to me."

"I will, miss," replied Oswald. "Will you stay here, Edward?"

"Yes," replied Edward.

He went out of the cottage door, and remained there while Oswald went to Mr. Heatherstone.

Oswald found him sensible, but in deep distress, as may be imagined. "The fire is all out, sir," said Oswald.

"I care not for that. My poor, poor child!"

"Your child is safe, sir," replied Oswald.

"Safe did you say?" cried Mr. Heatherstone, starting up. "Safe—where?"

"In my cottage. She has sent me for you."

Mr. Heatherstone rushed out, passed by Edward, who was standing at the door of the other cottage, and was in his daughter's arms. Oswald came out to Edward, who then detailed to him the way in which he had saved the girl.

"Had it not been for the ill-nature of that girl Phœbe in sending me to sleep where there was no straw, they would all have been burnt," observed Edward.

Oswald went into the cottage and returned with some salve, with which he dressed Edward's arm, which proved to be very severely burnt.

"How grateful the intendant ought to be—and will be, I have no doubt!" observed Oswald.

"And for that very reason I shall saddle my pony and ride home as fast as I can; and do you hear, Oswald, do not show him where I live."

Edward rode fast, for he was anxious to get home and ascertain the state of poor old Jacob; and, moreover, his burnt arm was very painful. He was met by Humphrey about a mile from the cottage, who told him that he did not think that the old man could last many hours, and that he was very anxious to see him. As the pony was quite tired with the fast pace that Edward had ridden, Edward pulled up to a walk, and, as they went along, acquainted Humphrey with what had passed.

"Thank God that you are come, Edward," said the old forester, "for I was anxious to see you before I die; and something tells me that I have but a short time to remain here."

"Why should you say so!—do you feel very ill?"

"No, not ill; but I feel that I am sinking fast. Recollect that I am an old man, Edward."

"Not so very old, Jacob; Oswald said that you were not more than sixty years old."

"Oswald knows nothing about it. I am past seventy-six, Edward. And now, Edward, I have but few words to say. Be careful—if not for your own sake, at least for your little sisters'. You are young, but you are strong and powerful above your years, and can better protect them than I could. I see darker days yet coming—but it is His will, and who shall doubt that that is right? I pray you not to make your birth and lineage known as yet—it can do no good, and it may do harm—and if you can be persuaded to live in the cottage, and to live on the farm, which will now support you all, it will be better. Do not get into trouble about the venison, which they now claim as their own. You will find some money in the bag in my chest, sufficient to buy all you want for a long while—but take care of it; for there is no saying but you may require it. And now, Edward, call your brother and sisters to me, that I may bid them farewell."

Edward summoned his sisters and Humphrey.

"Humphrey, my good boy," said Jacob. "Be careful, Humphrey, for you can ill be spared. Hold to the farm as it is now, it will support you all. My dear Alice and Edith, I am dying; very soon I shall be laid by your brothers, in my grave. Good-bye, and may God bless you.—Bless you, Edith; may you grow up as good and innocent as you are now. Farewell, Humphrey—farewell, Edward—my eyes are dim—pray for me, children. O God of mercy—pardon my many sins, and receive my soul, through Jesus Christ. Amen, amen."

CHAPTER 10

"Humphrey," said Edward, "the sooner all this is over the better. As long as poor Jacob's body remains in the cottage there will be nothing but distress with the poor girls."

"I agree with you," replied Humphrey; "where shall we bury him?"

"Under the great oak tree, at the back of the cottage," replied Edward. "One day the old man said to me that he should like to be buried under one of the oaks of the forest."

"Well, then, I will go and dig his grave tonight," replied Humphrey.

Humphrey went out, and having found his tools, set to the task—he worked hard, and before morning had finished. Edward helped him to drag the body on the cart to the grave. They laid it in.

"Are our sisters risen, do you think?"

"I am sure that they are," replied Humphrey, "and I will go to them."

Humphrey went to the door, and said, "Alice—Alice and Edith—come out immediately."

Edward took the Bible under his arm, and Alice by the hand. Humphrey led Edith until they arrived at the grave, when the two little girls saw the covered body of Jacob lying in it.

"Kneel down," said Edward, opening the Bible. And they all knelt down by the grave. Edward read the two Psalms, and then closed the book. The little girls took one last look at the body, and then turned away weeping to the cottage. Edward and Humphrey filled up the grave, and then followed their sisters home.

"I'm glad it's over," said Humphrey, wiping his eyes. "Poor old Jacob! I'll put a paling round his grave."

Edward and the children repeated the Lord's Prayer, and then rose up. They went to their respective employments, and the labour of the day soon made them composed, although then, for many days afterwards, it was but occasionally that a smile was seen upon their lips.

Thus passed a week, by which time Edward's arm was so far well that it gave him no pain, and he was able to assist Humphrey in the work on the farm. The snow had disappeared, and the spring, although it had been checked for a time, now made rapid advances. Constant occupation, and the return of fine weather, both had the effect of restoring the serenity of their minds; and while Humphrey was preparing the paling to fix round the grave of old Jacob, Alice and Edith collected the wild violets which now peeped forth on sheltered spots, and planted the roots over the grave. Edward also procured all the early flowers he could collect, and assisted his sisters in their task; and thus, in planting it, and putting up the paling, the grave of the old man became their constant work-ground; and when their labour was done they would still remain there and talk over his worth. As soon as the paling was finished, Humphrey put up a board against the oak tree, with the simple words carved on it, "Jacob Armitage."

Edward had, every day, expected that Oswald Partridge would have called upon him, as he had promised to do before the week was out; but Oswald had not made his appearance, much to Edward's surprise. A month passed away; Edward's arm was now quite well, and still Oswald came not. One morning, Humphrey and Edward were conversing upon many points—the principal of which was upon Edward going to Lymington, for they were now in want of flour and meal, when Edward thought of what old Jacob had told him relative to the money that he would find in his chest. He went into Jacob's room and opened the chest, at the bottom of which, under the clothes, he found a leather bag, which he brought out to Humphrey; on opening it they were much surprised to find in it more than sixty gold pieces, besides a great deal of silver coin.

"Surely this is a great sum of money," observed Humphrey.

"I think so too," replied Edward. "I wish Oswald Partridge would come, for I want to ask him many questions. I don't know the price of flour anything else we have to purchase, nor do I know what I ought to be paid for venison. I don't like to go to Lymington till I see him, for that reason. If he does not come soon, I shall ride over and see what is the matter."

Edward then replaced the money in the chest, and he and Humphrey went out to the farmyard to go on with their work.

It was not until six weeks after the death of old Jacob that Oswald Partridge made his appearance.

"How is the old man, sir?" was his first question.

"He was buried a few days after you left," replied Edward.

"I expected as much," said the forester. "Peace be with him; he was a good man. And how is your arm?"

"Nearly well," replied Edward. "Now, sit down, Oswald, for I have a great deal to say to you; and first let me ask you, what has detained you from coming here according to your promise?"

"Simply, and in a few words—murder."

"Murder!" exclaimed Edward.

"Yes, deliberate murder, sir; in short, they have beheaded the king—beheaded King Charles, our sovereign."

"Have they dared to do it?"

"They have," replied Oswald. "We know little that is going on, in the forest; but when I saw you last, I heard that he was then in London, and was to be tried."

"Tried!" exclaimed Edward. "How could they try a king? By the laws of our country, a man must be tried by his equals; and where were his equals?"

Edward was indeed in a state of mind which required calming down.

He quitted the cottage and walked out for some distance into the forest in deep thought. At last, more calm, he returned to the cottage, and listened to the details which Oswald now gave to him of what he had heard.

When Oswald had finished, Edward asked him whether the intendant had returned.

"Yes, or I should not have been here," replied Oswald. "He came back yesterday, looking most disconsolate and grave, and I hear that he returns to London in a few days. Indeed, he told me so himself, for I requested permission to come over to see your grandfather. He said that I might go, but must return soon, as he must go back to London. I believe from what Miss Patience told me, and what I have seen myself, that he is sincerely amazed and vexed at what has taken place; and so, indeed, are many more, who, although opposed to the king's method of government, never had an idea that things should have turned out as they have done. I have a message from him to you, which is, that he begs you will come to see him, that he may thank you for the preservation of his child."

"I will take his thanks from you, Oswald; that will do as well as if he gave them me in person."

"Yes, perhaps so; but I have another message from another party, which is the young lady herself. She desires me to tell you that she will never be happy till she has seen you, and thanked you for your courage and kindness; and that you have no right to put her under such an obligation, and not give her an opportunity of expressing what she feels. Now, Mr. Edward, I am certain that she is earnest in what she says, and she made me promise that I would persuade you to come. I could not refuse her, for she is a dear little creature. As her father will go to London in a few days you may ride over and see her, without any fear of being affronted by any offers which he may make to you."

Edward then put many questions to Oswald relative to the value of various articles, and to the best method of disposing of his venison.

"Humphrey," said Edward, as soon as Oswald was gone. "I have made up my mind to go to Lymington tomorrow. We must have some flour, and many other articles, which Alice says she can no longer do without."

"Why should we not both go, Edward?" replied Humphrey.

"No, not this time," replied Edward. "I have to find out many things and many people, and I had rather go by myself; besides, I cannot allow my sisters to be left alone. I do not consider there is any danger. I admit; but something might happen to them. I should never forgive myself. Still, it is necessary that you should go to Lymington with me some time or another, that you may know where to purchase and sell, if required. What I propose is, that I will ask Oswald to come and stay here a couple of days. We will then leave him in charge of our sisters, and go to Lymington together."

"You are right, Edward; that will be the best plan."

As Humphrey made this remark, Oswald re-entered the cottage.

"I will tell you why I have returned, Mr. Edward," said Oswald. "It is of no consequence whether I return now or tomorrow. It is now early, and as you intend going to Lymington it occurred to me that I had better go with you. I can then show you all you want, which will be much better than going by yourself."

The pony and cart were soon at the door, and Edward, having received further instructions from Alice, set off for Lymington, accompanied by Oswald.

CHAPTER 11

"Would you have found your way to Lymington?" said Oswald, as the pony trotted along.

"Yes; I think so," replied Edward.

As soon as they arrived at Lymington, Oswald directed the way to a small hostelry, to which the keepers and verderers usually resorted. They drove into the yard, and, giving the pony and cart in charge of the hostler, went into the inn, where they found the landlord, and one or two other people who were drinking.

"Well, Master Andrew, how fare you?" said Oswald.

"Let me see," said the corpulent landlord, throwing back his head, as he peered at Oswald; "why, Oswald Partridge, as I am a born man! Where have you been this many a day?"

"In the forest, Master Andrew, where there are no few chops and changes."

"Yes, I heard you have a sort of Parliamentary keeper, and who is this with you?"

"The grandson of an old friend of yours, now dead—poor old Jacob Armitage."

Oswald and Edward then entered with the landlord, and arrangements were made between Master Andrew and the latter for a regular supply of venison during the season at a certain price; but as it would now be dangerous to bring it into the town, it was agreed that when there was any ready Edward should come to Lymington and give notice, and the landlord would send out people to bring it in during the night. This bargain concluded, they went into the town to make the necessary purchases. Oswald took Edward to all the shops where the articles he required were to be purchased; some they carried away with them; others, which were too heavy, they left, to be called for with the cart as they went away. Among other articles Edward required powder and lead, and they went to a gunsmith's where it was to be procured. While making his purchases Edward perceived a sword, which he thought he had seen before, hanging up against the wall among other weapons.

"What sword is that?" said he to the man who was measuring out the powder.

"It's not my sword exactly," replied the man; "and yet I cannot return it to its owner or to the family. It was brought me to be cleaned by one of Colonel Beverley's people, and before it was called for the house was burnt, and every soul perished. It was one of the colonel's swords, I am sure, as there is E.B. on a silver plate engraved on it. I have a bill owing me for work done at Arnwood, and I have no chance of it being paid now; so, whether I am to sell the sword, or what to do, I hardly know."

Edward remained silent for some little while, for he could not trust himself to speak; at last he replied: "To be candid with you, I am, and all my family have been, followers of the Beverley family, and I should be sorry if the colonel's sword was to fall into any other hands. I think, therefore, if I pay the bill which is due, you may safely let me hold the sword as a security for the money, with the express understanding that if it is ever claimed by the Beverley family I am to give it up."

"Certainly," said Oswald; "nothing can be fairer or more clearly put."

"I think so, too, young man," replied the shopkeeper. "Of course, you will leave your name and address?"

"Yes; and my friend here will vouch for its being correct," replied Edward.

The shopkeeper then produced the account, which Edward paid; and, giving on the paper the name of Edward Armitage, he took possession of the sword. He then paid for the powder and lead, which Oswald took charge of, and, hardly able to conceal his joy, hastened out of the shop.

When they arrived at the inn, Oswald went out to the yard to get the cart ready, while Edward went into the landlord's room to make enquiries as to the quantity of venison he would be able to take off his hands at a time. Oswald had taken the sword from Edward, and had put it in the cart while he was fastening the harness, when a man came up to the cart, and looked earnestly at the sword. He then examined it, and said to Oswald:

"Why, that was Colonel Beverley's, my old master's sword. I knowed it again directly. I took it to Phillips, the gunmaker, to be cleaned."

"Indeed!" replied Oswald; "I pray what may be your name?"

"Benjamin White," replied the man; "I served at Arnwood till the night it was burned down; and I have been here ever since."

"Well, well, you stand by the pony, and look that nobody takes anything out of the cart while I go in for some parcels."

"Yes, to be sure I will; but, I say, forester, how came you by that sword?"

"I will tell you when I come out again," replied Oswald.

Oswald then went in to Edward, and told him what had occurred.

"He will certainly know you, sir, and you must not come out till I can get him away," said he.

"You are right, Oswald; but before he goes, ask him what became of my aunt and where she was buried."

Oswald, on his return, told Benjamin in what manner the sword had been procured from the shopman, by the grandson of old Armitage.

"I never knew that he had one," replied Benjamin; "nor did I know that old Jacob was dead."

"What became of the old lady who was at Arnwood?" enquired Oswald. "Was she not killed?"

"Yes; that is to say she killed herself, rather than not kill Southwold."

"Where was she buried?"

"In the churchyard, at St. Faith's, by the mayor and corporation; for there was not money enough found upon her person to pay the expenses of her burial."

"And so you are tapster at the 'Commonwealth.' Is it a good inn?"

"Can't say much for it. I shan't stay longer than I can help, I can tell you. Tell Jacob Armitage's grandson that I shall be glad to see him, for old Jacob's sake; and it's hard but I'll find him something to drink when he calls."

"I will: I shall see him tomorrow," replied Oswald, getting into the cart; "so good-bye, Benjamin," much to the satisfaction of Oswald, who thought that he would never go.

They went away at a rapid pace, to make up for lost time, and soon disappeared round the corner of the street. Oswald then got out again, summoned Edward, and, having called for the flour and other heavy articles, they set off on their return.

During the drive, Oswald made known to Edward the information which he had gained from Benjamin, and at a late hour they arrived safely at the cottage.

They stayed up but a short time, as they were tired; and Oswald had resolved upon setting off before daylight on the following morning, which he did without disturbing anyone; for Humphrey was up and dressed as soon as Oswald was, and gave him something to eat as he went along. All the others remained fast asleep. Humphrey walked about a mile with Oswald, and was returning to the farm, when he thought, as he had not examined his pitfall for many days, that he might as well look at it before he went back. He therefore struck out in the direction in which it lay, and arrived there just as the day began to dawn. —

It was the end of March, and the weather was mild for the season. Humphrey arrived at the pit, and it was sufficiently light for him to perceive that the covering had been broken in, and therefore, in all probability, something must have been trapped. He sat down and waited for daylight, but at times he heard a heavy breathing, and once a low groan. This made him more anxious, and he again and again peered into the pit, but could not for a long while discover anything, until at last he thought that he could make out a human figure lying at the bottom. Humphrey called out, asking if there was anyone there. A groan was the reply, and now Humphrey was horrified at the idea that somebody had fallen into the pit, and had perished, or was perishing, for want of succour. Recollecting that the rough ladder which he had made to take the soil up out of the pit was against an oak tree close at hand, he ran for it, and put it down the pit, and then cautiously descended. On his arrival at the bottom his fears were found to be verified, for he found the body of a lad half-clothed lying there. He turned it up, as it was lying with its face to the ground, and attempted to remove it and to ascertain if there was life in it, which he was delighted to find was the case. The lad groaned several times, and opened his eyes. Humphrey was afraid that he was not strong enough to lift him on his shoulders and carry him up the ladder; but on making the attempt, he found out, from exhaustion, the poor lad was light enough for him to carry him, which he did, and safely landed him by the side of the pit.

Recollecting the watering-place of the herd of cattle was not far off, Humphrey then hastened to it, and filled his hat half full of water. The lad, altough he could not speak, drank eagerly, and in a few minutes appeared much recovered. Humphrey gave him some more, and bathed his face and temples. The sun had now risen, and it was broad daylight. The lad attempted to speak, but what he did say was in so low a tone, and evidently in a foreign language, that Humphrey could not make him out. He therefore made signs to the lad that he was going away, and would be back soon; and having, as he thought, made the lad comprehend this, Humphrey ran away to the cottage as fast as he could; and as soon as he arrived he called for Edward, who came out; and when Humphrey told him in few words what had happened, Edward went into the cottage again for some milk and some cake, while Humphrey put the pony into the cart.

In a few moments they were off again, and soon arrived at the pitfall, where they found the lad still lying where Humphrey had left him. They soaked the cake in the milk, and as soon as it was soft gave him some; after a time he swallowed pretty freely, and was so much recovered as to be able to sit up. They then lifted him into the cart, and drove gentiy home to their cottage.

"What do you think he is, Edward?" said Humphrey.

"Some poor beggar lad, who has been crossing the forest."

"No, not exactly: he appears to me to be one of the Zingaros, or gipsies as they call them: he is very dark, and has black eyes and white teeth, just like those I saw once near Arnwood, when I was out with Jacob. Jacob said that no one knew where they came from, but that they were all over the country, and that they were great thieves, and told fortunes, and played all manner of tricks."

As soon as they arrived at the cottage, they lifted the lad out of the cart, and carried him into Jacob's room, and laid him on the bed, for he was too weak to stand.

Alice and Edith, who were much surprised at the new visitor, and the way in which he had been caught, hastened to get some gruel ready for him. As soon as it was ready, they gave it to the boy, who then fell back on the bed with exhaustion, and was soon in a sound sleep. He slept soundly all that night; and the next morning, when he awoke, he appeared much better, although very hungry. This last complaint was easy to remedy, and then the lad got up and walked into the sitting-room.

"What's your name?" said Humphrey to the lad.

"Pablo," replied the lad.

"Can you speak English?"

"Yes, little," replied he.

"How did you happen to fall into the pit?"

"Not see hole."

"Are you a gipsy?"

"Yes, Gitano—same thing."

Humphrey put a great many more questions to the lad, and elicited from him, in his imperfect English, the following particulars.

That he was in company with several others of his race, going down to the sea coast on one of their usual migrations, and that they had pitched their tents not far from the pitfall. That during the night he had gone out to set some snares for rabbits, and going back to the tents, it being quite dark, he had fallen into the hole. That he had remained there three days and nights, having in vain attempted to get out. His mother was with the party of gipsies to which he belonged; but he had no father. He did not know where to follow the gang, as they had not said where they were going, farther than the sea coast. That it was no use looking for them; and that he did not care much about leaving them, as he was very unkindly treated. In reply to the question as to whether he would like to remain with them, and work with them on the farm, he replied that he should like it very much if they would be kind to him, and not make him work too hard; that he could cook the dinner, and catch them rabbits and birds and make a great many things.

"Well, Pablo, we will try you, and if you are a good lad we will do all we can to make you happy," said Edward; "but if you behave ill, we shall be obliged to turn you out-of-doors; do you understand?"

"Be as good as I can," replied Pablo; and here the conversation ended for the present.

Pablo was a very short-built lad, of apparently fifteen or sixteen years of age, very dark in complexion, but very handsome in features, with beautiful white teeth and large dark eyes. Humphrey was particularly pleased with and interested about him, as the lad so nearly lost his life through his means.

"The lad may be very useful to us, and I sincerely hope that he may prove honest and true," said Humphrey. "When do you purpose going over to the keeper's cottage, Edward?"

"In a day or two; but I am not exactly in a humour now to be very civil to the Roundheads, although the one I have promised to visit is a lady, and a very amiable, pretty little girl in the bargain."

"Why, Edward, what has made you feel more opposed to them than usual?"

"In the first place, Humphrey, the murder of the king—for it was murder, and nothing better—I cannot get that out of my head; and yesterday I obtained what I considered as almost a gift from Heaven; and if it is so, it was not given but with the intention that I should make use of it."

"And what was that, Edward?"

"Our gallant father's sword, which he drew so nobly and so well in defence of his sovereign, Humphrey, and which I trust his son may one day wield with equal distinction, and, it may be, better fortune. Come in with me, and I will show it to you."

Edward and Humphrey went into the bedroom, and Edward brought out the sword, which he had placed by his side on the bed.

"See, Humphrey, this was our father's sword; and," continued Edward, kissing the weapon, "I trust I may be permitted to draw it to revenge his death, and the death of one whose life ever should have been sacred."

CHAPTER 12

Two days later, Edward announced his intention of visiting the attendant's house. "I think it is time that I keep my promise to Oswald," he said, "and go over to the intendant's house, and pay my visit to the young lady, as I presume she is—and certainly she has every appearance of being one."

"When will you set off?"

"Tomorrow morning; and I shall take my gun, although Oswald desired me not; I don't think it prudent to be unarmed; indeed, I do not feel comfortable without I have my gun at my side."

At sunrise Edward and Humphrey were both up; Alice came out when they tapped at her door, as she would not let Edward go without his breakfast. Edith joined them, and they went to prayers.

Edward threw his gun over his arm, and calling his puppy, which he had named Holdfast, bade Humphrey and his sisters farewell, and set off on his journey across the forest.

Holdfast, as well as Humphrey's puppy, which had been named Watch, had grown very fine young animals. The first had been named Holdfast, because it would seize the pigs by the ears and lead them into the sty, and the other because it was so alert at the least noise: but, as Humphrey said, Watch ought to have learnt to lead the pigs, it being more in his line of business than Holdfast's, which was to be brought up for hunting in the forest, while Watch was being educated as a house and farmyard dog.

Edward had refused to take the pony, as Humphrey required it for the farm work, and the weather was so fine that he preferred walking; the more so, as it would enable him on his return across the forest to try for some venison, which he could not have done if he had been mounted on

Billy's back. Edward walked quickly, followed by his dog, which he had taught to keep to heel. He felt happy, as people do who have no cares, from the fine weather, the deep green of the verdure chequered by the flowers in bloom, and the majestic scenery which met his eye on every side. His heart was as buoyant as his steps as he walked along, the light summer breeze fanning his face.

When he arrived at the intendant's house, the door was opened by Patience Heatherstone herself, who said, "Oh, how glad I am to see you! Come in." Edward took off his hat and bowed; Patience led the way into her father's study, where Edward had been first received.

"And now," said Patience, extending her hand to Edward, "thanks, many thanks, for your preserving me from so dreadful a death. You don't know how unhappy I have been at not being able to give you my poor thanks for your courageous behaviour."

Her hand still remained in Edward's while she said this.

"You rate what I did too highly," replied Edward; "I would have done the same for anyone in such distress; it was my duty as a—man"; cavalier he was about to say, but he checked himself.

"He who has preserved my life at the risk of his own becomes to me as a brother—at least I feel as a sister towards him: a debt is still a debt, whether indebted to a king or to a——"

"Forester, Mistress Patience, that is the real word that you should not have hesitated to have used: do you imagine that I am ashamed of my calling?"

"To tell you candidly the truth, then," replied Patience, "I cannot believe that you are what you profess to be. I mean to say, that although a forester now, you were never brought up as such. My father has an opinion allied to mine."

"I thank you both for your good opinion of me, but I fear that I cannot raise myself above the condition of a forester: nay, from your father's coming down here, and the new regulations, I have every chance of sinking down to the lower grade of a deer stealer and poacher; indeed, had it not been that I had my gun with me, I should have been seized as such this very day as I came over."

"But you were not shooting the deer, were you, sir?" enquired Patience.

"No, I was not; nor have I killed any since last I saw you."

"I am glad that I can say that to my father," replied Patience, "it will much please him. He said to me that he thought you capable of much higher employment than any that could be offered here, and only wished to know what you would accept. He has interest—great interest—although just now at variance with the rulers of this country, on account of the——"

"Murder of the king, you would or you should have said, Mistress Patience; I have heard how much he was opposed to that foul deed, and I honour him for it."

"How kind, how truly kind you are to say so!" said Patience, the tears starting in her eyes; "what pleasure to hear my father's conduct praised by you!"

"Why, of course, Mistress Patience, all of my way of thinking must praise him. Your father is in London, I hear?"

"Yes, he is; and that reminds me that you must want some refreshment after your walk. I will call Phœbe." So saying, Patience left the room.

The fact was, Mistress Patience was reminded that she had been sitting with a young man some time, and alone with him—which was not quite proper in those times and when Phœbe appeared with the cold viands, she retreated out of hearing, but remained in the room.

Edward partook of the meal offered him in silence, Patience occupying herself with her work, and keeping her eyes fixed on it, unless when they gave a slight glance at the table to see if anything was required. When the meal was over, Phœbe removed the tray, and then Edward rose to take his leave.

"Nay, do not go yet—I have much to say first; let me again ask you how we can serve you."

"I never can take any office under the present rulers of the nation; so that question is at rest."

"I was afraid you would answer so," replied Patience gravely; "do not think I blame you; for many are there already who would gladly retrace their steps if it were possible. They little thought, when they opposed the king, that affairs would have ended as they have done. Where do you live, sir?"

"At the opposite side of the forest, in a house belonging to me now, but which was inherited by my grandfather."

"You were brought up at Arnwood, you told my father; did you not?"

"Yes, I was brought up there, and remained there until the death of Colonel Beverley."

"And you were educated, were you not?"

"Yes; the chaplain taught me what little I do know."

"Then, if you were brought up in the house and educated by the chaplain, surely Colonel Beverley never intended you for a forester?"

"He did not; I was to have been a soldier as soon as I was old enough to bear arms."

"Perhaps you are distantly related to the late Colonel Beverley?"

"No; I am not *distantly* related," replied Edward, who began to feel uneasy at this close cross-examination; "but still, had Colonel Beverley been alive, and the king still required his services, I have no doubt that I should have been serving under him at this time. And now, Mistress Patience, that I have answered so many questions of yours, may I be permitted to ask a little about yourself in return? Have you any brothers?"

"None; I am an only child."

"Have you only one parent alive?"

"Only one."

"What families are you connected with?"

Patience looked up with surprise at this last question:

"My mother's name was Cooper; she was sister to Sir Anthony Ashley Cooper, who is a person well known."

"Indeed! then you are of gentle blood?"

"I believe so," replied Patience, with surprise.

"Thank you for your condescension, Miss Patience; and now, if you will permit me, I will take my leave."

"And when will you come and see my father?"

"I cannot say; I fear that I shall not be able very soon to look in his injured face, and it will not be well for a poacher to come near him," replied Edward: "however, some day I may be taken and brought before you as a prisoner, you know, and then he is certain to see me."

"I will not tell you to kill deer," replied Patience; "but if you do kill them no one shall harm you—or I know little of my power, or my father's. Farewell, then, sir; and more gratitude and thanks."

Patience held out her hand again to Edward, who this time, like a true cavalier, raised it respectfully to his lips. Patience coloured a little, but did not attempt to withdraw it, and Edward, with a low obeisance, quitted the room.

CHAPTER 13

Some days later, Humphrey was returning to the farm, having been on an errand with Billy and the cart. He was musing thoughtfully to himself, "I really think that I should be more comfortable if Edward was away. I am always in a fidget about him. I wish the new king, who is now in France, would raise an army and come over. It is better that Edward should be fighting in the field than remain here and risk being shot as a deer-stealer, or put in prison. The farm is sufficient for us all; and when I have taken in more ground it will be more than sufficient, even if I do not kill the wild cattle. I am fit for the farm, but Edward is not. He is thrown away, living in this obscurity, and he feels it. He was intended for a soldier, that is evident; and if ever he is one he will be in his element, and distinguish himself, if it pleases God to spare his life. I'll persuade him to stay at home a little while to help me to enclose the other piece of ground; and after that is done I'll dig a saw-pit and see if I can coax Pablo to saw with me. I must go to Lymington and buy a saw. If I once could get the trees sawed up into planks, what a quantity of things I could make, and how I could improve the place!"

Thus thought Humphrey as he went along; he was all for the farm and improvements, and was always calculating when he should have another calf, or a fresh litter of pigs. Humphrey's cogitations were interrupted by a halloo, and turning round in the direction of the voice he perceived Edward, and turned the cart to join him.

"You're just come in time, Humphrey; I have some provision for Alice's larder. I took my gun and came out on the path which I knew you would return on, and I have killed a young buck. He is good meat, and we are scarce of provisions."

Humphrey helped Edward to put the venison in the cart, and they returned to the cottage, which was not more than three miles off. Humphrey told Edward the result of his journey, and then proposed that Edward should stop at home for a few days and help him with the new enclosure. To this Edward cheerfully consented; and as soon as they arrived at the cottage, and Humphrey had had his breakfast, they took their axes and went out to fell at a cluster of small spruce-firs about a mile off.

"Now, Humphrey, what do you propose to do?"

"This," replied Humphrey: "I have marked out three acres or thereabouts of the land running in a straight line behind the garden. There is not a tree on it, and it is all good feedingground. What I intend to do enclose it with the spruce-fir posts and rails that we are about to cut down, and then set a hedge upon a low bank which I shall raise all round inside the rails. I know where there are thousands of seedling thorns, which I shall take up in the winter, or early in the spring, to put in, as the bank will be ready for them by that time."

"Well, that's all very good; but I fear it will be a long while before you have such a quantity of land dug up."

"Well, perhaps you are right, Edward," said Humphrey. "Why, here's Pablo coming after us; he's not coming to work, I presume, but to amuse himself by looking on."

"I don't think he is strong enough to do much hard work, Humphrey, although he appears very ingenious."

"No, I agree with you; and if he is to work, depend on it, it must not be by having work set out for him; he would take a disgust to it directly. I have another plan for him."

"And what is that, Humphrey?"

"I shall not set him anything to do, and shall make him believe that I do not think he is able to do anything. That will pique him, and I think by that means I shall get more work out of him than you would think, especially when, after he has done it, I express my wonder, and give him praise."

"Not a bad idea, that; you will work upon his pride, which is probably stronger than his laziness."

"I do not think him lazy, but I think him unused to hard work, and having lived a life of wandering and idleness, not very easy to be brought to constant and daily work, except by degrees, and by the means which I propose. Here we are," continued Humphrey, throwing his axe and billhook down, and proceeding to take off his doublet: "now for an hour or two's fulfilment of the sentence of our first parents—to wit, 'the sweat of the brow'."

Edward followed Humphrey's example in taking off his doublet; they selected the long, thin trees most fitted for rails, and were hard at work when Pablo came up to them. More than a dozen trees had fallen, and lay one upon the other, before they stopped a while to recover themselves a little.

"Hard work, Pablo," said Humphrey.

"Yes, very hard work; Pablo not strong enough."

"Oh no, you are not able to do anything of this kind, I know. No work this for gipsies; they take birds' nests and catch rabbits."

"Strong man cut down trees, weak man catch rabbits; both good," said Pablo.

"Yes, but strong man like work; not strong man not like work, Pablo. So now look on again, for we must have another spell."

"Strong man cut down trees, not strong man cut off branches," said Pablo, taking up the billhook and setting to work to cut off the boughs, which he did with great dexterity and rapidity.

Edward and Humphrey exchanged glances and smiles, and then worked away in silence till it was, as they supposed, dinnertime. They were not wrong in their supposition, although they had no other clock than their appetites, which, however, tell the time pretty correctly to those who work hard. Alice had the platters on the table, and was looking out to see if they were coming.

"Why, Pablo, have you been at work?" said Edith.

"Yes, little missy—work all the morning."

"Indeed he has, and has worked very well, and been very useful," said Edward.

After dinner they continued their labour, and by supper-time had so many trees cut down that they determined to carry them home the next day, and lay them along, to see how many more they would want. While they put the trees in the cart and took them home, Pablo contrived to lop off the boughs and prepare the poles for them to take away. As soon as they had cut down sufficient and carted them home, they then selected shorter trees for posts; and when Pablo had cleared them of the boughs, they sawed them out the proper lengths, and then carted them home. This occupied nearly the whole week, and then they proceeded to dig holes and set the posts in. The railing was then to be nailed to the posts, and that occupied them three days more; so that it was altogether a fortnight of hard work before the three acres were enclosed.

"If you don't want me any longer, Humphrey," said Edward, "I think I shall go over to see Oswald, and take Pablo with me. I want to know whether the intendant has come back; not that I shall go near him or his good little daughter, but I think I may as well go, and it will be a good opportunity of showing Pablo the way to Oswald's cottage."

"I think so too; and when you come back, Edward, one of us must go to Lymington, for I require some tools, and Pablo is very ragged. He must have some better clothes than these old ones of ours, if he is to be sent messages. Don't you think so?"

"Certainly I do."

"I want some more seeds sadly," said Humphrey, "and I must make out my list. I must go to Lymington myself this time, Edward; for you will be puzzled with all our wants."

"Not if I know exactly what you do want; but as I really do not, and probably should make mistakes, I think it will be better if you do go."

Early the next morning Edward took his gun, and with Pablo and Smoker set off for Oswald's cottage.

Edward talked a great deal with Pablo relative to his former life; and, by the answers which the boy gave him, was satisfied that, notwithstanding his doubtful way of bringing up, the lad was not corrupted, but was a well-minded boy. As they walked through a grove of trees, Edward still talking, Pablo stopped and put his hand before Edward's mouth, and then stooping down, at the same time seizing Smoker by the neck, he pointed with his finger. Edward at first could see nothing, but eventually he made out the horns of an animal just rising above a hillock. It was evidently one of the wild cattle. Edward cocked his gun and advanced cautiously, while Pablo remained where he was, holding Smoker. As soon as he was near enough to hit the head of the animal, Edward levelled and fired, and Pablo let Smoker loose, who bounded forward over the hillock. They followed the dog, and found him about to seize a calf which stood by a heifer that Edward had shot. Edward called him over and went up to the animal; it was a fine young heifer calf and the calf was not more than a fortnight old.

"We cannot stop now, Pablo," said Edward. "Humphrey would like to have the calf, and we must take our chance of its remaining by its mother till we come back. I think it will for a day or two, so let us push on."

No further adventure happened, and they arrived a little after noon at Oswald's cottage.

"I am glad that you have come, sir," said Oswald, as Edward extended his hand, "as I have just seen the intendant, and he has been asking many questions about you. I am certain he thinks that you are not the grandson of Jacob Armitage, and that he supposes I know who you are. He asked me where your cottage was, and whether I could not take him to it, as he wished to speak to you, and said that he felt great interest about you."

"And what did you say?"

"I said that your cottage was a good day's journey from here, and I was not certain that I knew the exact way, as I had been there but seldom; but that I knew where to find it, after I saw the forests of Arnwood. At that, the young mistress said that she would go with him, as you had told her that you had two sisters living with you, and she wished very much to see them and make their acquaintance."

"I am afraid that we shall not be able to prevent this visit, Oswald," replied Edward. "He is in command here, and the forest is in his charge. We must see to it. I only should like, if possible, to have notice of his coming, that we may be prepared."

"You need have no preparation, sir, if he should come," replied Oswald.

"Very true," said Edward; "we have nothing to conceal, and if he finds us in a pickle it is of no consequence."

"Rather the better, sir," replied Oswald. "Let your sisters be at the wash-tub, and you and your brother carting manure; he will then be more likely to have no suspicion of your being otherwise than what you assume to be."

Oswald's wife then put before him a large pie, and some wheaten bread. Edward helped Pablo to a large allowance, and then filled his own platter; while thus occupied, Oswald Partridge had left the cottage as agreed.

"What do you say, Pablo? do you think you can walk back tonight?"

"Once go one way, always know same way again."

"You are a clever fellow, Pablo, and I have a mind to try you. I think, Pablo, you shall go home, and tell Humphrey that I and Smoker will be where the heifer lies dead, and have it skinned by nine o'clock tomorrow morning; so if he comes he will find me there."

"Yes, I go now."

"Very well, then, if you wish it, you may go now," said Edward.

Pablo nodded his head, and disappeared.

A few minutes afterwards Oswald made his appearance.

"Is the boy gone?"

"Yes; he is gone back to the cottage." And Edward then stated how he had killed the heifer, and wanted to obtain the calf.

"You are right; and now for the news that I have to tell you. The Duke of Hamilton, the Earl of Holland, and Lord Capel have been tried, condemned, and executed."

Edward sighed. "More murder! but we must expect it from those who have murdered their king. Is that all?"

"No. King Charles the Second has been proclaimed in Scotland, and invited to come over."

Edward retired to bed, but not to sleep. The Scots had proclaimed the king, and invited him over. "He will surely come," thought Edward, "and he will have an army round him as soon as he lands." Edward made up his resolution to join the army as soon as he had heard that the king had landed; and what with considering how he should be able so to do, and afterwards building castles as to what he would do, it was long before he fell asleep; and when he did he dreamt of battles and victory—he was charging at the head of his troops—he was surrounded by the dying and the dead. He was wounded, and he was somehow or another well again as if by magic; and then the scene was changed, and he was rescuing Patience Heatherstone from his own lawless men, and preserving the life of her father, which was about to be sacrificed; and at last he awoke, and found that the daylight peeped through the windows, and that he had slept longer than he had intended to do. He arose and dressed himself quickly, and, not waiting for breakfast, went to the kennel, released Smoker from his durance, and set off on his return.

Before nine o'clock he had arrived at the spot where the heifer lay dead. He found the calf still by its side, bleating and walking round uneasily. As he approached with the dog, it went to a further distance, and there remained. Edward took out his knife, and commenced skinning the heifer, and then took out the inside. The animal was quite fresh and good, but not very fat, as may be supposed. While thus occupied, Smoker growled and then sprang forward, bounding away in the direction of the cottage, and Edward thought Humphrey was at hand. In a few minutes the pony and cart appeared between the trees, with Humphrey and Pablo in it, and Smoker leaping up at his friend Billy.

"Good morning, Humphrey," said Edward. "I am almost ready for you; but the question is, how are we to take the calf? It is as wild as a deer."

"It will be a puzzler, without Smoker can run it down," said Humphrey.

"I take him, with Smoker," said Pablo.

"How will you take it, Pablo?"

Pablo went to the cart, and took out a long small cord, which Humphrey had brought with them, and made a noose at one end; he coiled the rope in his hand, and then threw it out to its full length, by way of trial. "This way I take him, suppose I get near enough. This way take bulls in Spain: call him lasso. Now come with me." Pablo had his rope again coiled in his hand, and then went round to the other side of the calf, which still remained lowing at about two hundred yards' distance.

"Now tell Smoker," cried Pablo.

Humphrey set Smoker upon the calf, which retreated from the dog, presenting his head to run at it; and Pablo kept behind the animal, while Smoker attacked it, and drove it near to him.

As soon as the calf, which was so busy with the dog that it did not perceive Pablo, came sufficiently near to him, Pablo threw his rope, and caught the loop round the animal's neck. The calf set off galloping towards Humphrey, and dragging Pablo after him, for the latter was not strong enough to hold it.

Humphrey went to his assistance, and then Edward, and the calf was thrown down by Smoker, who seized it by the neck, and it was tied and put on the cart in a few minutes.

"Well done, Pablo! you are a clever fellow," said Edward, "and this calf shall be yours."

"It is a cow-calf," said Humphrey, "which I am glad of. Pablo, you did that well, and, as Edward says, the calf belongs to you."

Pablo looked pleased, but said nothing.

Humphrey was very anxious to go to Lymington, and was not sorry that he had some meat to take with him: he determined to get off the next morning; and Edward proposed that he should take Pablo with him. Humphrey and Pablo went away after breakfast with Billy, and the meat and skin of the heifer in the cart. Humphrey had also a large basket of eggs and three dozen of chickens from Alice to be disposed of, and a list, as long as the tail of a kite, of articles which she and Edith required. As soon as they were gone, Edward, who was still castle-building, instead of offering his services to Alice, brought out his father's sword and commenced cleaning it. When he had polished it up to his satisfaction, he felt less inclined than ever to do anything; so after dinner he took his gun and walked out into the forest, that he might indulge in his reveries. He walked on, quite unconscious of the direction in which he was going, and more than once finding his hat knocked off his head by the branch of a tree which he had not perceived—when his ears were saluted with the neighing of a horse. He looked up, and perceived that he was near to a herd of forest ponies, the first that he had heard since he had lived in the forest.

This roused him, and he looked about him. "Where can I have been wandering to?" thought Edward: "I never fell in with any of the forest ponies before; I must therefore have walked in a direction quite contrary to what I usually do. I do not know where I am; the scenery is new to me. What a fool I am! It's lucky that nobody except Humphrey digs pitfalls, or I should probably have been in one by this time; and I've brought out my gun and left the dog at home. Well, I suppose I can find my way back." Edward then surveyed the whole herd of ponies, which were at no great distance from him.

"Now I'll puzzle Humphrey when I go back," thought Edward. "He says that Billy is getting old, and that he wishes he could get another pony. I will tell him what a plenty there are, and propose that he should invent some way of catching one. That will be a poser for him; yet I'm sure that he'll try, for he is very ingenious."

Edward then hurried in a direction which he considered might lead him homeward, and walked fast. Thus he went on, again absorbed in the news which he had gained from Oswald, till on a sudden, he again recollected himself, and perceived that he had lost sight of the copse of trees on a high hill, to which he had been directing his steps. Where was it? He turned round and round, and at last found out that he had been walking away from it. "The best thing I can do is to decide upon taking some straight line, and continue in it; I must then get out of the forest at last, even if I walk right across it. That will be better than going backwards and forwards, or round and round, as I otherwise shall do, just like a puppy running after its own tail. So now shine out, stars!" Edward waited until he could make out Charles's Wain, which he well knew, and then the Polar Star. As soon as he was certain of that, he resolved to travel by it due north, and he did so, sometimes walking fast, and at others keeping up a steady trot for half a mile without stopping. As he was proceeding on his travels, he observed, under some trees ahead of him, a spark of fire emitted; he thought it was a glowworm at first, but it was more like the striking of a flint against steel; and as he saw it a second time, he stopped that he might ascertain what it might be before he advanced farther.

CHAPTER 14

It was now very dark, as there was no moon, and the stars were often obscured by the clouds, which were heavy, and borne along by the wind, which was very high. The light again appeared, and this time Edward heard the clash of the flint against the steel, and he was certain that it was somebody striking a light. He advanced very cautiously, and arrived at a large tree, behind which he remained to reconnoitre. The people, whoever they might be, were not more than thirty yards from him; a light spread its rays for a moment or two, and he could make out a figure kneeling and holding his hat to protect it from the wind; then it burnt brighter, and he saw that a lantern had been lighted, and then, of a sudden, all was dark again: so Edward immediately satisfied himself that a dark lantern had been lighted and then closed. Who the parties might be, he, of course, had no idea; but he was resolved that he would ascertain, if he could, before he accosted them and asked his way.

"They have no dog," thought Edward, "or it would have growled before this; and it's lucky that I have none either." Edward then crept softly nearer to them: the wind, which was strong, blew from where they were to where Edward stood, so that there was less chance of their hearing his approach.

Edward went on his hands and knees, and crawled through the fern until he gained another tree, and within ten yards of them, and from where he could hear what they might say. He was thus cautious, as he had been told by Oswald that there were many disbanded soldiers who had taken up their quarters in the forest, and had committed several depredations upon the houses adjacent to it, always returning to the forest as a rendezvous. Edward listened, and heard one say:

"It is not time yet! No, no: too soon by half an hour or more. The people from Lymington who buy him what he wants always bring it to him at night, that his retreat may not be discovered. They sometimes do not leave the cottage till two hours after dark, for they do not leave Lymington to go there till it is dark."

"Do you know who it is who supplies him with food?"

"Yes, the people at the inn in Parliament Street—I forget the sign."

"Oh! I know. Yes, the landlord is a downright malignant in his heart! We might squeeze him well, if we dared show ourselves in Lymington."

"Yes, but they would squeeze our necks tighter than would be agreeable, I expect," replied the other.

"Are you sure that he has money?"

"Quite sure, for I peeped in through the chinks of the window-shutters, and I saw him pay for the things brought to him; it was from a canvas bag, and it was gold that he took out."

"And where did he put the bag, after he had paid them?"

"That I can't tell, for as I knew that they would come out as soon as they were paid, I was obliged to beat a retreat, lest I should be seen."

"Well, then, how is it to be managed?"

"We must first tap at the door, and try if we can get in as benighted travellers; if that won't do, and I fear it will not, while you remain begging for admittance at the door, and keep him occupied, I will try the door behind, that leads into the garden; and if not the door, I will try the window. I have examined them both well, and have been outside when he has shut up his shutters, and I know the fastenings. With a pane out I could open them immediately."

"Is there anybody else beside him in the cottage?"

"Yes, a lad who attends him, and goes to Lymington for him."

"No women?"

"Not one."

"But do you think we two are sufficient! Had we not better get more help? There is Broom, and Black, the gipsy, at the rendezvous. I can go for them, and be back in time: they are stout and true."

"Stout enough but not true. No, no, I want no shares in this business, and you know how ill they behaved in the last affair. I'll swear that they only produced half the swag. I like honour between gentlemen and soldiers, and that's why I have chosen you. I know I can trust you, Benjamin. It's time now—what do you say? We are two to one, for I count the boy as nothing. Shall we start?"

"I am with you. You say there's a bag of gold, and that's worth fighting for."

"Yes, Ben, and I'll tell you; with what I've got buried, and my share of that bag, I shall have enough, I think, and I'll start for the Low Countries, for England's getting rather too warm for me."

"Well, I shan't go yet," replied Benjamin; "I don't like your foreign parts. Come, let's be off; if we get the money you shall go to the Low Countries, Will, and I'll start for the north, where they don't know me—for if you go I won't stay here."

The two men then rose up; and the one whose name appeared to be Will first examined if the candle in his dark lantern burnt well, and then they both set off, followed by Edward, who had heard quite enough to satisfy him that they were bent upon a burglary—if not murder. Edward followed them, so as to keep their forms indistinctly in sight, which was as much as he could do at twenty yards' distance; fortunately the wind was so high that they did not hear his footsteps, although he often trod upon a rotten stick, which snapped as it broke in twain. As near as Edward could guess, he had tracked them for about three miles, when they stopped, and he perceived that they were examining their pistols, which they took from their belts. They then went on again, and entered a small plantation of oak trees, of about forty years' growth—very thick and very dark, with close underwood below. They followed each other through a narrow path, until they came to a cleared place in the middle of the plantation, in which there stood a low cottage, surrounded with covert on every side, with the exception of some thirty yards of land around it. All was still, and as dark as pitch; Edward remained behind the trees, and when the two men again stopped he was not six feet from them. They consulted in a low tone, but the wind was so high that he could not distinguish what they said. At last they advanced to the cottage, and Edward, still keeping within the trees, shifted his position so that he should be opposite the gable end of the cottage. He observed one man go up to the front door, while the other went round to the door behind, as had been agreed. Edward threw open the pan of the lock of the gun, and reprimed it, that he might be sure, and then waited for what was to follow. He heard the man Will at the front door, talking and asking for shelter in a plaintive but loud voice; and shortly afterwards he perceived a light through the chinks of the shutters—for Edward was continually altering his position to see what was going on in the front and in the back. At one time he thought of levelling his gun and killing one of the men at once; but he could not make up his mind to do that, as a burglary, although intended, had not yet been committed; so he remained passive until the attack was really made, when he resolved that he would come to the rescue. After some minutes of entreaty that they would open the door, the man in front commenced thumping and beating against it, as if he would make them open the door by force; but this was to attract the attention of those within, and divert it from the attempts that the other was making to get in behind. Edward was aware of this; he now kept his eye upon what was going on at the back. Advancing nearer, which he ventured to do now that both men were so occupied, he perceived that the fellow had contrived to open the window close to the back door, and was remaining quite close to it with a pistol in his hand, apparently not wishing to run the risk of climbing in. Edward slipped under the eaves of the cottage, not six feet from the man, who remained with his back partly turned towards him. Edward then, finding he had obtained this position unperceived, crouched down with his gun ready pointed.

As Edward remained in this position, he heard a shrill voice cry out, "They are getting in behind!" and a movement in the cottage. The man near him, who had his pistol in his hand, put his arm through the window and fired inside. A shriek was given, and Edward fired his gun into the body of the man who immediately fell. Edward lost no time in reloading his gun, during which he heard the bursting open of the front door and the report of firearms; then all was silent for a moment excepting the wailing of somebody within. As soon as his gun was reloaded, Edward walked round to the front of the cottage, where he found the man who was called Ben lying across the threshold of the open door. He stepped across the body, and looking into the room within, perceived a body stretched on the floor, and a young lad weeping over it.

"Don't be alarmed, I am a friend," said Edward, going in to where the body lay; and taking the light, which was at the farther end of the chamber, he placed it on the floor, that he might examine the state of the person, who was breathing heavily, and apparently badly wounded. "Rise up, my lad," said Edward, "and let me see if I can be of any use."

"Ah, no!" cried the boy, throwing back his long hair from his temples, "he bleeds to death!"

"Bring me some water quick," said Edward, "there's a good lad, while I see where he is hurt."

The boy ran up to fetch the water, and Edward discovered that the ball had entered the neck, above the collar-bone, and that the blood poured out of the man's mouth, who was choking with the effusion. Although ignorant of surgery Edward thought that such a wound must be mortal; but the man was not only alive but sensible, and although he could not utter a word, he spoke with his eyes, and with signs. He raised his hand and pointed to himself first, and shook his head, as if to say that it was all over with him; and then he turned round his head, as if looking for the lad, who was now returning with the water. When the lad again knelt by his side, weeping bitterly, the man pointed to him, and gave such an imploring look that Edward immediately comprehended what he wished; it was to ask protection for the boy. It could not be misunderstood; and could Edward do otherwise than promise it to the dying man? His generous nature could not refuse it, and he said, "I understand you; you wish me to take care of your boy when you are gone. Is it not so?"

The man signified assent.

"I promise you I will do so. I will take him into my own family, and he shall share with us."

The man raised his hand again, and a gleam of joy passed over his features as he took the hand of the lad and put it into that of Edward. His eyes were then fixed upon Edward, as if to scrutinize into his character by his features, while the former bathed his temples and washed the blood from his mouth with the water brought by the boy, who appeared in a state of grief so violent as to paralyse his senses. After a minute or two, another effusion of blood choked the wounded man, who, after a short struggle, fell back dead.

"He is gone," thought Edward, "and now what is to be done? I must first ascertain whether the two villains are dead or not." Edward took a light and examined the body of Ben, lying over the threshold of the door; the man was quite dead, the ball having entered his brain. He was proceeding round the outside of the cottage to examine the state of the other man, whom he had shot himself; but the wind nearly blew out the light, and he therefore returned to the chamber and placed it on the floor, near to where the boy lay insensible over the corpse of the man who had died in the arms of Edward; and then went out without a light, and with his gun, to the other side of the cottage, where the other robber had fallen. As he approached the man, a faint voice was heard to say:

"Ben, Ben! some water, for the love of God! Ben, I'm done for!"

Edward, without giving an answer, went back to the room for the water, which he took round to the man, and put it to his lips; he felt that he was bound by humanity so to do to a dying man, scoundrel though he might be. It was still dark, but not so dark as it had previously been, for the late moon was just rising.

The man drank the water eagerly, and said, in broken sentences, "I feel —that I am bleeding to death—inside." The man again attempted to drink out of the basin proffered by Edward; but as he made the attempt he fell back with a groan.

Edward, perceiving that he was dead, returned to the cottage to look after the lad, who still remained prostrate and embracing the corpse in the chamber. Edward then reflected upon what had best be done. After a time he decided upon dragging away the body of the robber named Ben outside of the threshold, and then securing the door. This, with some trouble, he effected, and then he made fast the window that had been forced open behind. Before he removed the boy, who lay with his face buried on the corpse, and appeared to be in a state of insensibility, Edward examined the corpse as it lay. Although plainly dressed, yet it was evident that it was not the body of a rustic; the features were fair, and the beard was carefully cut; the hands were white, and the fingers long, and evidently had never been employed in labour. That the body was that of some superior person disguised as a rustic was evident, and this was corroborated by the conversation which took place between the two robbers. "Alas!" thought Edward, "the family of Arnwood appear not to be the only people who are in disguise in this forest. That poor boy! he must not remain there." Edward looked round, and perceived that there was a bed in the adjoining room, the door of which was open; he lifted up the boy, and carried him, still insensible, into the room, and laid him on the bed.

Edward then returned to the other room, and recollected, or rather was reminded, that he had had no supper, and it was now nearly dawn of day. He looked into a cupboard and found plenty of provisions, and some flasks of wine. "I have earned my supper," thought he, "and I will not, therefore, deny myself." So he brought out the viands, and made a hearty meal. He then sank into one of his reveries, which lasted till he fell into a slumber. When he woke up it was the voice of the boy, who in his sleep cried out "Father!" Edward started up, and found that the sun was an hour high, and that he must have slept some time. He gently opened the cottage door, looked at the bodies of the two men, and then walked out to survey the locality of the cottage, which he had but faintly made out during the night. He found that it was surrounded by a thicket of trees and underwood so close and thick, that there appeared to him no outlet in any direction. "What a place for concealment!" thought Edward, "but still these prowling thieves discovered it. Why, troops of horse might scour the forest for months and never discover such a hiding place." Edward walked round by the side of the thicket to find out the track by which the robbers had entered when he followed them, and at last succeeded in doing so. He followed the path through the thicket until he was clear of it, and again in the forest, but the scenery outside was unknown to him, and he had not an idea as to what part of the forest it was in. "I must question the boy," thought Edward. "I will go back and wake him up, for it is time that I was moving." As he was again turning into the thicket he heard a dog giving tongue, as if on a scent. It came nearer and nearer to him, and Edward remained to see what it might be. In a moment more he perceived his own dog, Smoker, come bounding out of a neighbouring copse, followed by Humphrey and Pablo. Edward hallooed. Smoker sprang towards him, leaping up, and loading him with caresses, and in another moment he was in Humphrey's arms.

"Oh, Edward, let me first thank God!" said Humphrey as the tears started and rolled down his cheeks. "What a night we have passed! What has happened? That dear fellow, Pablo, thought of putting Smoker on the scent; he brought out your jacket and showed it to Smoker, and gave it him to smell, and then led him along till he was on your footsteps; and the dog followed him it seems, although it has been round and round in every direction, till at last he has brought us to you."

Edward shook hands with Pablo, and thanked him. "How far are we from the cottage, Humphrey?"

"About eight miles I should say, Edward; not more."

"Well, I have much to tell you, and I must tell it to you in few words before I go farther, and afterwards I will tell you all in detail."

The proposal of Edward, that Humphrey should go over and make known the circumstances to Oswald, that they might be communicated to the intendant, was readily acceded to; and Pablo, it was agreed, should go home and tell Alice and Edith that Edward was safe.

Humphrey and Pablo both set off, and then Edward went to waken the boy, still lying on the bed.

"Come, you must get up now. You know that what's done cannot be undone; and if you are a good boy, and have read the Bible, you must know that we must submit to the will of God, who is our kind Father in heaven."

"Ah me!" said the boy, who was awake when Edward went to him, "I know well it is my duty, but it is a hard duty, and I am heart-broken. I have lost my father, the only friend I had in the world: who is there to love and cherish me now? What will become of me?"

"I promised your father, before he died, that I would take care of you, my poor fellow; and a promise is sacred with me, even if it were not made to a dying man. I will do my best, depend upon it, for I have known myself what it is to want and to find a protector. You shall live with me and my brother and sisters, and you shall have all we have."

"Have you sisters, then?" replied the boy.

"Yes; I have sent for the cart to take you away from this, and tonight you shall be in our cottage; but now tell me—I do not ask who your father was, or why he was living here in secret, as I found it out by what I overheard the robbers say to one another--but how long have you lived here?"

"More than a year."

"Whose cottage is it?"

"My father bought it when he came, as he thought it safer, so that he might not be discovered or betrayed; for he had escaped from prison after having been condemned to death by the Parliament."

"Then he was a loyal man to his king?"

"Yes, he was, and that was his only crime."

"Then fear not, my good boy; we are all loyal as well as he was, and will never be otherwise. I tell you this that you may safely trust us. Now, if the cottage was his, the furniture and property were his also."

"Yes; all was his."

"And it is now yours, is it not?"

"I suppose so," said the boy, bursting into tears.

"Then listen to me;—your father is safe from all persecution now; he is, I trust, in heaven; and you they cannot touch, as you have done nothing to offend them; but still they will take possession of your father's property as soon as the know of his death, and find out who he was. This, for your sake, I wish to prevent them from doing, and have therefore sent for the cart that I may remove to my cottage everything that is of value, that it may be held for your benefit; some day or another you may require it. The murder having been committed in the forest, and I having been a witness, and, moreover, having shot one of the robbers, I have considered it right to send over to the intendant of the forest to give him notice of what has taken place within his jurisdiction. I do not think he is so bad a man as the rest; but still, when he comes here, he may consider it his duty to take possession of everything for the Parliament, as I have no doubt such are his orders, or will be when he communicates with the Parliament. Now this is a robbery which I wish to prevent, by carrying away your property before they come over, which they will tomorrow, and I propose that you shall accompany me, with all that you can take away, or that may be useful, this evening."

"You are very kind," replied the boy. "I will do all you wish; but I feel very weak, and very unwell."

"You must not exert yourself, for your own sake, my poor fellow. Come now, sit up and put all your own clothes together. Collect everything in this room, while I look about the house. And tell me, had not your father some money? for the robbers said that they saw him counting it out of a sack, through the chinks of the shutters, and that was why they made the attack."

"Hateful money!" cried the boy. "Yes, he had, I believe, a great deal of money; but I cannot say how much."

"Now get up, and do as I request, my dear boy," said Edward raising him up in his arms; "when your grief is lessened, you may have many happy days yet in store for you; you have a Father in heaven that you must put your trust in, and with Him you will find peace."

CHAPTER 15

EDWARD THEN took the counterpane off the bed, and went with it into the next room. He gently drew the body to the corner of the room, and covered it up with the counterpane and then proceeded to examine the cupboards, &c. In one he found a good store of books, in another there was linen of all sorts, a great many curious arms, two suits of bright armour such as was worn in those times, pistols and guns, and ammunition. On the floor of one of the cupboards was an iron chest about two feet by eighteen inches. It was locked. Edward immediately concluded that this chest held the money of the unfortunate man; but where was the key? Most likely about his person. He did not like to afflict the poor boy by putting the question to him, but he went to the body and examined the pockets of the clothes; he found a bunch of several keys, which he took, and then replaced the coverlid. He tried one of the keys, which appeared to be of the right size, to the lock of the iron chest, and found that it fitted it. Satisfied with this, he did not raise the lid of the chest, but dragged it out into the room. There were many things of value about the room; the candlesticks were silver, and there were goblets of the same metal. Edward collected all these articles, and a timepiece, and put them into a basket, of which there were two large ones at the end of the room, apparently used for holding firewood. Everything that he thought could be useful, or of value, he gathered together for the benefit of the poor orphan boy. He afterwards went into another small room, where he found sundry small trunks and cases locked up. These he brought out without examining, as he presumed that they contained what was of value, or they would not be locked. When he had collected everything, he found that he had already more than the cart could carry in one trip; and he wanted to take some bedding with him, as he had not a spare bed in the cottage to give to the boy. Edward decided in his own mind that he would take the most valuable articles away that night, and return with the cart for the remainder early on the following morning. It was now past noon, and Edward took out of the cupboard what victuals were left, and then went into the chamber where the boy was, and begged that he would eat something. The poor boy said that he had no appetite; but Edward insisted, and at last prevailed upon him to eat some bread and drink a glass of wine, which proved of great service to him. The poor fellow shuddered as he saw the body covered up in the corner of the room, but said nothing. Edward was trying to make him eat a little more, when Pablo made his appearance at the door.

Edward and Pablo pulled the body of the robber on one side of the doorway, and threw over it some dried fern which lay by; they then backed the cart down to the door; the iron chest was first got in, then all the heavy articles, such as armour, guns, and books, &c., and by that time the cart was more than half-loaded. Edward then went into the chamber, and brought out he packages the boy had made up, and put them all in the cart until it was loaded high up; they brought out some blankets and laid over all, to keep things steady; and then Edward told the boy that all was ready, and that they had better go.

"No room for cart to get through wood," said Pablo; "hard work, cart empty—more hard work, cart full."

And so it proved to be: and it required all the united efforts of Billy, Edward and Pablo to force a passage for the cart through the narrow pathway; but at last it was effected, and then they went on at a quick pace, and in less than two hours the cottage was in sight. When within two hundred yards of it, Edith, who had been on the watch, came bounding out, and flew into Edward's arms, and covered him with kisses.

"You naughty Edward, to frighten us so!"

"Look, Edith, I have brought you a nice little play-fellow. Welcome him, dearest."

Edith extended her hand as she looked into the boy's face.

"He is a pretty boy, Edward, much prettier than Pablo."

"No, Missy Edith," said Pablo; "Pablo more man than he."

"Yes, you may be more man, Pablo; but you are not so pretty."

They arrived at the cottage, and Edward and Pablo were busy unpacking the cart, and putting all the contents into the inner chamber, where Pablo now slept, when Alice, who, with Edith, had been talking to the boy, came to Edward and said:

"Edward, she's a girl!"

"A girl!" replied Edward, astonished.

"Yes, she told me so, and wished me to tell you."

"But why does she wear boy's clothes?"

"It was her father's wish, as he was very often obliged to send her to Lymington to a friend's house, and he was afraid of her getting into trouble; but she has not told me her story as yet, she says that she will tonight."

"Well then," replied Edward, "you must make up a bed for her in your room tonight. Take Pablo's bed, and he shall sleep with me. Tomorrow morning I will bring some more bedding from her cottage."

At last everything was out of the cart, the iron chest dragged into Pablo's room, and Billy put into his stable and given his supper, which he had well earned, for the cart had been very heavily loaded. They then all sat down to supper, Edward saying to their new acquaintance:

"So I find that I am to have another sister instead of another brother. Now you will tell me your name?"

"Yes; Clara is my name."

"And why did you not tell me that you are a girl?"

"I did not like, because I was in boy's clothes, and felt ashamed; indeed I was too unhappy to think about what I was. My poor dear father!" and she burst into tears.

Alice and Edith kissed her and consoled her, and she became calm again. After supper was over they busied themselves making arrangements for her sleeping in their room, and then they went to prayers.

They were up on the following morning at day dawn, and, putting Billy in the cart, set off for the cottage of Clara. They found everything as they had left it, and, having loaded the cart with what had been left behind the day before, and bedding for two beds, with several articles of furniture which Edward thought might be useful, there being still a little room left, Edward packed up in a wooden case with dried fern all the wine that was in the cupboard; and, having assisted Pablo in forcing the cart once more through the path in the wood, he left him to return home with the cart, while he remained to await the arrival of Humphrey, and whoever might come with him from the intendant's. About ten o'clock, as he was watching outside of the wood, he perceived several people approaching him, and soon made out that Humphrey, the intendant, and Oswald were among the number.

The intendant left his horse to the care of one of the verderers, and went through the wood on foot with the rest of the party, preceded by Edward. He appeared to be very grave and thoughtful, and Edward thought that there was a coolness in his manner towards himself—for it must be recollected that Mr. Heatherstone had not seen Edward since he had rendered him such service in saving the life of his daughter. The consequence was that Edward felt somewhat indignant, but he did not express his feelings, by his looks even, but conveyed the party in silence to the cottage. On their arrival Edward pointed to the body of the robber, which had been covered with fern, and the verderers exposed it.

"By whose hand did that man fall?" said the intendant.

"By the hand of the party who lived in the cottage."

Edward then led the way round to the back of the cottage where the other robber lay.

"And this man was slain by my hand," replied Edward. "We have one more body to see," continued Edward, leading the way into the cottage, and uncovering the body of Clara's father.

Mr. Heatherstone looked at the face and appeared much moved. "Cover it up," said he, turning away; and then sitting down on a chair close to the table,—"And how was this found?" he said.

When Edward then commenced by stating, "that he was out in the forest and had lost his way, and was seeking his way home——"

"You were out in the forest during the night?"

"Yes, sir, I was."

"With your gun?"

"I always carry my gun," replied Edward.

"In pursuit of game?"

"No, sir, I was not. I have never been out in pursuit of game during night-time in my life."

Edward met with no more interruption in his narrative. He stated briefly all that had taken place, from the time he fell in with the robbers till the winding up of the catastrophe.

The clerk took down all that Edward had stated and then read it over to him, to ascertain if he had written it down correctly, and then enquired of Edward if he could read or write.

"I should hope so," replied Edward, taking the pen and signing his name.

The clerk stared, and then said, "People in your condition do not often know how to read and write, Mr. Forester, and therefore you need not be offended at the question."

"Very true," replied Edward. "May I ask if my presence is considered any longer to be necessary?"

"You stated that there was a boy in the house, young man," said the intendant: "what has become of him?"

"He is removed to my cottage."

"Why did you do so?"

"Because when his father died I promised to him that I would take care of his child; and I intend to keep my word."

The intendant paused, and then said, "I perceive that some articles have been removed, the bedding, for instance; have you taken anything away?"

"I have removed bedding, for I had no bed to offer to the lad, and he told me that the cottage and furniture belonged to his father; of course by his father's death it became his, and I felt that I was warranted in so doing."

"May I ask, did you remove any papers?"

"I cannot tell; the lad packed up his own things; there were some boxes removed, which were locked up, and the contents are to me wholly unknown. I could not leave the boy here in this scene of death, and I could not well leave the property belonging to him to be at the mercy of any other plunderers of the forest. I did as I considered right for the benefit of the boy, and in accordance with the solemn promise which I made to his father."

"Still, the property should not have been removed. The party who now lies dead there is a well-known malignant."

"How do you know that, sir?" interrupted Edward, "did you recognize him when you saw the body?"

"I did not say that I did," replied the intendant.

"You either must have so done, sir," replied Edward, "or you must have been aware that he was residing in this cottage: you have to choose between."

"You are bold, young man," replied the intendant, "and I will reply to your observation. I did recognize the party when I saw his face, and I knew him to be one who was condemned to death, and who escaped from prison a few days before the one appointed for his execution. I heard search had been made for him, but in vain, and it was supposed that he had escaped beyond the seas. Now his papers may be the means of giving the Parliament information against others as well as himself."

"And enable them to commit a few more murders," added Edward.

"Silence, young man; the authorities must not be spoken of in so irreverent a manner. Are you aware that your language is treasonable?"

"According to act of parliament, as at present constituted, it may be," replied Edward; "but as a loyal subject of King Charles the Second, I deny it."

"I have no concern with your loyalty, young man, but I will not admit any language to be uttered in my presence against the ruling powers. The inquest is over. Let everyone leave the house except Edward Armitage, to whom I would speak alone."

"Excuse me one moment, sir," said Edward, "and I will return."

Edward went out with the rest, and calling Humphrey aside, said to him, "Contrive to slip away unperceived; here are the keys; haste to the cottage as fast a you can, look for all the papers you can find in the packages taken there; bury them and the iron chest in the garden, or anywhere where they cannot be discovered."

Humphrey nodded, and turned away, and Edward re-entered the cottage.

He found the intendant was standing over the corpse; he had removed the coverlid, and was looking mournfully down on the face disfigured with blood. Perceiving the entrance of Edward, he again took his seat at the table, and after a pause said:

"Edward Armitage, I will now answer for myself and thousands more. You are too young a man to have known the cause of the insurrection, or rather opposition to the unfortunate King Charles. He attempted to make himself absolute and to wrest the liberties from the people of England; that his warmest adherents will admit. When I joined the party which opposed him, I little thought that matters would have been carried so far as they have been; I always considered it lawful to take up arms in defence of our liberties, but at the same time I equally felt that the person of the king was sacred."

"I have heard so, sir."

"Yes, and in truth; for never did any people strive more zealously to prevent the murder of the king—for murder it was—than my relative Ashley Cooper and myself. So much so, indeed, as to have incurred not only the suspicion but the illwill of Cromwell, who, I fear, is now making rapid advances towards that absolute authority for which the king has suffered, and which he would now vest in his own person. Thousands who took an active part against the king will, when the opportunity is ripe, retrace their steps; but I expect that we have much to suffer before that time will come. And now, Edward Armitage, I have said more to you than I have to any person breathing, except my own kinsman."

"I thank you for your confidence, sir, which not only will not be betrayed, but will act as a warning to guide my future conduct."

"I meant it should. Be no longer rash and careless in avowing your opinions. You can do no good to the cause, and may do yourself much harm. And now I must ask another question, which I could not before the other people. You have surprised me by stating that Major Ratcliffe had a son here; there must be some mistake, or the boy must be an impostor. He had a daughter, an only daughter, as I have, but he never had a son."

"It is a mistake that I fell into, sir, by finding a boy here, as I stated to you at the inquest; and I considered it to be a boy until I brought her home, and she then discovered to my sisters that she was a girl dressed in boy's clothes. I did not give that as explanation at the inquest, as it was not necessary."

"I am right, then. I must relieve you of that charge, Edward Armitage; she shall be to me as a daughter, and I trust that you will agree with me, without any disparagement to your feelings, that my house will be a more fit residence for her than your cottage."

"I will not prevent her going, if she wishes it, after your explanation and confidence, Mr. Heatherstone."

"One thing more. As I said to you before, Edward Armitage, I believe many of these verderers, all of whom have been selected from the army, are spies upon me: I must therefore be careful. You said that you were not aware that there were any papers?"

"I saw none, sir; but I suspect, from the many locked-up trunks and small boxes, that there may be; but when I went out with the others from the inquest, I dispatched my brother Humphrey to the cottage, advising him to open all the locks and to remove any papers which he might find."

"Well, then, I have but one word more to say—recollect, if I appear harsh and severe in the presence of others, it is only assumed towards you, and not real. You understand that?"

"I do, sir, and beg you will exercise your discretion."

The intendant then went out and said to the party, "It appears from what I can extract from this lad Armitage that there are boxes which he removed to his cottage; we will go there to see what they may contain. It is now noon. Have you any refreshment to offer us in your cottage, young man, when we arrive?"

"I keep no hostelry, sir," replied Edward somewhat gloomily; "my own labour, and my brother's, is sufficient for the support of my own family, but no more."

"Let us move on; and two of you keep your eye upon that young man," said the intendant, aside.

They then proceeded through the wood; the intendant mounted his horse, and they set off for the cottage, where they arrived at about two o'clock in the afternoon.

CHAPTER 16

HUMPHREY CAME out as soon as he perceived the intendant and his party approaching, and whispered to Edward that all was safe. The intendant dismounted, and, ordering everybody but his clerk to wait outside, was ushered into the cottage by Edward. Alice, Edith, and Pablo were in the room; the two girls were not a little flushed and frightened by the unusual appearance of so large a body of strangers.

The boxes were brought out, opened, and examined by the intendant and his clerk, but of course no papers were found in them.

"I must now send in two of my people to search the house," said the intendant. "Had you not better go to the little girl, that she may not be frightened?"

"I will go to her," said Alice.

Two of the people, assisted by the clerk, then searched the house; they found nothing worthy of notice, except the weapons and armour which Edward had removed and which he stated to the intendant that he took away as valuable property belonging to the little girl.

"It is sufficient," said the intendant to his clerk—"undoubtedly there are no papers; but I must, before I go, interrogate this child, who has been removed thus; but she will be frightened, and I shall obtain no answer from her if we are so many, so let everybody leave the cottage while I speak to her."

The clerk and the others left the cottage, and the intendant desired Edward to bring Clara from the bedroom. She came out accompanied by, and clinging indeed to Alice, for she was much alarmed.

"Come here, Clara," said the intendant gently; "you do not know perhaps that I am sincere friend, and now that your father is dead I want you to come and live with my daughter, who will be delighted to have you as a companion. Will you go with me, and I will take care of you and be a father to you?"

"I do not like to leave Alice and Edith; they treat me so kindly, and call me sister," replied Clara, sobbing.

"I am sure they do, and that you must be fond of them already, but still it is your duty to come with me, and if your father could speak to you now, he would tell you so. I will not force you away, but remember you are born a lady, and must be brought up and educated as a lady, which cannot be the case in this cottage, although they are very kind to you, and very nice young people. You do not recollect me, Clara, but you often sat on my knee when you were a little girl, and when your father lived in Dorsetshire. You recollect the great walnut tree by the sitting-room window, which looked out into the garden, don't you?"

"Yes," replied Clara, with surprise.

"Yes, so do I too, and how you used to sit on my knee; and do you remember Jason, the big mastiff, and how you used to ride upon his back?"

"Yes," replied Clara, "I do; but he died a long while ago."

"He did, when you were not more than six years old. And now tell me, where did the old gardener bury him?"

"Under the mulberry tree," replied Clara.

"Yes, so he did, and I was there when poor Jason was buried. You don't recollect me. But I will take off my hat, for I did not wear the same dress as I do now. Now look, Clara, and see if you remember me."

Clara, who was no longer alarmed, looked on the intendant's face, and then said, "You called my father Philip, and he used to call you Charles."

"You are right, my sweet one," replied the intendant, pressing Clara to his bosom; "I did so, and we were great friends. Now, will you come with me? and I have a little girl, older than you by three or four years, who will be your companion, and love you dearly."

The intendant then went out of the cottage, and joined his people outside. Edward went out after him; and as the intendant mounted his horse, he said very coldly to Edward—"I shall keep a sharp lookout on your proceedings, sir, depend upon it; I tell you decidedly, so fare you well."

With these words the intendant put the spurs to his horse, and rode away.

The two brothers had a long conversation that evening, in which Edward made Humphrey acquainted with all that had passed between him and the intendant.

The next day they dug up the iron chest and the box into which Humphrey had put all the papers he had collected together. Edward opened the iron chest, and found in it a considerable quantity of gold in bags, and many trinkets and jewels which he did not know the value of. The papers he did not open, but resolved that they should be given to the intendant, for Edward felt that he could trust in him. The other boxes and trunks were also opened and examined, and many other articles of apparent value discovered.

"I should think all these jewels worth a great deal of money, Humphrey," said Edward; "if so, all the better for poor little Clara. I am sorry to part with her, although we have known her so short a time; she appears to be such an amiable and affectionate child."

"That she is; and certainly the handsomest little girl I ever saw. What beautiful eyes! Do you know that on one of her journeys to Lymington she was very nearly taken by a party of gipsies? And by what Pablo can make out, it would appear that it was by the party which he belonged to."

"I wonder at her father's permitting her to go alone such a distance."

"Her father could not do otherwise. Necessity has no law. He could trust no other person, so he put her in boy's clothes that there might be less risk. Still, she must have been very intelligent to have done the office."

"She is thirteen years old, although she is small," replied Edward. "And intelligent she certainly is, as you may see by her countenance.

Who would ever have imagined that our sisters would have been able to do what they are doing now? It's an old saying, 'We never know what we can do till we try.' By the by, Humphrey, I met a famous herd of forest ponies the other day, and I said to myself, 'I wonder whether Humphrey will be clever enough to take one of them, as he has the wild cattle?' For Billy is getting old, and we want a successor."

"We want more than a successor to Billy, Edward, we want two more to help him; and I have the means of maintaining two more ponies, if I could catch them."

Three days after this conversation, Oswald Partridge made his appearance, having been sent by the intendant to tell Edward that he should come over on the following day to take away little Clara.

"And how is she to go?" said Edward.

"He will bring a little nag for her, if she can ride; if she cannot, she must ride in the cart which will come for that baggage."

"Clara, can you ride a horse?"

"Yes," replied Clara, "if it does not jump about too much. I always rode one when I lived in Dorsetshire."

"This won't jump about, my little lady," said Oswald, "for he is thirty years old, I believe, and as steady as an old gentleman ought to be."

"I have had some conversation with Master Heatherstone," continued Oswald to Edward. "He is much pleased with you, I can tell you. He said, that in times like these, he required young men like you about him; and that as you would not take the berth of verderer, he must find one better suited for you, for he said that you were too good for such an office."

"Many thanks to him for his good opinion," replied Edward; "but I do not think that he has any office in his gift which I can accept."

"So I thought, but I said nothing. He again asked many questions relative to old Jacob Armitage, and he pressed me very hard. He said that Humphrey was as much above his position in appearance as you were; but as he was brought up at Arnwood, he presumed that he had had the same advantages. And then he said 'But were his two sisters brought up at Arnwood also?' I replied that I believed not, although they were often there, and were allowed to play with the children of the house. He looked at me steadfastly, as if he would read my thoughts, and then went on writing. I cannot help thinking that he has a suspicion that you are not the grandchildren of old Jacob; but at the same time I do not think that he has an idea who you really are."

"I trust to you, Oswald, and so there's an end of the matter. But tell me, Oswald, what do they say of his taking charge of this little girl?"

"Why, they did begin to talk about it; but when he gave out that it was the order of Parliament that the child should remain with him until further directions, of course they said nothing, for they dared not. It seems that the Ratcliffe property is sequestrated, but not yet granted to anyone; and the Parliament will most likely, as soon as she is old enough, give her as a wife, with the property, to one of their party; they have done it before now as it secures the property under all changes."

As Oswald had informed them, the intendant made his appearance in the forenoon of the following day, and was accompanied by his daughter, who rode by his side. A groom, on another horse, led a pony for Clara to ride; and a cart for the luggage followed at some distance. Edward went out to assist Miss Heatherstone to dismount, and she frankly extended her hand to him as she reached the ground. Edward was a little surprised as well as pleased at this condescension on her part towards a forester.

"You do me much honour, Mistress Patience," said he, bowing.

"I cannot forget that I owe my life to you, Master Armitage," replied Patience, "and I cannot be too grateful. May I request another favour of you?"

"Certainly, if it is in my power to do as you wish."

"It is this, said she, in a low voice; "that you will not hastily reject any overtures which may be made to you by my father; that is all. And now let me go in and see your sisters, for my father has praised them very much, and I wish to know them."

Edward then told the intendant that there was an iron chest with a good deal of money in it, and jewels also; and many other articles of value in the other boxes.

"I fear, sir, that the cart will hardly hold all the goods."

"I do not intend to take away the heavy or more bulky articles, such as the bedding, armour, etc. I will only take Clara's own packages, and the valuables and papers. The remainder may stay here, as they can be of no use, till they are demanded from you. Where is Oswald Partridge?"

"In the stable with the horses, sir," replied Humphrey.

"Then, when the cart is loaded—and it had better be done by you while the men are in the stable—Oswald shall take charge of it, and take the things to my house."

"Here are the keys, sir," said Edward, presenting them.

"Good. And now, Edward Armitage, that we are alone, I want to have a little conversation with you. You are aware how much I feel indebted to you for the service you have rendered me, and how anxious I am to show my gratitude. You are born for better things than to remain an obscure forester, and perhaps a deer-stalker. I have now an offer to make to you, which, I trust, upon reflection, you will not refuse—and I say reflection, because I do not wish you to give an answer till you have well reflected. I know that you will not accept anything under the present government, but a private situation you can raise no objection to; the more so, as, so far from leaving your family, you will be more in a position to protect them. I am in want of a secretary, and I wish you to accept the office, to live entirely in my house, and to receive a handsome salary for your services, which will not, I trust, be too heavy. You will be near to your family here in the cottage, and be able to protect them and assist them; and, what is more, you will mix with the world and know what is going on, as I am in the confidence of the government. Of course I put implicit confidence in you, or I would not offer the situation. But you will not always be down here: I have my correspondents and friends, to whom I shall have to send you occasionally on most trusty commissions. You, I am sure, will suit me in every respect, and I hope you will undertake the post which I now offer you. Give me no answer just now; consult with your brother, and give the offer due consideration, and when you have made up your mind you can let me know."

Edward bowed, and the intendant went into the cottage.

"Mistress Alice, many thanks for your hospitality; and now, farewell. Edith, good-bye dear. Now, Clara, are you quite ready?"

They all went out of the cottage. The intendant put Clara on the pony, after she had kissed Alice and Edith. Edward assisted Patience, and when she was mounted she said:

"I hope you will accept my father's offer—you will oblige me so much if you do."

"It will give it every consideration it deserves," replied Edward. "Indeed, it will depend more upon my brother than myself whether I accept it or not."

"Your brother is a very sensible young man, sir, therefore I have hopes," replied Patience.

Edward bowed, and then turned to the intendant, who had apparently been waiting while the conversation was going on. The intendant bade him a cordial farewell; Edward shook Clara by the hand, and the cavalcade set off. They all remained outside of the cottage till the party were at some distance, and then Edward walked apart with Humphrey, to communicate to him the offer made by the intendant, and to ask his opinion.

"My opinion is made up, Edward; which is, that you should accept it immediately. You are under no obligation to the government, and you have already conferred such an obligation upon the intendant that you have a right to expect a return. Why stay here, when you can safely mix with the world and know how things are going on? I do not require your assistance, now that I have Pablo, who is more useful every day. Do not lose such an opportunity of making a friend for yourself and all of us—a protector, I may say; and who is, by what he has confided to you, anything but approving of the conduct of the present government. He has paid you a deserved compliment by saying that he can and will trust you. You must not refuse the offer, Edward, it would really be folly if you did."

"You are right, Humphrey, and I will accept the offer; I can but return to you if things do not go on well."

"I thank you sincerely for your decision, Edward," replied Humphrey. "What a sweet girl that Patience Heatherstone is! I think I never saw such an enchanting smile!"

Edward thought of the smile she gave him when they parted but an hour ago, and agreed with Humphrey, but he replied:

"Why, brother, you are really in love with the intendant's daughter."

"Not so, my dear fellow; but I am in love with her goodness and sweetness of disposition, and so are Alice and Edith, I can tell you. She has promised to come over and see them, and bring them flowers for their garden, and I hardly know what; and I am very glad of it, as my sisters have been buried here so long that they cannot but gain by her company now and then. No! I will leave Mistress Heatherstone for you; I am in love with little Clara."

"Not a bad choice, Humphrey: we both aspire high, for two young foresters, do we not? However, they say 'Every dog has his day', and Cromwell and his parliament may have theirs. King Charles may be on his throne again now, long before—you catch a forest pony, Humphrey."

"I hope he will, Edward; but recollect how you laughed at the idea of my catching a cow—you may be surprised a second time. 'Where there is a will there is a way', the saying is. But I must go and help Alice with the heifer; she is not very quiet yet, and I see her going out with her pail."

The brothers then parted, and Edward walked about, turning over in his mind the events of the day, and very often finding his thoughts broken in upon by sudden visions of Patience Heatherstone—and certainly the remembrance of her was to him the most satisfactory and pleasing portion of the prospect in his offered situation.

CHAPTER 17

EDWARD REMAINED at the cottage, expecting to hear some message from the intendant. He was right in his conjecture, for, on the third day, Oswald Partridge came over to say that the intendant would be happy to see him, if he could make it convenient to go over; which Edward assented to do on the following day. Oswald had ridden over on a pony: Edward arranged to take Billy and return with him. They started early the next morning, and Edward asked Oswald if he knew why the intendant had sent for him.

"Not exactly," replied Oswald; "but I think, from what I heard Miss Patience say, it is to offer you some situation, if you could be prevailed upon to accept it."

"Very true," replied Edward, "he offers me the post of secretary. What do you think?"

"Why, sir, I think I would accept it; at all events, I would take it on trial—there can be no harm done: if you do not like it, you can only go back to the cottage again. One thing I am sure of, which is, that Master Heatherstone will make it as pleasant to you as he can, for he is most anxious to serve you."

"That I really believe," replied Edward; "and I have pretty well made up my mind to accept the office. It is a post of confidence, and I shall know all that is going on, which I cannot do while I am secluded in the forest; and depend upon it, we shall have stirring news."

"I suppose you think that the king will come over?" replied Oswald.

"I feel certain of it, Oswald; and that is the reason why I want to be where I can know all that is going on."

"Well, sir, it is my opinion that the king will come over, as well as yours; yet I think at present he stands but a poor chance; but Master Heatherstone knows more on that score than anyone, I should think; but he is very close."

The conversation then changed, and after a ride of eight hours they arrived at the intendant's house. Edward gave Billy into Oswald's charge, and knocked at the door. Phœbe let him in, and asked him into the sitting-room, where he found the intendant alone.

"Edward Armitage, I am glad to see you; and shall be still more so if I find that you have made up your mind to accept my proposition. What is your reply?"

"I am very thankful to you for the offer, sir," replied Edward; "and I will accept it if you think that I am fitting for it, and if I find that I am equal to it: I can but give it a trial, and leave if I find it too arduous or too irksome."

"Too arduous it shall not be—that shall be my concern; and too irksome I hope you will not find it. My letters are not so many but that I could answer them myself, were it not that my eyes are getting weak, and I wish to save them as much as possible. You will therefore have to write chiefly what I shall dictate; but it is not only for that I require a person that I can confide in. I very often shall send you to London instead of going myself, and to that I presume you will have no objection?"

"Certainly none, sir."

"Well, then, it is no use saying any more just now; you will have a chamber in this house, and you will live with me, and at my table altogether. Neither shall I say anything just now about remuneration, as I am convinced that you will be satisfied. All that I require now is to know the day that you will come, that everything may be ready."

"I suppose, sir, I must change my attire?" replied Edward, looking at his forester's dress. "That will hardly accord with the office of secretary."

"I agree with you that it will be better to keep that dress for your forest excursions, as I presume you will not altogether abandon them," replied the intendant. "You can provide yourself with a suit at Lymington. I will furnish you the means."

"I thank you, sir, I have means, much more than sufficient," replied Edward, "although not quite so wealthy as little Clara appeared to be."

"Wealthy, indeed!" replied the intendant. "I had no idea that poor Ratcliffe possessed so much ready money and jewels. Well, then, this is Wednesday; can you come over next Monday?"

"Yes, sir," replied Edward, "I see no reason to the contrary."

Mr. Heatherstone then opened the door, and saying to his daughter Patience, "My dear, I leave you to entertain Edward Armitage till dinner-time," he ushered Edward in, and closed the door again. Clara ran up to Edward as soon as he went in, and having kissed her, Edward then took Patience's offered hand.

"You will be able to watch over your sisters, Mr. Armitage, as well here, almost, as if you were at the cottage. You do not return till tomorrow? How did you come over?"

"I rode the pony Billy, Mistress Patience."

"Why do you call her Mistress Patience, Edward?" said Clara. "You call me Clara; why not call her Patience?"

"You forget that I am only a forester, Clara," replied Edward, with a grave smile.

"No, you are a secretary now," replied Clara.

"Mistress Patience is older than you by several years. I call you Clara because you are but a little girl; but I must not take that liberty with Mistress Heatherstone."

"Do you think so, Patience?" said Clara.

"I certainly do not think that it would be a liberty in a person, after being well acquainted with me, to call me Patience," replied she; "especially when that person lives in the house with us, eats and associates with us as one of the family, and is received on an equality; but I daresay, Clara, that Master Armitage will be guided by his own feelings, and act as he considers to be proper."

"But you give him leave, and then it is proper," replied Clara.

"Yes, if he gave himself leave, Clara," said Patience. "But we will now show him his own room, Clara," continued Patience, wishing to change the subject of conversation. "Will you follow us, sir?" said Patience, with a little mock ceremony.

Edward did so without reply, and was ushered into a large airy room, very neatly furnished.

"You sleep here tonight, I think my father said?" enquired Patience.

"He did make the proposal, and I shall gladly avail myself of it, as I am not to trust to Phœbe's ideas of comfort this time," said Edward, smiling.

"Yes, that was a cross action of Phœbe's; and I can tell you, Master Armitage, that she is ashamed to look you in the face ever since; but how fortunate for me that she was cross, and turned you out as she did! You must forgive her, as she was the means of your performing a noble action; and I must forgive her as she was the means of my life being saved."

"I have no feeling except kindness towards Phœbe," replied Edward; "indeed I ought to feel grateful to her; for if she had not given me so bad a bed that night. I never should have been so comfortably lodged as it is proposed that I shall be now."

"I hope you are hungry, Edward," said Clara; "dinner is almost ready."

Mr. Heatherstone, as was usual at that time with the people to whose party he ostensibly belonged, said a grace before meat, of considerable length, and then they sat down to table. As soon as the repast was over, Mr. Heatherstone returned to his study, and Edward went out to find Oswald Partridge, with whom he remained the large portion of the afternoon, going to the kennel and examining the dogs, and talking of matters connected with the chase.

"I have not two men that can stalk a deer," observed Oswald; "the men appointed here as verderers and keepers have not one of them been brought up to the business. Most of them are men who have been in the army, and I believe have been appointed to these siuations to get rid of them, because they were troublesome; and they are anything but good characters; the consequence is, that we kill but few deer, for I have so much to attend to here, as none of them know their duties, that I can seldom take my own gun out. I stated so to the intendant, and he said that if you accepted an offer he had made you, and came over here, we should not want venison; so it is clear that he does not expect you to have your pen always in your hand."

Edward did not sleep much that night. The novelty of his situation, the novelty of his prospects, and his speculations thereon, kept him awake till near morning; he was, however, up in good time, and having assisted at the morning prayers, and afterwards eaten a most substantial breakfast, he took his leave of the intendant and the two girls, and set off on his return to the cottage, having renewed his promise of coming on the following Monday to take up his abode with them. Billy was fresh, and cantered gaily along, so that Edward was back early in the afternoon, and once more welcomed by his household.

He stated to Humphrey all that had occurred, and Humphrey was much pleased at Edward having accepted the offer of the intendant. Alice and Edith did not quite so much approve of it, and a few tears were shed at the idea of Edward leaving the cottage. The next day, Edward and Humphrey set off for Lymington, with Billy in the cart.

"Do you know, Edward," said Humphrey, "what I am going to try and purchase? I will tell you:—as many kids as I can, or goats and kids, I don't care which."

"Why, have you not stock enough already? You will this year have four cows in milk, and you have two cow-calves bringing up."

"That is very true, but I do not intend to have goats for their milk, but simply for eating in lieu of mutton. Sheep I cannot manage, but goats, with a little hay in winter, will do well, and will find themselves in the forest all the year round. I won't kill any of the females for the first year or two, and after that I expect we shall have a flock sufficent to meet any demand upon it."

On their arrival at Lymington they went straight to the hostelry, and found the landlord at home. He recommended a tailor to Edward, who sent for him to the inn, and was measured by him for a plain suit of dark cloth. Edward and Humphrey then went out, as Edward had to procure boots, and many other articles of dress, to correspond with the one which he was about to assume.

"I am most puzzled about a hat, Humphrey," said Edward; "I hate those steeple-crowned hats, worn by the Roundheads; yet the hat and feather is not proper for a secretary."

"I would advise you to submit to wear the steeple-crowned hats, nevertheless," said Humphrey. "Your dress, as I consider, is a sort of disgrace to a cavalier born, and the heir of Arnwood; why not, therefore, take its hat as well? As secretary to the intendant you should dress like him; if not, you may occasion remarks, especially when you travel on his concerns."

"You are right, Humphrey, I must not do things by halves; and unless I wear the hat I might be suspected."

Edward chose a hat and a plain sword-belt, paid for them, and desired the man to carry them to the hostelry.

While all these purchases on the part of Edward, and many others by Humphrey, such as nails, saws, tools, and various articles which Alice required for the household, were gathered together, the landlord had sent out to enquire for the goats, and found out at what price they were to be procured. Humphrey left Edward to put away these in the cart, while he went out a second time to see the goats; he made an agreement with the man who had them for sale, for a male and three females with two kids each at their sides, and ten more female kids wich had just been weaned. The man engaged to drive them from Lymington, as far as the road went into the forest, on the following day; when Humphrey would meet them, pay him his money, and drive them to the cottage, which would be only three miles from the place agreed upon. Having settled that satisfactorily, he returned to Edward, who was all ready, and they went back home.

"We have dipped somewhat into the bag today, Edward," said Humphrey; "but the money is well spent."

"I think so, Humphrey; but I have no doubt that I shall be able to replace the money very soon, as the intendant will pay me for my services. The tailor had promised the clothes on Saturday without fail, so that you or I must go for them."

"I will go, Edward; my sisters will wish you to stay with them now, as you are so soon to leave them; and I will take Pablo with me, that he may know his way to the town; and I will show him where to buy things, in case he goes there by himself."

Humphrey was off the next morning, with Pablo, at an early hour, to meet the farmer of whom he had purchased the goats and kids. He found them punctual to the time at the place agreed upon; and, being satisfied with the lot, paid the farmer his money, and drove them home through the forest.

CHAPTER 18

THE FLOCKS of goats were much admired, and the next morning were driven out into the forest to feed, attended by Pablo and Holdfast. When it was dinner-time, Pablo drove the flock near to the cottage, telling the dog to mind them. The sensible animal remained at once with the goats until Pablo's return from dinner; and it may be as well to observe here that in a few days the dog took charge of them altogether, driving them home to the yard every evening. As soon as the goats were put into the yard, the dog had his supper; the dog took care, therefore, not to be too late. To return to our narrative.

On Saturday, Humphrey and Pablo went to Lymington, to bring home Edward's clothes, and Humphrey made Pablo acquainted with all that he wanted to know, in case it might be necessary to send Pablo there alone.

On Monday morning, Edward, to please his sisters, put on his new clothes, and put his forester's dress in the bundle with his linen. Alice and Edith thought he looked very well in them, and said that it reminded them of the days of Arnwood. The fact was, that Edward appeared as he was, a gentleman born; that could not well be concealed under a forester's dress, and in his present attire it was undeniable. After breakfast, Billy was harnessed and brought to the cottage door. Edward's linen was put in the cart, and as he had agreed with Humphrey he took only Smoker with him, leaving the puppy at the cottage. Pablo went with him to bring back the cart. Edward kissed his sisters, who wept at the idea of his leaving them, and shaking hands with Humphrey he set off to cross the forest.

When Edward arrived at the intendant's house, he was very kindly received by the intendant and the two girls. Having deposited his wardrobe in his bedroom, he went out to Oswald and put Smoker in the kennel, and on his return found Pablo sitting on the carpet in the sitting-room talking to Patience and Clara, and they all three appeared much amused. When Pablo and Billy had both had something to eat, the cart was filled with pots of flowers, and several other little things as presents from Patience Heatherstone, and Pablo set off on his return.

"Why do you always call Patience Mistress Heatherstone? Ought he not to call her Patience, sir?" said Clara, appealing to the intendant.

"That must depend upon his own feelings, my dear Clara," replied Mr. Heatherstone. "It is my intention to waive ceremony as much as possible. Edward Armitage has come to live with us as one of the family, and he will find himself treated by me as one of us. I shall, therefore, in future address him as Edward, and he has my full permission, and I may say it is my wish, that he should be on the same familiar terms with us all. When Edward feels inclined to address my daughter, as he does you, by her name of baptism, he will, I dare say, now that he has heard my opinion, do so; and reserve 'Mistress Heatherstone' for the time when they have a quarrel."

"Then I hope he will never again address me that way," observed Patience; "for I am under too great obligations to him to bear even the idea of being on bad terms with him."

"Do you hear that, Edward?" said Clara.

"Yes, I do, Clara; and after such a remark, you may be sure that I shall never address her in that way again."

In a few days Edward became quite at home. In the forenoon Mr. Heatherstone dictated one or two letters to him, which he wrote; and after that his time was at his own disposal, and was chiefly passed in the company of Patience and Clara. With the first he had now become on the most intimate and brotherly footing; and when they addressed each other, Patience and Edward were the only appellations made use of. Once Mr. Heatherstone asked Edward whether he would not like to go out with Oswald to kill deer, which he did; but the venison was hardly yet in season. There was a fine horse in the stable at Edward's order, and he often rode out with Patience and Clara; indeed, his time passed so agreeably that he could hardly think it possible that a fortnight had passed away, when he asked permission to go over to the cottage and see his sisters.

With the intendant's permission Patience and Clara accompanied him; and the joy of Alice and Edith was great when they made their appearance. Oswald had, by Edward's request, gone over a day or two before, to tell them that they were coming, that they might be prepared; and the consequence was, that it was a holiday at the cottage. Alice had cooked her best dinner, and Humphrey and Pablo were at home to receive them.

"How pleasant it will be, if we are to see you and Clara whenever we see Edward!" said Alice to Patience. "So far from being sorry that Edward is with you, I shall be quite glad of it."

"I water the flowers every day," said Edith, "and they make the garden look so gay."

"I will bring you plenty more in the autumn, Edith; this is not the right time for transplanting," replied Patience. "And now, Alice, you must take me to see your farm, for when I was here last I had no time; let us come now, and show me everything."

In the meantime, Edward and Humphrey, after the first greetings were over, had walked out to converse, while Pablo had taken the horses into the stable.

"Well, Humphrey, how do you get on?"

"Very well," replied Humphrey. "I have just finished a very tough job. I have dug out the sawpit, and have sawed the slabs for the sides of the pit, and made it quite secure. The large fir tree that was blown down is now at the pit, ready for sawing up into planks, and Pablo and I are to commence tomorrow. At first we made but a bad hand of sawing off the slabs, but before we had cut them all we got on pretty well. Pablo don't much like it, and, indeed, no more do I much, it is such mechanical work, and so tiring; but he does not complain. I do not intend that he shall saw more than two days in a week; that will be sufficient; we shall get on fast enough."

"You are right, Humphrey; it is an old saying, that you must not work a willing horse to death. Pablo is very willing, but hard work he is not accustomed to."

"Well, now you must come and look at my flock of goats, Edward, they are not far off. I have taught Holdfast to take care of them, and he never leaves them now, and brings them home at night. Watch always remains with me, and is an excellent dog, and very intelligent."

"You have indeed a fine flock, Humphrey!" said Edward.

"Yes, and they are improved in appearance already since they have been here. Alice has got her geese and ducks, and I have made a place large enough for them to wash in, until I have time to dig them out a pond."

"I thought we had gathered more hay than you required; but now I think you will find none to spare before the spring."

"So far from it, that I have been mowing down a great deal more, Edward, and it is almost ready to carry away. Poor Billy has had hard work of it, I assure you, since he came back, with one thing and another."

"Poor fellow, but it won't last long, Humphrey," said Edward, smiling; "the other horses will soon take his place."

"I trust they will," said Humphrey, "at all events by next spring; before that I do not expect that they will."

CHAPTER 19

THE SUMMER had now advanced, when Oswald one day said to Edward, "Have you heard the news, sir?"

"Nothing very particular," replied Edward; "I know that General Cromwell is over in Ireland, and they say very successful; but I have cared little for particulars."

"They say a great deal more, sir," replied Oswald; "they say that the king is in Scotland, and that the Scotch have raised an army for him."

"Indeed!" replied Edward, "that is news indeed! The intendant has never mentioned it to me."

"I dare say not, sir, for he knows your feelings, and would be sorry to part with you."

"I will certainly speak to him on the subject," said Edward, "at the risk of his displeasure; and join the army I will, if I find what you say is true. I should hold myself a craven to remain here while the king is fighting for his own, and not be at his side."

"Well, sir, I think it is true, for I heard that the Parliament had sent over for General Cromwell to leave Ireland, and lead the troops against the Scotch army."

"You drive me mad, Oswald! I will go to the intendant immediately!"

Edward, much excited by the intelligence, went into the room where he usually sat with the intendant. The latter, who was at his desk, looked up, and saw how flushed Edward was, and said very quietly:

"Edward, you are excited, I presume, from hearing the news which has arrived?"

"Yes, sir, I am very much so; and I regret very much that I should be the last to whom such important news is made known."

"It is, as you say, important news," replied the intendant; "but if you will sit down, we will talk a little upon the subject."

Edward took a chair, and the intendant said:

"I have no doubt that your present feeling is to go to Scotland, and join the army without delay?"

"Such is my intention, I candidly confess, sir. It is my duty."

"Perhaps you may be persuaded to the contrary before we part," replied the intendant. "The first duty you owe is to your family in their present position; they depend upon you; and a false step on your part would be their ruin. How can you leave them, and leave my employ, without it being known for what purpose you are gone? It is impossible! I must myself make it known, and even then it would be very injurious to me, the very circumstance of my having one of your party in my service. I am suspected by many already, in consequence of the part I have taken against the murder of the late king, and also of the lords who have since suffered. But, Edward, I did not communicate this intelligence to you for many reasons. I knew that it would soon come to your ears, and I thought it better that I should be more prepared to show you that you may do yourself and me harm, and can do no good to the king. I will now show you that I do put confidence in you; and, if you will read these letters, they will prove to you that I am correct in what I assert."

The intendant handed three letters to Edward, by which it was evident that all the king's friends in England were of opinion that the time was not ripe for the attempt, and that it would be only a sacrifice to stir in the matter; that the Scotch army raised was composed of those who were the greatest enemies to the king, and that the best thing that could happen for the king's interest would be that they were destroyed by Cromwell; that it was impossible for the English adherents of Charles to join them, and that the Scotch did not wish them so to do.

"You are no politician, Edward," said the intendant, smiling, as Edward laid down the letters. "You must admit, that on showing these letters, I have put the utmost confidence in you?"

"You have, indeed, sir; and, thanking you for having so done I hardly need add that your confidence will never be betrayed."

"That I am sure of; and I trust you will now agree with me and my friends, that the best thing is to remain quiet?"

"Certainly, sir, and in future I will be guided by you."

"That is all I require of you; and after that promise you shall hear all the news as soon as it arrives. There are thousands who are just as anxious to see the king on the throne again as you are, Edward, and you now know that I am one of them; but the time is not yet come, and we must bide our time. Depend upon it, that General Cromwell will scatter that army like chaff. He is on his march now. After what has passed between us this day, Edward, I shall talk unreservedly to you on what is going on."

"I thank you, sir, and I promise you faithfully, as I said before, not only to be guided by your advice, but to be most secret in all that you may trust me with."

"I have confidence in you, Edward Armitage; and now we will drop the subject for the present; Patience and Clara want you to walk with them, so good-bye for the present."

Edward left the intendant, much pleased with the interview. The intendant kept his word, and concealed nothing from Edward. All turned out as the intendant had foretold. The Scotch army were cut to pieces by Cromwell. The king retreated to the Highlands; and Edward felt satisfied that he could do no better than be guided by the intendant in all his future undertakings.

Edward continued at the intendant's, and gave great satisfaction to Mr. Heatherstone. He passed his time very agreeably, sometimes going out to shoot deer with Oswald, and often supplying venison to his brother and sisters at the cottage. During the autumn Patience very often went to the cottage, and occasionally Mr. Heatherstone paid them a visit; but after the winter set in Edward came over by himself, shooting as he went; and when he and Smoker came to the cottage, Billy always had a journey to go for the venison left in the forest. Patience sent Alice many little things for the use of her and Edith, and some very good books for them to read; and Humphrey, during the evenings, read with his sister, that they might learn what he could teach them.

CHAPTER 20

THE WINTER set in very severe, and the falls of snow were very heavy and frequent. It was fortunate that Humphrey had been so provident in making so large a quantity of hay, or the stock would have been starved. The flock of goats, in great part, subsisted themselves on the bark of trees and moss; at night they had some hay given to them, and they did very well. It was hardly possible for Edward to come over and see his brother and sisters, for the snow was so deep as to render such a long journey too fatiguing for a horse. Twice or thrice after the snow fell he contrived to get over, but after that they knew that it was impossible, and did not expect him. Humphrey and Pablo had little to do except attending to the stock, and cutting firewood to keep up their supply, for they now burnt it very fast. The snow lay several feet high around the cottage, being driven against it by the wind. A sharp frost and clear weather succeeded to the snow-storms, and there appeared no chance of the snow melting away. The nights were dark and long, and their oil for their lamp was getting low. Humphrey was anxious to go to Lymington, as they required many things; but it was impossible to go anywhere except on foot, and walking was, from the depth of the snow, a most fatiguing exercise. There was one thing, however, that Humphrey had not forgotten, which was that he had told Edward that he would try and capture some of the forest ponies; and during the whole of the time since the heavy fall of snow had taken place he had been making his arrangements. The depth of the snow prevented the animals from obtaining any grass, and they were almost starved, as they could find nothing to subsist upon except the twigs and branches of trees which they could reach. Humphrey went out with Pablo and found the herd, which was about five miles from the cottage, and near to Clara's cottage. He and Pablo brought with them as much hay as they could carry, and strewed it about so as to draw the ponies nearer to them, and then Humphrey looked for a place which would answer his purpose. About three miles from the cottage he found what he thought would suit him; there was a sort of avenue between two thickets, about a hundred yards wide; and the wind blowing through this avenue, during the snow-storm, had drifted the snow at one end of it, and right across it raised a large mound several feet high. By strewing small bundless of hay, he drew the herd of ponies into this avenue; and in the avenue he left them a good quantity to feed upon every night, for several nights, till at last the herd went there every morning.

"Now, Pablo, we must make a trial," said Humphrey. "You must get your lassoes ready, in case they should be required. We must go to the avenue before daylight with the two dogs, tie one upon one side of the avenue, and the other on the other, that they may bark and prevent the ponies from attempting to escape through the thicket. Then we must get the ponies between us and the drift of snow which lies across the avenue, and try if we cannot draw them into the drift. If so, they will plunge in so deep that some of them will not be able to get out before we have thrown the ropes around their necks."

Before daylight they went with the dogs and a large bundle of hay, which they strewed nearer to the mound of drift snow. They then tied the dogs up on each side, ordering them to lie down and be quiet. Then they walked through the thicket so as not to be perceived, until they considered that they were far enough from the drift snow. About daylight the herd came to pick up the hay as usual, and after they had passed them Humphrey and Pablo followed in the thicket, not wishing to show themselves till the last moment. While the ponies were busy with the hay, they suddenly ran into the avenue and separated, so as to prevent the ponies from attempting to gallop past them. Shouting as loud as they could, as they ran up to the ponies, and calling to the dogs, who immediately set up barking on each side; the ponies, alarmed at the noise, and the appearance of Humphrey and Pablo, naturally set off in the only direction which appeared to them to be clear, and galloped away over the mound of drift snow, with their tails streaming, snorting and plunging in the snow as they hurried along; but as soon as they arrived at the mound of drift snow, they plunged first up to their bellies, and afterwards, as they attempted to force their way where the snow was deeper, many of them stuck fast altogether, and attempted to clear themselves in vain. Humphrey and Pablo, who had followed them as fast as they could run, now came up with them and threw the lasso over the neck of one, and ropes with slip nooses over two more, which were floundering in the snow together. The remainder of the herd, after great exertions, got clear of the snow, by turning round and galloping back through the avenue. The three ponies captured made a furious struggle; but by drawing the ropes tight round their necks they were choked, and soon unable to move. They then tied their forelegs, and loosed the ropes round their necks, that they might recover their breath.

"Got them now, Massa Humphrey," said Pablo.

"Yes; but our work is not yet over, Pablo, we must get them home; how shall we manage that?"

"Suppose they no eat today and tomorrow, get very tame."

"I believe that will be the best way; they cannot get loose again, do all they can."

"No, sir; but get one home today. This very fine pony; suppose we try him."

Pablo then put the halter on, and tied the end short to the foreleg of the pony, so that it could not walk without keeping its head close to the ground—if it raised its head it was obliged to lift up its leg. Then he put the lasso round its neck to choke it if it was too unruly, and, having done that, he cast loose the ropes which had tied its forelegs together.

"Now, Massa Humphrey, we get him home somehow. First I go loose the dogs; he 'fraid of the dog, and run t'other way."

The pony, which was an iron-grey and very handsome, plunged furiously and kicked behind; but it could not do so without falling down, which it did several times before Pablo returned with the dogs. Humphrey held one part of the lasso on one side and Pablo on the other, keeping the pony between them; and with the dogs barking at it behind, they contrived, with a great deal of exertion and trouble, to get the pony to the cottage. The poor animal, driven in this way on three legs, and every now and then choked with the lasso, was covered with foam before they arrived. Billy was turned out to make room for the newcomer, who was fastened securely to the manger and then left without food that he might become tame. It was too late then, and they were too tired themselves to go for the other two ponies; so they were left lying on the snow all night, and the next morning they found they were much tamer than the first; and during the day, following the same plan, they were both brought to the stable and secured alongside of the other. Alice and Edith were delighted with the new ponies, and Humphrey was not a

98

little pleased that he had succeeded in capturing them, after what had passed between Edward and him. After two days' fasting the poor animals were so tame that they ate out of Pablo's hand and submitted to be stroked and caressed; and before they were a fortnight in the stable Alice and Edith could go up to them without danger. They were soon broken in; and, after a month, they were all three tolerably quiet to ride.

The snow was so deep all over the country that there was little communication with the metropolis. The intendant's letter spoke of King Charles raising another army in Scotland, and that his adherents in England were preparing to join him as soon as he marched southward.

"I think, Edward," said the intendant, "that the king's affairs do now wear a more promising aspect; but there is plenty of time yet. I know your anxiety to serve your king, and I cannot blame it. I shall not prevent your going, although of course I must not be cognizant of your having done so. When the winter breaks up I shall send you to London. You will then be able to judge better of what is going on, and your absence will not create any suspicion; but you must be guided by me."

It was soon after this conversation that a messenger arrived from London with letters, announcing that King Charles had been crowned in Scotland, with great solemnity and magnificence.

"The plot thickens," said the intendant; "and by this letter from my correspondent, Ashley Cooper, I find that the king's army is well appointed, and that David Leslie is Lieutenant-General: Middleton commands the horse, and Wemyss the artillery. Now, Edward, I shall send you to London, and I will give you letters to those who will advise you how to proceed. You may take the black horse, he will bear you well. You will of course write to me, for Sampson will go with you, and you can send him back when you consider that you do not require or wish for his presence; there is no time to be lost, for, depend upon it, Cromwell, who is still at Edinburgh, will take the field as soon as he can. Are you ready to start tomorrow morning?"

"Yes, sir, quite ready."

"I fear that you cannot go over to the cottage to bid farewell to your sisters; but perhaps it is better that you should not."

"I think so too, sir," replied Edward; "now that the snow has nearly disappeared I did think of going over, having been so long absent, but I must send Oswald over instead."

"Well, then, leave me to write my letters, and do you prepare your saddlebags. Patience and Clara will assist you. Tell Sampson to come to me."

Edward had left the room, and having obtained the saddlebags from Phœbe, had gone up to his chamber. The first thing that he laid hold of was his father's sword; he took it down, and having wiped it carefully he kissed it, saying, "God grant that I may do credit to it, and prove as worthy to wield it as was my brave father!" He had uttered these words aloud; and again taking the sword, and laying it down on the bed, turned round, and perceived that Patience had, unknown to him, entered the room, and was standing close to him. Edward was not conscious that he had spoken aloud, and therefore merely said, "I was not aware of your presence, Patience. Your foot is so light."

"Whose sword is that, Edward?"

"It is mine; I brought it at Lymington."

"But what makes you have such an affection for the sword?"

"Affection for it?"

"Yes; as I came into the room, you kissed it as fervently as——"

"As a lover would his mistress, I presume you would say," replied Edward.

"Nay, I meant not to use such vain words. I was about to say as a Catholic would a relic. I ask you again, why so? A sword is but a sword. You are about to leave this on a mission of my father's. You are not a soldier, about to engage in strife and war; if you were, why kiss your sword?"

"I will tell you. I do love this sword. I purchased it, as I told you, at Lymington, and they told me that it belonged to Colonel Beverley. It is for his sake that I love it. You know what obligations our family were under to him."

"This sword was, then, wielded by Colonel Beverley, the celebrated cavalier, was it?" said Patience, taking it from off the bed, and examining it.

"Yes it was; and here, you see, are his initials upon the hilt."

"And why do you take it to London with you? Surely it is not the weapon which should be worn by a secretary, Edward; it is too large, and cumbrous, and out of character."

"Recollect, that till these last few months I have been a forester, Patience, and not a secretary. Indeed I feel that I am more fit for active life than the situation which your father's kindness has bestowed upon me. I was brought up, as you have heard, to follow to the wars, had my patron lived."

Patience made no reply. Clara now joined them, and they commenced the task of examining the linen; and Edward left the room, as he wished to speak with Oswald. They did not meet again till dinner-time. Edward's sudden departure had spread a gloom over them all,—even the intendant was silent and thoughtful. In the evening he gave Edward the letters which he had written, and a considerable sum of money, telling him where he was to apply if he required more for his expenses.

"If you should leave London there will be no occasion, nay, it would be dangerous, to write to me. I shall take it for granted that you will retain Sampson till your departure, and when he returns here, I shall presume that you have gone north. I will not detain you longer; may Heaven bless and protect you!"

So saying, the intendant went away to his own room.

"Kind and generous man!" thought Edward, "how much did I mistake you when we first met!"

Taking up the letters and bag of money, which still remained on the table, Edward went to his room, and, having placed the letters and money in the saddlebag, he commended himself to the Divine Protector, and retired to rest.

Before daylight the sound of Sampson's heavy travelling boots below roused up Edward, and he was soon dressed. Taking his saddlebags on his arm he walked softly downstairs, that he might not disturb any of the family; but when he was passing the sitting-room he perceived that there was a light in it, and on looking in, that Patience was up and dressed. Edward looked surprised, and was about to speak, when Patience said:

"I rose early, Edward, because when I took leave of you last night I forgot a little parcel that I wanted to give you before you went. It will not take much room, and may beguile a weary hour. It is a little book of meditations. Will you accept it, and promise me to read it when you have time?"

"I certainly will, my dear Patience—if I may venture on the expression—read it, and think of you."

"Nay, read it and think of what it contains," replied Patience.

"I will, then. I shall not need the book to remind me of Patience Heatherstone, I assure you."

"And now, Edward, I do not pretend to surmise the reason of your departure, nor would it be becoming in me to attempt to discover what my father thinks proper to be silent upon; but I must beg you to promise one thing."

"Name it, dear Patience," replied Edward; "my heart is so full at the thought of leaving you that I feel I can refuse you nothing."

"It is this,—I have a presentiment, I know not what, that you are about to encounter danger. If so, be prudent—be prudent for the sake of your dear sisters, be prudent for the sake of all your friends who would regret you—promise me that."

"I do promise you, most faithfully, Patience, that I will ever have my sisters and you in my thoughts, and will not be rash under any circumstances."

"Thank you, Edward; may God bless you, and preserve you!"

Edward first kissed Patience's hand, that was held in his own, but perceiving the tears starting in her eyes he kissed them off, without any remonstrance on her part, and then left the room. In a few moments more he was mounted on a fine powerful black horse, and followed by Sampson, on his road to London.

We will pass over the journey, which was accomplished without any event worthy of remark. Edward had, from the commencement, called Sampson to his side, that he might answer the questions he had to make upon all that he saw. Sampson was a very powerful man, of cool and silent character, by no means deficient in intelligence, and trustworthy withal. He had long been a follower of the intendant, and had served in the army. He was very devout; and generally, when not addressed, was singing hymns in a low voice.

On the evening of the second day they were close to the metropolis, and Sampson pointed out to Edward St. Paul's Cathedral and Westminster Abbey, and other objects of note.

"And where are we to lodge, Sampson?" enquired Edward.

"The best hotel that I know of is the 'Swan with Three Necks,' in Holborn. It is not over-frequented by roisterers, and you will there be quiet, and, if your affairs demand it, unobserved."

The following morning he examined the letters which had been given to him by the intendant, and enquired of Sampson if he could direct him on his way. Sampson knew London well; and Edward set out to Spring Gardens, to deliver a letter, which the intendant informed him was confidential, to a person of the name of Langton. Edward knocked and was ushered in, Sampson taking a seat in the hall while Edward was shown into a handsomely furnished library, where he found himself in the presence of a tall, spare man, dressed after the fashion of the Roundheads of the time. He presented the letter.

"You are right welcome, Master Armitage," said Mr. Langton; "I find that, young as you appear to be, you are in the whole confidence of our mutual friend, Master Heatherstone. He hints at your being probably obliged to take a journey to the north, and that you will be glad to take charge of any letters which I may have to send in that direction. I will have them ready for you; and in case of need they will be such as will give a colouring to your proceeding, provided you may not choose to reveal your true object. How wears our good friend Heatherstone and his daughter?"

"Quite well, sir."

"And he told me in one of his former letters that he had the daughter of our poor friend Ratcliffe with him. Is it not so?"

"It is, Master Langton; and as gentle a child as you wish to see."

"When did you arrive in London?"

"Yesterday evening, sir."

"It is my opinion, Master Armitage, that the less you are seen in this city, the better, there are hundreds employed to find out newcomers, and to discover from their people, or by other means, for what purpose they may have come; for you must be aware, Master Armitage, that the times are dangerous and people's minds are various. In attempting to free ourselves from what we considered despotism, we have created for ourselves a worse despotism, and one that is less endurable. It is to be hoped that what has passed will make not only kings, but subjects wiser than they have been. Do you propose to leave this instantly?"

"Certainly, if you think it advisable."

"My advice, then, is to leave London immediately. I will give you letters to some friends of mine in Lancashire and Yorkshire; in either

102

county you can remain unnoticed, and make what preparations you think necessary. But do nothing in haste—consult well, and be guided by them, who will, if it is considered advisable and prudent, join with you in your project. I need say no more. Call upon me tomorrow morning, an hour before noon, and I will have letters ready for you."

Edward rose to depart, and thanked Mr. Langton for his kindness.

"Farewell, Master Armitage," said Langton; "tomorrow at the eleventh hour!"

Edward then quitted the house, and delivered the other letters of credence. The only one of importance at the moment was the one of credit; the others were to various members of the Parliament, desiring them to know Master Armitage as a confidential friend of the intendant, and in case of need to exert their good offices in his behalf. The letter of credit was upon a Hamburg merchant, who asked Edward if he required money. Edward replied that he did not at present, but that he had business to do for his employer in the north, and might require some when there, if it was possible to obtain it so far from London.

Edward then returned to the hotel. Before he went to bed, he told Sampson that he found that he had to leave London on Mr. Heatherstone's affairs, and might be absent some time; he concluded by observing that he did not consider it necessary to take him with him, as he could dispense with his services, and Mr. Heatherstone would be glad to have him back.

"As you wish, sir," replied Sampson. "When am I to go back?"

"You may leave tomorrow as soon as you please. I have no letter to send. You may tell them that I am well, and will write as soon as I have anything positive to communicate."

At the hour appointed on the following day Edward repaired to Mr. Langton, who received him very cordially.

"I am all ready for you, Master Armitage; there is a letter to two Catholic ladies in Lancashire, who will take great care of you; and here is one to a friend of mine in Yorkshire. The ladies live about four miles from the town of Bolton, and my Yorkshire friend in the city of York. You may trust to either of them. And now, farewell; and, if possible, leave London before nightfall—the sooner the better. Where is your servant?"

"He has returned to Master Heatherstone this morning."

"You have done right. Lose no time to leave London; and don't be in a hurry in your future plans. You understand me. If anyone accosts you on the road, put no trust in any professions. You, of course, are going down to your relations in the north. Have you pistols?"

"Yes, sir; I have a pair which did belong to the unfortunate Mr. Ratcliffe."

"Then they are good ones, I'll answer for it; no man was more particular about his weapons, or knew how to use them better. Farewell, Master Armitage, and may success attend you!"

CHAPTER 21

EDWARD WAS certain that Mr. Langton would not have advised him to leave London if he had not considered that it was dangerous to remain. He therefore first called on the Hamburg merchant, who, upon his explanation, gave him a letter of credit to a friend who resided in the city of York, and then returned to the hotel, packed up his saddlebags, paid his reckoning, and, mounting his horse, set off on the northern road. As it was late in the afternoon before he was clear of the metropolis, he did not proceed farther than Barnet, where he pulled up at the inn. Having procured a bed, and given his saddlebags into the charge of the hostess, he sat down by the fire, which, although it was warm weather, was nevertheless kept alight.

Edward had made no alteration in the dress which he had worn since he had been received in the house of Mr. Heatherstone. It was plain, although of good materials. He wore a high-crowned hat, and, altogether, would, from his attire, have been taken for one of the Roundhead party. His sword and shoulder-belt were indeed of more gay appearance than those usually worn by the Roundheads, but this was the only difference.

When Edward first entered the room, there were three persons in it, whose appearance was not very prepossessing. They were dressed in what had once been very gay attire, but which now exhibited tarnished lace, stains of wine, and dust from travelling. They eyed him as he entered, and one of them said:

"That's a fine horse you were riding, sir. Has he much speed?"

"He has," replied Edward, as he turned away, and went into the bar to speak with the hostess, and give his property into her care.

"Going north, sir?" enquired the same person when Edward returned.

"Not exactly," replied Edward, walking to the window to avoid further conversation.

"The Roundhead is on stilts," observed another of the party.

"Yes," replied the first; "it is easy to see that he has not been accustomed to be addressed by gentlemen; for half a pin I would slit his ears!"

Edward did not choose to reply; he folded his arms, and looked at the man with contempt.

The hostess, who had overheard the conversation, now called for her husband, and desired him to go into the room and prevent any further insults to the young gentleman who had just come in. The host, who knew the parties, entered the room, and said:

"Now you'll clear out of this as fast as you can; be off with you to the stables, or I'll send for somebody you will not like."

The three men rose and swaggered, but obeyed the host's orders, and left the room.

"I am sorry, young Master, that these roisterers should have affronted you, as my wife tells me that they have. We cannot well refuse to take in their horses; but we know well who they are, and if you are travelling far, you had better ride in company."

"Thank you for your caution, my good host," replied Edward; "I thought they were highwaymen, or something of the sort."

"You have made a good guess, sir; but nothing has yet been proved against them, or they would not be here. You have a good sword, there sir, I have no doubt; but I trust that you have other arms."

"I have," replied Edward, opening his doublet, and showing his pistols.

"That's right. Will you take anything before you retire?"

"Indeed I will, for I am hungry; anything will do."

As soon as he had supped, Edward asked the hostess for his saddlebags, and went up to his bed.

Early the next morning he rose and went to the stable to see his horse fed. The three men were in the stables, but they did not say anything to him. Edward returned to the inn, called for breakfast, and, as soon as he had finished, took out his pistols to renew the priming. While so occupied he happened to look up, and perceived one of the men with his face against the window, watching him. "Well, now, you see what you have to expect if you try your trade with me," thought Edward. "I am very glad that you have been spying." Having replaced his pistols, Edward paid his reckoning, and went to the stable, desiring the ostler to saddle his horse and fix on his saddlebags. As soon as this was done, he mounted and rode off. Before he was well clear of the town the highwaymen cantered past him on three well-bred, active horses. "I presume we shall meet again," thought Edward, who for some time cantered at a gentle pace, and then, as his horse was very fresh, he put him to a faster pace, intending to do a long day's work. He had ridden about fifteen miles when he came to a heath, and, as he continued at a fast trot, he perceived the three highwaymen about a quarter of a mile in advance of him; they were descending a hill which was between them, and he soon lost sight of them again. Edward now pulled up his horse to let him recover his wind, and walked him gently up the hill. He had nearly gained the summit when he heard the report of firearms, and soon afterwards a man on horseback, in full speed, galloped over the hill towards him. He had a pistol in his hand, and his head turned back. The reason for this was soon evident, as immediately after him appeared the three highwaymen in pursuit. One fired his pistol at the man who fled, and missed him. The man then fired in return, and with true aim, as one of the highwaymen fell. All this was so sudden that Edward had hardly time to draw his pistol, and put spurs to his horse, before the parties were upon him, and were passing him. Edward levelled at the second highwayman as he passed him, and the man fell. The third highwayman, perceiving this, turned his horse to the side of the road, cleared a ditch, and galloped away across the heath. The man who had been attacked had pulled up his horse when Edward came to his assistance, and now he rode up to him saying:

"I have to thank you, sir, for your timely aid; for these rascals were too many for me."

"You are not hurt, I trust, sir?" replied Edward.

"No, not the least; the fellow singed my curls though, as you may perceive. They attacked me about half a mile from here. I was proceeding north when I heard the clatter of hoofs behind me; I looked round, and saw at once what they were, and I sprang my horse out of the road to a thicket close to it, that they might not surround me. One of the three rode forward to stop my passage, and the other two rode round to the back of the thicket to get behind me. I then saw that I had separated them, and could gain a start upon them by riding back again, which I did as fast as I could, and they immediately gave chase. The result you saw. Between us we have broken up the gang; for both these fellows seem dead, or nearly so."

"What shall we do with them?"

"Leave them where they are," replied the stranger. "I am in a hurry to get on. I have important business at the city of York, and cannot waste my time in depositions, and such nonsense."

"I am also going north," replied Edward, "and am anxious to get there as soon as I can."

"With your permission we will ride together," said the stranger. "I shall be the gainer, as I shall feel that I have one with me who is to be trusted to in case of any further attacks."

There was such a gentlemanlike, frank, and courteous air about the stranger that Edward immediately assented to his proposal of their riding in company for mutual protection. He was a powerful, well-made man, of apparently about one or two and twenty, remarkably handsome in person, dressed richly, but not gaudily, in the cavalier fashion, and wore a hat with a feather. As they proceeded, they entered into conversation on indifferent matters for some time, neither party attempting by any question to discover who his companion might be. Edward had more than once, when the conversation flagged for a minute, considered what reply he should give in case his companion asked the cause of his journey, and at last had made up his mind what to say.

A little before noon they pulled up to bait their horses at a small village—the stranger observing that he avoided St. Albans and all other large towns, as he did not wish to satisfy the curiosity of the people, or to have his motions watched; and therefore, if Edward had no objection, he knew the country so well that he could save time by allowing him to direct their path. Edward was, as may be supposed, very agreeable to this; and during their whole journey they never entered a town, except they rode through it after dark, and put up at humble inns on the roadside, where, if not quite so well attended to, they were free from observation.

It was, however, impossible that this reserve could continue long, as they became more and more intimate every day. At last the stranger said:

"Master Armitage, we have travelled together for some time, inter-changing thoughts and feelings, but with due reserve as respects ourselves and our own plans. Is this to continue? If so, of course, you have but to say so; but if you feel inclined to trust me, I have the same feeling towards you. By your dress I should imagine that you belong to a party to which I am opposed, but your language and manners do not agree with your attire; and I think a hat and feathers would grace that head better than the steeple-crowned affair which now covers it. It may be that the dress is only assumed as a disguise: you know best. However, as I say, I feel confidence in you, to whatever party you may belong, and I give you cre-dit for your prudence and reserve in these troubled times. I am a little older than you, and may advise you; and I am indebted to you, and can-not therefore betray you—at least, I trust you believe so."

"I do believe it," replied Edward; "and I will so far answer you, Master Chaloner, that this attire of mine is not the one which I would wear if I had my choice."

"I believe that," replied Chaloner; "and I cannot help thinking that you are bound north on the same business as myself, which is, I confess to you honestly, to strike a blow for the king. If you are on the same errand, I have two old relations in Lancashire, who are staunch to the cause; and I am going to their house to remain until I can join the army. If you wish it, you shall come with me, and I will promise you kind treatment and safety while under their roof."

"And the names of these relatives of yours, Master Chaloner?" said Edward.

"Nay, you shall have them; for when I trust, I trust wholly. Their name is Conynghame."

Edward took his letters from out of his side-pocket, and handed one of them to his fellow-traveller. The address was, "To the worthy, Mistress Conynghame, of Portlake, near Bolton, county of Lancaster."

Chaloner burst out with a loud laugh.

"This is excellent! Two people meet, both bound on the same business, both going to the same rendezvous, and for three days do not venture to trust each other."

"The times require caution," replied Edward.

"You are right," answered Chaloner, "and you are of my opinion. I know now that you have both prudence and courage. The first quality has been scarcer with us Cavaliers than the last; however, now, all reserve is over, at least on my part."

"And on mine also," replied Edward.

Chaloner then talked about the chances of the war. He stated that King Charles's army was in a good state of discipline, and well found in everything; that there were hundreds in England who would join it, and that everything promised well.

"My father fell at the battle of Naseby, at the head of his retainers," said Chaloner, after a pause; "and they have contrived to fine the property, so that it has dwindled from thousands down to hundreds. Indeed, were it not for my good old aunts, I should be but a poor gentleman."

"Your father fell at Naseby? Were you there?"

"I was," replied Chaloner.

"My father also fell at Naseby," said Edward.

"Your father did?" replied Chaloner. "I do not recollect the name—Armitage—he was not in command there, was he?" continued Chaloner.

"Yes, he was," replied Edward.

"There was none of that name among the officers that I can recollect, young sir," replied Chaloner, with an air of distrust. "Surely you have been misinformed."

"I have spoken the truth," replied Edward; "and have now said so much that I must, to remove your suspicion, say more than perhaps I should have done. My name is not Armitage, although I have been so called for some time. You have set me the example of confidence, and I will follow it. My father was Colonel Beverley, of Prince Rupert's troop."

Chaloner started with astonishment.

"I'm sure that what you say is true," at last he said; "for I was thinking who it was that you reminded me of. You are the very picture of your father. Although a boy at the time, I knew him well, Master Beverley; a more gallant Cavalier never drew sword. Come, we must be sworn friends in life and death, Beverley."

Edward was much delighted at this tribute paid to his father's memory, and the tears more than once started into his eyes as Chaloner renewed his praise.

Late in the evening they arrived at Portlake, a grand old mansion situated in a park crowded with fine old timber. Chaloner was recognized, as they rode up the avenue, by one of the keepers, who hastened forward to announce his arrival; and the domestics had opened the door for them before they arrived at it. In the hall they were met by the old ladies, who expressed their delight at seeing their nephew, as they had great fear that something had happened to him.

"And something did very nearly happen to me," replied Chaloner, "had it not been for the timely assistance of my friend here, who, notwithstanding his Puritan attire, I hardly need tell you is a Cavalier devoted to the good cause, when I say he is the son of Colonel Beverley, who fell at Naseby with my father."

"No one can be more welcome, then," replied the old ladies, who extended their hands to Edward. They then went into a sitting-room, and supper was ordered to be sent up immediately.

"And where is the army at this moment?" enquired Edward.

"They will be but a few miles from us tonight, their march is so rapid; tomorrow we will join if it pleases."

"Most willingly," replied Edward.

After an hour's more conversation, they were shown into their rooms, and retired for the night.

CHAPTER 22

THE NEXT morning, before they had quitted their beds, a messenger arrived with letters from General Middleton, and from him they found that the king's army had encamped on the evening before not six miles from Portlake. As they hastily dressed themselves, Chaloner proposed to Edward that a little alteration in his dress would be necessary; and taking him to a wardrobe in which had been put aside some suits of his own, worn when he was a younger and slighter-made man than he now was, he requested Edward to make use of them. Edward, who was aware that Chaloner was right in his proposal, selected two suits of colours which pleased him most; and dressing in one, and changing his hat for one more befitting his new attire, was transformed into a handsome Cavalier. As soon as they had broken their fast they took leave of the old ladies, and mounting their horses set off for the camp. An hour's ride brought them to the outposts; and, communicating with the officer on duty, they were conducted by an orderly to the tent of General Middleton, who received Chaloner with great warmth as an old friend, and was very courteous to Edward as soon as he heard that he was the son of Colonel Beverley.

"I have wanted you, Chaloner," said Middleton; "we are raising a troop of horse; the Duke of Buckingham commands it, but Massey will be the real leader of it; you have influence in this county, and will, I have no doubt, bring us many good hands."

"Where is the Earl of Derby?"

"Joined us this morning; we have marched so quick that we have not had time to pick our adherents up."

"And General Leslie?"

"Is by no means in good spirits: why, I know not. We have too many ministers with his army, that is certain, and they do harm; but we cannot help ourselves. His Majesty must be visible by this time; if you are ready, I will introduce you."

General Middleton then walked with them to the house in which the king had taken up his quarters for the night; and after a few minutes' waiting they were admitted into his presence.

"Allow me, your Majesty," said General Middleton, after the first salutations, "to present to you Major Chaloner, whose father's name is not unknown to you."

"On the contrary, well known to us," replied the king, "as a loyal and faithful subject, whose loss we must deplore. I have no doubt that his son inherits his courage and his fidelity."

The king held out his hand, and Chaloner bent his knee and kissed it.

"And now, your Majesty will be surprised that I should present to you one of a house supposed to be extinct—the oldest son of Colonel Beverley."

"Indeed!" replied his Majesty; "I heard that all his family perished at the ruthless burning of Arnwood. I hold myself fortunate, as a king, that even one son of so loyal and so brave a gentleman as Colonel Beverley has escaped. You are welcome, young sir—most welcome to us; you must be near us; the very name Beverley will be pleasing to our ears, by night or day."

Edward knelt and kissed his Majesty's hand, and the king said: "What can we do for a Beverley? Let us know, that we may show our feelings towards his father's memory."

"All I request is, that your Majesty will allow me to be near you in the hour of danger," replied Edward.

"A right Beverley reply," said the king, "and so we shall see to it, Middleton."

After a few more courteous words from his Majesty, they withdrew; but General Middleton was recalled by the king for a minute or two to receive his commands. When he rejoined Edward and Chaloner, he said to Edward:

"I have orders to send in for his Majesty's signature your commission as captain of horse, and attached to the king's personal staff; it is a high compliment to the memory of your father, sir, and, I may add, your own personal appearance. Chaloner will see to your uniforms and accoutrements; you are well mounted, I believe; you have no time to lose, as we march tomorrow for Warrington, in Cheshire."

"Has anything been heard of the Parliamentary army?"

"Yes; they are on the march towards London by the Yorkshire road, intending to cut us off if they can. And now, gentlemen, farewell; for I have no idle time, I assure you."

When they arrived at Warrington, they found a body of horse drawn up to oppose their passage onwards. These were charged, and fled with a trifling loss; and as they were known to be commanded by Lambert, one of Cromwell's best generals, there was great exultation in the king's army; but the fact was, that Lambert had acted upon Cromwell's orders, which were, to harass and delay the march of the king as much as possible, but not to risk with his small force anything like an engagement. After this skirmish it was considered advisable to send back the Earl of Derby and many other officers of importance into Lancashire, that they might collect the king's adherents in that quarter and in Cheshire. Accordingly, the earl, with about two hundred officers and gentlemen, left the army with that intention. It was then considered that it would be advisable to march the army direct to London; but the men were so fatigued with the rapidity of the march up to the present time, and the weather was so warm, that it was decided in the negative; and as Worcester was a town well affected to the king, and the country abounded with provisions, it was resolved that the army should march there, and wait for English reinforcements. This was done; the city opened the gates with every mark of satisfaction, and supplied the army with all that it required. The first bad news which reached them was the dispersion and defeat of the whole of the Earl of Derby's party by a regiment of militia, which had surprised them at Wigan during the night, when they were all asleep, and had no idea that any enemy was near to them. Although attacked at such a disadvantage they defended themselves till a large portion of them were killed and the remainder were taken prisoners.

"This is bad news, Chaloner," said Edward; "we have lost our best officers, who never should have left the army; and now the consequences of the defeat will be that we shall not have any people come forward to join us. The winning side is the right side in this world; and there is more evil than that; the Duke of Buckingham has claimed the command of the army, which the king has refused; so that we are beginning to fight among ourselves. General Leslie is evidently dispirited, and thinks bad of the cause. Middleton is the only man who does his duty. Depend upon it, we shall have Cromwell upon us before we are aware of it; and we are in a state of sad confusion—officers quarrelling, men disobedient, much talking, and little doing. Here we have been five days, and the works which have been proposed to be thrown up as defences not yet begun. I cannot but admire the patience of the king with so much to harass him."

Several more days passed, during which no defences were thrown up, and the confusion and quarrelling in the army continued to increase, until at last news arrived that Cromwell was within half a day's march of them, and that he had collected all the militia on his route, and was now in numbers nearly double to those in the king's army. All was amazement and confusion—nothing had been done—no arrangements had been made— and Chaloner told Edward that all was lost if immediate steps were not taken.

On the 3rd of October, the army of Cromwell appeared in sight. Edward had been on horseback, attending the king, for the best part of the night; the disposition of the troops had been made as well as it could; and it was concluded, as Cromwell's army remained quiet, that no attempt would be made on that day. About noon the king returned to his lodging, to take some refreshment after his fatigue. Edward was with him; but before on hour had passed the alarm came that the armies were engaged. The king mounted his horse, which was ready saddled at the door; but before he could ride out of the city, he was met and nearly beaten back by the whole body almost of his own cavalry, who came running on with such force that he could not stop them. His Majesty called to several of the officers by name, but they paid no attention; and so great was the panic, that both the king and his staff were nearly overthrown and trampled underfoot.

Cromwell had passed a large portion of his troops over the river without the knowledge of the opponents, and when the attack was made in so unexpected a quarter, a panic ensued. Where General Middleton and the Duke of Hamilton commanded, a very brave resistance was made; but Middleton being wounded, the Duke of Hamilton having his leg taken off by a round shot, and many gentlemen having fallen, the troops, deserted by the remainder of the army, gave way, and the rout was general, the foot throwing away their muskets before they were discharged.

His Majesty rode back into the town, and found a body of horse, who had been persuaded by Chaloner to make a stand. "Follow me," said his Majesty; "we will see what the enemy are about. I do not think they pursue, and if so, we may yet rally from this foolish panic."

His Majesty, followed by Edward, Chaloner, and several of his personal staff, then galloped out to reconnoitre; but to his mortification he found that the troops had not followed him, but gone out of the town by the other gate, and that the enemy's cavalry in pursuit were actually in the town. Under such circumstances, by the advance of Chaloner and Edward, his Majesty withdrew, and turning his horse's head, he made all haste to leave Worcester. After several hours' riding the king found himself in company of about 4,000 of the cavalry who had so disgracefully fled; but they were still so panicstruck that he could put no confidence in them, and having advised with those about him, he resolved to quit them. This he did without mentioning his intentions to any of his staff, not even Chaloner or Edward; leaving at night with two of his servants, whom he dismissed as soon as it was daylight, considering that his chance of escape would be greater if he was quite alone.

It was not till the next morning that they discovered that the king had left them and then they determined to separate, and, as the major portion were from Scotland, to make what haste they could back to that country. And now Chaloner and Edward consulted as to their plans.

"It appears to me," said Edward, laughing, "that the danger of this campaign of ours will consist in getting back again to our own homes; for I can most safely assert that I have not as yet struck a blow for the king."

"That is true enough, Beverley. When do you purpose going back to the New Forest? I think, if you will permit me, I will accompany you," said Chaloner. "All the pursuit will be to the northward to intercept and overtake the retreat into Scotland. I cannot therefore go to Lancashire; and indeed, as they know that I am out, they will be looking for me everywhere."

"Then come with me," said Edward. "I will find you protection till you can decide what to do. Let us ride on away from this, and we will talk over the matter as we go; but depend upon it, the farther south we get the safer we shall be; but still not safe, unless we can change our costume. There will be a strict search for the king to the south, as they will presume that he will try to get safe to France. Hark! what is that? I heard the report of arms. Let us ride up this hill, and see what is going on."

They did so, and perceived that there was a skirmish between a party of Cavaliers and some of the Parliamentary cavalry, at about a quarter of a mile distant.

"Come, Chaloner, let us at all events have one blow."

"Agreed," replied Chaloner spurring his horse; and down they went at full speed, and in a minute were in the *mêlée,* coming on the rear of the Parliamentary troops.

This sudden attack from behind decided the affair. The Parliamentary troopers, thinking that there were more than two coming upon them, made off after another minute's combat, leaving five or six of their men on the ground.

"Thanks, Chaloner! thanks, Beverley!" said a voice, which they immediately recognized. It was that of Grenville, one of the king's pages. "These fellows with me were just about to run, if you had not come to our aid. I will remain with them no longer, but join you if you will permit me."

"At all events, remain here till they go; I will send them off."

"My lads, you must all separate, or there will be no chance of escape. No more than two should ride together. Depend upon it, we shall have more of the troops here directly."

The men, about fifteen in number, who had been in company with Grenville, considered that Chaloner's advice was good, and without ceremony set off, with their horses' heads to the northward, leaving Chaloner, Edward and Grenville together on the field of the affray. About a dozen men were lying on the ground, either dead or severely wounded; seven of them were of the king's party, and the other five of the Parliamentary troops.

"Now what I propose," said Edward, "is this,—let us do what we can for those who are wounded, and then strip off the dresses and accoutrements of those Parliamentary dragoons who are dead, and dress ourselves in them, accoutrements and all. We can then pass through the country in safety, as we shall be supposed to be one of the parties looking for the king."

"That is a good idea," replied Chaloner, "and the sooner it is done the better."

"Well," said Edward, wiping his sword which he still held drawn, and then sheathing it, "I will take the spoils of this fellow nearest to me; he fell by my hand, and I am entitled to them by all the laws of war and chivalry."

They tied their horses to a tree, and having given what assistance they could to the wounded men, they proceeded to strip three of the Parliamentary troopers; and then laying aside their own habiliments, they dressed themselves in the uniform of the enemy, and mounting their horses, made all haste from the place. Having gained about twelve miles, they pulled up their horses, and rode at a more leisurely pace. It was now eight o'clock in the evening, but still not very dark; they therefore rode on another five miles, till they came to a small village, where they dismounted at an alehouse, and put their horses into the stable.

"We must be brutal in our manners, or we shall be suspected."

"Very true," said Grenville, giving the ostler a kick and telling him to bestir himself, if he did not want his ears cropped.

They entered the alehouse, and soon found out they were held in great terror. In the morning they set off again, by Chaloner's advice paying for nothing that they had ordered, although they had all of them plenty of money. They now rode fast, enquiring at the places which they passed through whether any fugitives had been seen, and if they came to a town, enquiring, before they entered, whether there were any Parliamentary troops. So well did they manage, that after four days they had gained the skirts of the New Forest, and concealed themselves in a thicket till night-time, when Edward proposed that he should conduct his fellow travellers to the cottage.

His great object was to ward off any suspicion of where he had been, and of course any idea that the intendant had been a party to his acts; and the fortunate change of his dress enabled him now to do so with success. He had decided to conduct his two friends to the cottage that night and the next morning to ride over in his Parliamentary costume to the intendant's house, and bring the first news of the success of Cromwell and the defeat at Worcester.

As they had travelled along, they found that the news of Cromwell's success had not yet arrived; and Edward thought it very probable that he would be the first to communicate the intelligence to the intendant and those who resided near him.

As soon as it was dusk the three travellers left their retreat, and, guided by Edward, soon arrived at the cottage. Their appearance at first created no little consternation, for Humphrey and Pablo happened to be in the yard when they heard the clattering of the swords and accoutrements, and through the gloom observed, as they advanced, that the party were troopers. At first Humphrey was for running in and barring the door, but on a second reflection, he felt that he could not do a more imprudent thing, if there was danger; and he therefore contented himself with hastily imparting the intelligence to his sisters, and then remaining at the threshold to meet the coming of the parties. The voice of Edward calling his name dissipated all alarm, and the next minute he was in the arms of his brother and sisters.

"First let us take our horses to the stable, Humphrey," said Edward, after the first greeting was over, "and then we will come and partake of anything that Alice can prepare for us, for we have not fared over well for the last three days."

Accompanied by Humphrey and Pablo, they all went to the stables, and turned out the ponies to make room for the horses; and as soon as they were all fed and littered down, they returned to the cottage, and Chaloner and Grenville were introduced. Supper was soon on the table, and they were too hungry to talk while they were eating, so that but little information was gleaned from them that night. However, Humphrey ascertained that all was lost, and that they had escaped from the field, previous to Alice and Edith leaving the room to prepare beds for the newcomers. When the beds were ready, Chaloner and Grenville retired and

114

then Edward remained half an hour with Humphrey, to communicate to him what had passed.

"And now, Humphrey, my advice is this. My two friends cannot remain in this cottage, for many reasons; but we have the key of Clara's cottage, and they can take up their lodging there and we can supply them with all they want, until they find means of going abroad, which is their intention. I must be off to the intendant tomorrow, and the day after I will come over to you. In the meantime our guests can remain here, while you and Pablo prepare the cottage for them; and when I return everything shall be settled, and we will conduct them to it. I do not think there is much danger of their being discovered while they remain there, certainly not so much as if they were here; for we must expect parties of troops in every direction now, as they were when the king's father made his escape from Hampton Court."

The next morning, long before their guests were awake, Edward had been called by Humphrey, and found Pablo at the door with his horse. Edward, who had put on his Parliamentary accoutrements, bade a hasty farewell to them, and set off across the forest to the house of the intendant, where he arrived before they had left their bedrooms. The first person he encountered was, very fortunately, Oswald, who was at his cottage door. Edward beckoned to him, being then about one hundred yards off; but Oswald did not recognize him at first, and advanced towards him in a very leisurely manner, to ascertain what the trooper might wish to enquire. But Edward called him Oswald, and that was sufficient. In a few words Edward told him how all was lost, and how he had escaped by changing clothes with one of the enemy.

Edward put spurs to his horse, and arrived at the intendant's at full speed, making no small clatter in the yard below as he went in, much to the surprise of Sampson, who came out to ascertain what was the cause, and who was not a little surprised at perceiving Edward, who threw himself off the horse, and desiring Sampson to take it to the stable, entered the kitchen, and disturbed Phœbe, who was preparing breakfast. Without speaking to her, Edward passed on to the intendant's room, and knocked.

"Who is there?" said the intendant.

"Edward Armitage," was the reply, and the door was opened. The intendant started back at the sight of Edward in the trooper's costume.

"My dear Edward, I am glad to see you in any dress; but this requires explanation. Sit down and tell me all."

"All is soon told, sir," replied Edward, taking off his iron skull-cap, and allowing his hair to fall down on his shoulders.

He then, in a few words, stated what had happened, and by what means he had escaped, and the reason why he had kept on the trooper's accoutrements, and made his appearance in them.

"You have done very prudently," replied the intendant, "and you have probably saved me; at all events you have warded off all suspicion, and those who are spies upon me will now have nothing to report expect to

115

my favour. Your absence has been commented upon, and made known at high quarters, and suspicion has arisen in consequence. Your return as one of the Parliamentary forces will now put an end to all illnatured remarks. My dear Edward, you have done me a service. As my secretary and having been known to have been a follower of the Beverleys, your absence was considered strange, and it was intimated at high quarters that you had gone to join the king's forces, and that with my knowledge and consent. This I have from Langton; and it has in consequence injured me not a little; but now your appearance will make all right again. Now we will first to prayers and then to breakfast. Patience and Clara will not be sorry to recover their companion; but how they will like you in that dress I cannot pretend to say."

"I will, with your permission, sir, not quit this costume for one day, as it may be as well that I should be seen in it."

"You are right, Edward; for this day retain it. Go down to the parlour; you will find Patience and Clara anxiously waiting for you, I have no doubt. I will join you there in ten minutes."

Edward left the room, and went downstairs. It hardly need be said how joyfully he was received by Patience and Clara. The former expressed her joy in tears, the latter in wild mirth.

CHAPTER 23

It was only to Oswald that Edward made known what had occurred; he knew that he was to be trusted. The next day Edward resumed his forester's dress, while another one was preparing for him, and went over to the cottage, where, with the consent of the intendant, he proposed remaining for a few days. Of course Edward had not failed to acquaint the intendant with his proposed plans relative to Chaloner and Grenville, and received his consent; at the same time advising that they should gain the other side of the Channel as soon as they possibly could. Edward found them all very anxious for his arrival. Humphrey and Pablo had been to the cottage, which they had found undisturbed since the capture of the robbers, and made everything ready for the reception of the two Cavaliers; as, on their first journey, they took with them a cartload of what they knew would be necessary. Chaloner and Grenville appeared to be quite at home already, and not very willing to shift their quarters. They, of course, still retained their troopers' clothes, as they had no other to wear until they could be procured from Lymington. As soon as he could get away, Edward went out with Humphrey to have some conversation with him.

"What very agreeable, pleasant young men are Master Chaloner and Grenville," observed Humphrey.

"Chaloner I know well," replied Edward; "he is to be trusted, and he is the only one in whom I have been able to place confidence, and therefore I was most fortunate in falling in with him as I did on my first starting. Grenville I know little about; we met often, it is true, but it was in the presence of the king, being both of us on his staff; at the same time, I must acknowledge that I know nothing against him; and this I do know, which is, that he is brave."

Edward then narrated how well satisfied the intendant had been with his *ruse* in returning to him in the dress of a trooper.

"Talking about that, Edward, do you not think it likely that we shall have the troopers down here in search of the king?"

"I wonder you have not had them already," replied Edward.

"And what shall we do if they arrive?"

"That is all prepared for," replied Edward; "although, till you mentioned it, I had quite forgotten it. The intendant was talking with me on the subject last night, and here is an appointment for you as verderer, signed by him, which you are to use as you may find necessary; and here is another missive, ordering you to receive into your house two of the troopers who may be sent down here, and find quarters and victuals, but not to be compelled to receive more. Until the search is over, Chaloner and Grenville must retain their accoutrements and remain with us. And, Humphrey, if you have not made any use of the clothes which I left here, I will put them on now, as, should any military come here as scouters to the intendant, I shall have some authority over them."

"They are in your chest, where you left them, Edward. By the by, you have not told me what you think of Alice and Edith, after your long absence."

"I think they are both very much grown and very much improved," replied Edward; "but I must confess to you that I think it is high time that they were removed from their present homely occupations, and instructed as young ladies should be."

"I have not enquired about Patience, brother; how is she?"

"She is as good and as handsome as ever, and very much grown; indeed, she is becoming quite womanly."

"And Clara?"

"Oh, I do not perceive any difference in her; I think she is grown, but I hardly observed her. Here comes Chaloner; we will tell him of our arrangements in case we are disturbed by the military parties."

"It is a most excellent arrangement," said Chaloner, when Edward had made the communication; "and it was a lucky day when I first fell in with you, Beverley."

"Not Beverley, I pray you; that name is to be forgotten; it was only revived for the occasion."

"Very true; then, Master Secretary Armitage, I think the arrangement excellent; the only point will be to find out what troops are sent in this direction, as we must of course belong to some other regiment, and have been pursued from the field of battle. I should think Lambert's squadrons will not be this way."

"We will soon ascertain that; let your horses be saddled and accoutred, so that should any of them make their appearance, the horses may be at the door. It is my opinion that they will be here some time today."

"I fear that it will be almost impossible for the king to escape," observed Chaloner. "I hardly know what to think of his leaving us in that way."

"I have reflected upon it," replied Edward, "and I think it was perhaps prudent; some were to be trusted, and some not; he therefore trusted nobody. Besides, his chance of escape, if quite alone, is greater than if in company. And yet I feel a little mortified that he did not trust me; my life was at his service."

"He could no more read your heart than he could mine or others," observed Chaloner; "and any selection would have been invidious: on the whole, I think he acted wisely, and I trust that it will prove so. One thing is certain, which is, that all is over now, and that for a long while: we may let our swords rest in their scabbards. Indeed, I am sickened with it, after what I have seen, and would gladly live here with you, and help to till the land—away from the world and all its vexations. What say you, Edward; will you and your brother take me as a labourer after all is quiet again?"

"You would soon tire of it, Chaloner; you were made for active exertion and bustling in the world."

"Nevertheless, I think, under two such amiable and pretty mistresses, I could stay well contented here: it is almost Arcadian. But still it is selfish for me to talk in this way; indeed, my feelings are contrary to my words."

"How do you mean, Chaloner?"

"To be candid with you, Edward, I was thinking what a pity it is that two such sweet girls as your sisters should be employed here in domestic drudgery, and remain in such an uncultivated state—if I may be pardoned for speaking so freely; but I do so because I am convinced that if in proper hands, they would grace a court; and you must feel that I am right."

"Do you not think that the same feelings have passed in my mind, Chaloner? Indeed, Humphrey will tell you that we were speaking on the same subject but an hour ago. You must, however, be aware of the difficulty I am in: were I in possession of Arnwood and its domain, then indeed—but that is all over now, and I presume I shall shortly see my own property, whose woods are now in sight of me, made over to some Roundhead, for good services against the Cavaliers at Worcester."

"Edward," replied Chaloner, "I have this to say to you, and I can say it because you know that I am indebted to you for my life, and that is a debt that nothing can cancel: if at any time you determine upon removing your sisters from this, recollect my maiden aunts at Portlake. They cannot be in better hands, and they cannot be in the hands of any persons who will more religiously do their duty towards them. They are rich, in spite of exactions; but in these times women are not fined and plundered as men are, and they have been well able to afford all that has been taken from them, and all that they have voluntarily given to the assistance of our party. They are alone, and I really believe that nothing would make them more happy than to have the care of the two sisters of Edward Beverley—be sure of that. But I will be more sure of it, if you will find means of sending to them a letter, which I shall write to them. I tell you that you will do them a favour, and that if you do not accept the offer you will sacrifice your sisters' welfare to your own pride,—which I do not think you would do."

"Most certainly I will not do that," replied Edward; "and I am fully sensible of your kind offer; but I can say no more until I hear what your good aunts may reply to your letter. You mistake me much, Chaloner, if you think that any sense of obligation would prevent me from seeing my sisters removed from a position so unworthy of them, but which circumstances have driven them to. That we are paupers in undeniable; but I cannot forget that my sisters are the daughters of Colonel Beverley."

"I am delighted with your reply, Edward, and I fear not that of my good aunts. It will be a great happiness to me when I am wandering abroad to know that your sisters are under their roof, and are being educated as they ought to be."

"What's the matter, Pablo?" said Humphrey to the former, who came running, out of breath.

"Soldiers," said Pablo; "plenty of them, gallop this way."

"Now, Chaloner, we must get ourselves out of this scrape; and I trust that afterwards all will be well," said Edward. "Bring the horses out to the door; and, Chaloner, you and Grenville must wait within; bring my horse out also, as it will appear as if I had just ridden over. I must in to change my dress. Humphrey, keep a lookout and let us know when they come."

Chaloner and Edward went in, and Edward put on his dress of secretary. Shortly afterwards, a party of cavalry were seen galloping towards the cottage. They soon arrived there, and pulled up their horses. An officer who headed them addressed Humphrey in a haughty tone, and asked him who he was.

"I am one of the verderers of the forest, sir," replied Humphrey.

"And whose cottage is that? and who have you there?"

"The cottage is mine, sir; two of the horses at the door belong to two troopers who have come in quest of those who fled from Worcester: the other horse belongs to the secretary of the intendant of the forest, Master Heatherstone, who has come over with directions from the intendant as to the capture of the rebels."

At this moment Edward came out and saluted the officer.

"This is the secretary, sir, Master Armitage," said Humphrey.

"What regiment do the troopers belong to that you have here?"

"I believe to Lambert's troop; but they shall answer for themselves. Tell those men to come out," said Edward to Humphrey.

"Yes, sir; but they are hard to wake, for they have ridden from Worcester; but I will rouse them."

"Nay, I cannot wait," replied the officer. "I know none of Lambert's troops, and they have no information to give. Forward! men," continued the officer, saluting Edward as he passed on; and in a minute or two they were far in the distance.

"That's well over," observed Edward. "Chaloner and Grenville are too young-looking, and too good-looking for Lambert's villains; and a sight of them might have occasioned suspicion. We must, however, expect more visits. Keep a good lookout, Pablo."

For three or four days the Parliamentary forces continued to scour the forest, and another visit or two was paid to the cottage, but without suspicion being created, in consequence of the presence of Edward and his explanation. The parties were invariably sent in another direction. Edward wrote to the intendant, informing him what had occurred, and requesting permission to remain a few days longer at the cottage; and Pablo, who took the letter, returned with one from the intendant acquainting him that the king had not yet been taken; and requesting the utmost vigilance on his part to ensure his capture, with directions to search various places, in company with the troopers who had been stationed at the cottage; or if he did not like to leave the cottage, to show the letter to any officer commanding parties in search, that they might act upon the suggestions contained in it. This letter Edward had an opportunity of showing to one or two officers commanding parties, who approached the cottage, and to whom Edward went out to communicate with, thereby preventing their stopping there.

At last, in about a fortnight, there was not a party in the forest, all of them having gone down to the seaside, to look out for the fugitives, several of whom were taken.

Humphrey took the cart to Lymington, to procure clothes for Chaloner and Grenville, and it was decided that they should assume those of verderers of the forest, which would enable them to carry a gun. As soon as Humphrey had obtained what was requisite, Chaloner and Grenville were conducted to Clara's cottage, and took possession. Humphrey lent them Holdfast as a watch, and they took leave of Alice and Edith with much regret.

CHAPTER 24

For several days Edward remained at home, anxiously awaiting every news which arrived; expecting every time that the capture of the king would be announced, and, with great joy, finding that hitherto all efforts had been unsuccessful. But there was a question which now arose in Edward's mind and which was the cause of deep reflection. Since the proposal of sending his sisters away had been started, he left the great inconvenience of his still representing himself to the intendant as the grandson of Armitage. His sisters, if sent to the ladies at Portlake, must be sent

120

without the knowledge of the intendant; and if so, the discovery of their absence would soon take place, as Patience Heatherstone would be constantly going over to the cottage; and he now asked himself the question, whether after all the kindness and confidence which the intendant had shown him, he was right in any longer concealing from him his birth and parentage.

That he was justified in so doing at first, he felt; but since joining the king's army, and the events which had followed, he considered that he was treating the intendant ill, and he now resolved to take the first opportunity of making the confession. But to do it formally, and without some opportunity which might offer, he felt awkward. At last he thought that he would at once make the confession to Patience under the promise of secrecy. That he might do at once; and, after he had done so, the intendant could not tax him with want of confidence altogether. He had now analysed his feelings towards Patience; and he felt how dear she had become to him. During the time he was with the army she had seldom been out of his thoughts; and although he was often in the society of well-bred women, he saw not one that, in his opinion, could compare with Patience Heatherstone; but still what chance had he of supporting a wife? At present, at the age of nineteen, it was preposterous. Thoughts like these ran in his mind, chasing each other, and followed by others as vague and unsatisfactory; and, in the end, Edward came to the conclusion that he was without a penny, and that being known as the heir of Beverley would be to his disadvantage; that he was in love with Patience Heatherstone, and had no chance at present of obtaining her; and that he had done well up to the present time in concealing who he was from the intendant, who could safely attest that he knew not that he was protecting the son of so noted a Cavalier; and that he would confess to Patience who he was, and give as a reason for not telling her father that he did not wish to commit him by letting him know who it was that was under his protection.

Edward was already satisfied that he was not quite looked upon with indifference by Patience Heatherstone; and he was not yet certain whether it was not a grateful feeling that she had towards him more than any other; that she believed him to be beneath her in birth, he felt convinced, and therefore she could have no idea that he was Edward Beverley. It was not till several days after he had made up his mind that he had an opportunity of being with her alone, as Clara Ratcliffe was their constant companion. However, one evening Clara went out, and stayed out so long, carelessly wrapped up, that she caught cold; and the following evening she remained at home, leaving Edward and Patience to take their usual walk unaccompanied by her. They had walked for some minutes in silence, when Patience observed:

"You are very grave, Edward, and have been very grave ever since your return; have you anything to vex you beyond the failure of the attempt?"

"Yes, I have, Patience. I have much on my conscience, and do not know how to act. I want an adviser and a friend, and know not where to find one."

"Surely my father is your sincere friend, and not a bad adviser."

"I grant it; but the question is between your father and me, and I cannot advise with him for that reason."

"Then advise with me, Edward, if it is not a secret of such moment that it is not to be trusted to a woman: it will be the advice of a sincere friend; you will give me credit for that."

"Yes, and for much more; for I think I shall have good advice, and will therefore accept your offer. I feel, Patience, that although I was justified, on my first acquaintance with your father, in not making known to him a secret of some importance, yet now that he has put such implicit confidence in me, I am doing him and myself an injustice in not making the communication—that is, as far as confidence in him is concerned; I consider that he has a right to know all, and yet feel that it would be prudent on my part that he should not know all, as the knowledge might implicate him with those with whom he is at present allied. A secret sometimes is dangerous; and if your father could not say that on his honour he knew not of the secret, it might harm him if the secret became afterwards known. Do you understand me?"

"I cannot say that I do; you have a secret that you wish to make known to my father, and you think the knowledge of it may harm him. I cannot imagine what kind of a secret that may be."

"Well, I can give you a case in point. Suppose now that I knew that King Charles was hidden in your stable-loft: such might be the case, and your father be ignorant of it, and his assertion of his ignorance would be believed; but if I were to tell your father that the king was there, and it was afterwards discovered, do you not see that by confiding such a secret to him, I should do harm, and perhaps bring him into trouble?"

"I perceive now, Edward. Do you mean to say that you know where the king is concealed? For if you do, I must beg of you not to let my father know anything about it. As you say, it would put him in a difficult position, and must eventually harm him much. My father wishes the king well, I believe, but at the same time, he will not take an active part, as you have already seen; at the same time, I am convinced that he would never betray the king if he knew where he was. I say, therefore, if that is your secret, keep it from him, for his sake and for mine, Edward, if you regard me."

"You know not how much I regard you, Patience. I saw many high-born women when I was away, but none could I see equal to Patience Heatherstone in my opinion; and Patience was ever in my thoughts during my long absence."

"I thank you for your kind feelings towards me," replied Patience; "but, Master Armitage, we talked of your secret."

"Master Armitage!" rejoined Edward; "how well you know how to remind me, by that expression, of my obscure birth, whenever I am apt to forget the distance which I ought to observe!"

"You are wrong," replied Patience; "but you flattered me so grossly, that I called you Master Armitage to show that I disliked flattery; that was all. I dislike flattery from those who are above me in rank, as well as those who are below me; and I should have done the same to any other person, whatever his condition might be. But forget what I said, I did not mean to vex you, only to punish your for thinking me so silly as to believe such nonsense."

"Your humility may construe that into flattery which was said by me in perfect sincerity and truth—that I cannot help," replied Edward. "I might have added much more, and yet have been sincere; if you had not reminded me of my not being of gentle birth I might have had the presumption to have told you much more; but I have been rebuked."

Edward finished speaking, and Patience made no reply; they walked on for several moments without exchanging another syllable. At last Patience said:

"I will not say who is wrong, Edward, but this I do know, that the one who first offers the olive branch after a misunderstanding cannot but be right. I offer it now, and ask you whether we are to quarrel about one little word. Let me ask you, and give me a candid answer. Have I ever been so base as to treat as an inferior one to whom I have been so much obliged?"

"It is I who am in fault, Patience," replied Edward. "I have been dreaming for a long while, pleased with my dreams; and forgetting that they were dreams and not likely to be realized. I must now speak plainly. I love you, Patience; love you so much that to part from you would be misery—to know that my love was rejected, as bitter as death. That is the truth, and I can conceal it no longer. Now I admit you have a right to be angry."

"I see no cause for anger, Edward," replied Patience. "I have not thought of you but as a friend and benefactor; it would have been wrong to have done otherwise; I am but a young person, and must be guided by my father. I would not offend him by disobedience. I thank you for your good opinion of me, and yet I wish you had not said what you have."

"Am I to understand from your reply, that if your father raised no objection, my lowly birth would be none in your opinion?"

"Your birth has never come into my head, except when reminded of it by yourself."

"Then, Patience, let me return for the present to what I had to confide to you. I was——"

"Here comes my father, Edward," said Patience. "Surely I have done wrong, for I feel afraid to meet him."

Mr. Heatherstone now joined them, and said to Edward:

"I have been looking for you; I have news from London which has rejoiced me much. I have at last obtained what I have some time been trying for; and, indeed, I may say, that your prudence in returning home as a trooper, added to your conduct in the forest, has greatly advanced, and ultimately obtained for me my suit."

They walked to the house, and the intendant as soon as he had gained his own room, said to Edward:

"There is a grant to me of a property which I have long solicited for my services—read it."

Edward took up the letter, in which the Parliament informed Mr. Heatherstone that his application for the property of Arnwood had been acceded to, and signed by the Commissioners; and that he might take immediate possession. Edward turned pale as he laid the document down on the table.

"We will ride tomorrow, Edward, and look it over. I intend to rebuild the house."

Edward made no reply.

"Are you not well?" said the intendant with surprise.

"Yes, sir," replied Edward. "I am well, I believe; but I will confess to you that I am disappointed. I did not think that you would have accepted a property from such a source, and so unjustly sequestrated."

"I am sorry, Edward," replied the intendant, "that I should have fallen in your good opinion; but allow me to observe that you are so far right, that I never would have accepted a property to which there were living claimants; but this is a different case. For instance, the Ratcliffe property belongs to little Clara and is sequestrated. Do you think I would accept it? Never! But here is a property without an heir. There is no living claimant! It must be given to somebody, or remain with the government. This property, therefor, and this property only, out of all sequestrated, I selected; as I felt that, in obtaining it, I did harm to no one. I have been offered others, but have refused them. I would accept of this, and this only; and that is the reason why my applications have hitherto been attended with no success. I trust you believe me, Edward, in what I assert?"

"First answer me one question, Mr. Heatherstone. Suppose it were proved that the whole of the family did not, as it is supposed, perish at the conflagration of Arnwood? Suppose a rightful heir to it should at any time appear, would you then resign the property to him?"

"As I hope for heaven, Edward, I would!" replied the intendant, solemnly raising his eyes upwards as he spoke. "I then should think that I had been an instrument to keep the property out of other hands less scrupulous, and should surrender it as a trust which had been confided to me for the time only."

"With such feelings, Mr. Heatherstone, I can now congratulate you upon your having acquired the property," replied Edward.

"And yet I do not deserve so much credit, as there is little chance of my sincerity being put to the test, Edward. There is no doubt that the family all perished; and Arnwood will become the dower of Patience Heatherstone."

Edward's heart beat quick. A moment's thought told him his situation.

He had been prevented by the interruption of Mr. Heatherstone, from making his confession to Patience; and now he could not make it to anybody without a rupture with the intendant, or a compromise by asking what he so earnestly desired—the hand of Patience. Mr. Heatherstone, observing to Edward that he did not look so well, said supper was ready, and that they had better go into the next room. Edward mechanically followed. At supper he was tormented by the incessant enquiries of Clara as to what was the matter with him. He did not venture to look at Patience and made a hasty retreat to bed; complaining, as he well might do, of a severe headache.

Edward threw himself on his bed, but to sleep was impossible. He thought of the events of the day, over and over again. Had he any reason to believe that Patience returned his affection? No: her reply was too calm, too composed, to make him suppose that; and now that she would be an heiress there would be no want of pretenders to her hand, and he would lose her and his property at the same time. It was true that the intendant had declared that he would renounce the property if the true heir appeared, but that was easy to say upon the conviction that no heir would appear; and even if he did renounce it, the Parliament would receive it again, rather than it should fall into the hands of a Beverley. "Oh, that I had never left the cottage!" thought Edward. "I might then at least have become resigned and contented with my lot. Now I am miserable, and, whichever way I turn, I see no prospect of being otherwise. One thing only I can decide upon, which is, that I will not remain any longer than I can help under this roof. I will go over and consult with Humphrey; and if I can only place my sisters as I want, Humphrey and I will seek our fortunes."

Edward rose at daylight, and, dressing himself, went down and saddled his horse. Desiring Sampson to tell the intendant that he had gone over to the cottage, and would return by the evening, he rode across the forest, and arrived just as they were sitting down to breakfast. His attempts to be cheerful before his sisters did not succeed, and they were all grieved to see him look so pale and haggard. As soon as breakfast was over, Edward made a sign, and he and Humphrey went out.

"What is the matter, my dear brother?" said Humphrey.

"I will tell you all. Listen to me," replied Edward, who then gave him the detail of all that had passed, from the time he had walked out with Patience Heatherstone till he went to bed. "Now you know all; and what shall I do? Remain there I cannot!"

"If Patience Heatherstone had professed regard for you," replied Humphrey, "the affair would have been simple enough. Her father could have no objections to the match; and he would at the same time have acquitted his conscience as to the retaining of the property; but you say she showed none."

"Where there is such a sense of propriety, there can be little affection."

"I know nothing about these things, Edward," replied Humphrey; "but

I have been told that a woman's heart is not easily read. What do you propose to do?"

"What I fear you will not approve of, Humphrey; it is to break up our establishment altogether. If the answer is favourable from the Ladies Conynghame, my sisters shall go to them; but that we had agreed upon already. Then for myself—I intend to go abroad, and obtain employment in some foreign service."

"That is the worst part of it, Edward; but if your peace of mind depends upon it, I will not oppose it."

"You, Humphrey, may come with me and share my fortunes, or do what you think more preferable."

"I think then, Edward, that I shall not decide rashly. I must have remained here with Pablo, if my sisters had gone to the Ladies Conynghame and you had remained with the intendant: I shall, therefore, till I hear from you, remain where I am, and I shall be able to observe what is going on here, and let you know."

"Be it so," replied Edward; "let me only see my sisters well placed, and I shall be off. It is misery to remain there now."

After some more conversation, Edward mounted his horse and returned to the intendant's. He did not arrive till late, for supper was on the table. The intendant gave him a letter for Mr. Chaloner, which was enclosed in one from Mr. Langton; and further informed Edward that news had arrived of the king having made his escape to France.

"Thank God for that!" exclaimed Edward. "With your leave, sir, I will tomorrow deliver this letter to Mr. Chaloner, as I know it to be of consequence."

The following morning Edward, who had not slept an hour during the night, set off for Clara's cottage, and found Chaloner and Grenville still in bed. At the sound of his voice the door was opened, and he gave Chaloner the letter; the latter read it and then handed it to Edward. The Ladies Conynghame were delighted at the idea of receiving the two daughters of Colonel Beverley, and would treat them as their own; they requested that they might be sent to London immediately, where the coach would meet them to convey them down to Lancashire.

"I am much indebted to you, Chaloner," said Edward. "I will send my brother off with my sisters as soon as possible. You will soon think of returning to France; and, if you will permit me, I will accompany you."

"You, Edward? That will be delightful; but you had no idea of the kind when last we met. What has induced you to alter your mind?"

"I will tell you by and by; I do not think I shall be here again for some days. I must be a great deal at the cottage when Humphrey is away; for Pablo will have a great charge upon him—more indeed than he can attend to; but as soon as Humphrey returns I will come to you and make preparations for our departure. Till then, farewell, both of you."

Although Alice and Edith had been somewhat prepared for leaving the cottage, yet the time was so very uncertain that the blow fell heavy upon them. They were to leave their brothers, whom they loved so dearly, to go to strangers; and when they understood that they were to leave in two days, and that they should not see Edward again, their grief was very great; but Edward reasoned with Alice and consoled her, although with Edith it was a more difficult task. She not only lamented her brothers, but her cow, her pony, and her kids—all the dumb animals were friends and favourites of Edith; and even the idea of parting with Pablo was the cause of a fresh burst of tears. Having made every arrangement with Humphrey, Edward once more took his leave, promising to come over and assist Pablo as soon as he could.

The next day Humphrey was busied in his preparations. They supplied provisions to Clara's cottage; and when Pablo took them over in the cart, Humphrey rode to Lymington and provided a conveyance to London for the following day. We may as well observe that they set off at the hour appointed, and arrived safely at London in three days. There, at an address given in the letter, they found the coach waiting; and having given his sisters into the charge of an elderly waiting woman, who had come up in the coach to take charge of them, they quitted him with many tears, and Humphrey hastened back to the New Forest.

On his return, he found to his surprise that Edward had not called at the cottage as he had promised; and, with a mind foreboding evil, he mounted a horse and set off across the forest to ascertain the cause. As he was close to the intendant's house he was met by Oswald, who informed him that Edward had been seized with a violent fever, and was in a very dangerous state, having been delirious for three or four days.

Humphrey hastened to dismount, and knocked at the door of the house; it was opened by Sampson, and Humphrey requested to be shown up to his brother's room. He found Edward in the state described by Oswald, and wholly unconscious of his presence; the maid, Phœbe, was by his bedside.

"You may leave," said Humphrey abruptly; "I am his brother."

Phœbe retired, and Humphrey was alone with his brother.

"It was, indeed, an unhappy day when you came to this house," exclaimed Humphrey, as the tears rolled down his cheeks: "my poor, poor Edward!"

Edward now began to talk incoherently, and attempted to rise from the bed, but his efforts were unavailing—he was too weak; but he raved of Patience Heatherstone, called himself Edward Beverley more than once, and talked of his father and of Arnwood.

"If he has raved in this manner," thought Humphrey, "he has not many secrets left to disclose. I will not leave him, and will keep others away if I can."

Humphrey had been sitting an hour with his brother when the surgeon came to see his patient. He felt his pulse, and asked Humphrey if he was nursing him.

"I am his brother, sir," replied Humphrey.

"Then, my good sir, if you perceive any signs of perspiration—and I think now that there is a little—keep the clothes on him and let him perspire freely. If so, his life will be saved."

The surgeon withdrew, saying that he would return again late in the evening.

Humphrey remained for another two hours at the bedside, and then feeling that there was a sign of perspiration, he obeyed the injunctions of the surgeon, and held on the clothes, against all Edward's endeavours to throw them off. For a short time the perspiration was profuse and Edward subsided into a deep slumber.

"Thank Heaven! there are then hopes."

"Did you say there were hopes?" repeated a voice behind him.

Humphrey turned, and perceived Patience and Clara behind him, who had come in without his observing it.

"Yes," replied Humphrey, looking reproachfully at Patience, "there are hopes, by what the surgeon says, that he may yet be able to quit this house, which he was so unfortunate as to enter."

This was a harsh and rude speech of Humphrey's; but he considered that Patience Heatherstone had been the cause of his brother's dangerous state, and that she had not behaved well.

Patience made no reply, but falling down on her knees by the bedside prayed silently; and Humphrey's heart smote him for what he had said to her. "She cannot be so bad," thought Humphrey, as Patience and Clara quitted the room without the least noise.

Shortly afterwards the intendant came up into the room, and offered his hand to Humphrey, who pretended not to see it, and did not take it.

"He has got Arnwood; that is enough for him," thought Humphrey; "but my hand in friendship he shall not receive."

The intendant put his hand within the clothes, and feeling the high perspiration which Edward was in, said:

"I thank thee, O God, for all thy mercies, and that thou hast been pleased to spare this valuable life! How are your sisters, Master Humphrey? my daughter bade me enquire. I will send over to them and let them know that your brother is better, if you do not leave this for the cottage yourself after the surgeon has called again."

"My sisters are no longer at the cottage, Master Heatherstone," replied Humphrey; "they have gone to some friends who have taken charge of them. I saw them safe to London myself, or I should have known of my brother's illness and have been here before this."

"You indeed tell me news, Master Humphrey," replied the intendant. "With whom, may I ask, are your sisters placed, and in what capacity are they gone?"

This reply of the intendant's reminded Humphrey that he had somewhat committed himself, as being supposed to be the daughters of a forester, it was not to be thought that they had gone up to be educated; and he therefore replied:

"They found it lonely in the forest, Master Heatherstone, and wished to see London; so we have taken them there, and put them into the care of those who have promised that they shall be well placed."

The intendant appeared to be much disturbed and surprised; but he said nothing, and soon afterwards quitted the room. He almost immediately returned with the surgeon, who, as soon as he felt Edward's pulse, declared that the crisis was over, and that when he awoke he would be quite sensible. Having given directions as to the drink of his patient, and some medicine which he was to take, the surgeon then left, stating that he should not call until the next evening, unless sent for, as he considered all danger over.

Edward continued in a quiet slumber for the major portion of the night. It was just break of day when he opened his eyes. Humphrey offered him some drink, which Edward took greedily; and seeing Humphrey said:

"Oh, Humphrey, I had quite forgotten where I was—I'm so sleepy!" and with these words his head fell on the pillow, and he was again asleep.

When it was daylight Oswald came into the room:

"Master Humphrey, they say that all danger is over now, but that you have remained here all night. I will relieve you now, if you will let me. Go and walk in the fresh air, it will revive you."

"I will, Oswald, and many thanks. My brother has woke up once, and, I thank God, is quite sensible. He will know you when he wakes again, and then do you send for me."

Humphrey left the room, and was glad after a night of close confinement in a sickroom to feel the cool morning air fanning his cheeks. He had not been long out of the house before he perceived Clara coming towards him.

"How d'ye do, Humphrey?" said Clara; "and how is brother this morning?"

"He is better, Clara, and I hope now out of danger."

"But, Humphrey," continued Clara, "when we came into the room last night, what made you say what you did?"

"I do not recollect that I said anything."

"Yes, you did; you said that there were now hopes that your brother would be able soon to quit this house, which he had been so unfortunate as to enter. Do you recollect?"

"I may have said so, Clara," replied Humphrey; "it was only speaking my thoughts aloud."

"But why do you think so, Humphrey? Why has Edward been unfortunate in entering this house? Patience cried so much after she left the room because you said that. Why did you say so? You did not think so a short time ago."

"No, my dear Clara, I did not, but I do now, and I cannot give you my reasons; so you must say no more about it."

Clara was silent for a time, and then said:

"Patience tells me that your sisters have gone away from the cottage. You told her father so."

"It is very true; they have gone."

"But why have they gone? What have they gone for? Who is to look after the cows and goats and poultry? Who is to cook your dinner, Humphrey? What can you do without them, and why did you send them away without letting us know that they were going, so that at least we might have bidden them farewell?"

"My dear Clara," replied Humphrey—who, feeling no little difficulty in replying to all these questions, resolved to cut the matter short by appearing to be angry—"you know that you are the daughter of a gentleman, and so is Patience Heatherstone. You are both of gentle birth; but my sisters, you know, are only the daughters of a forester, and my brother Edward and I are no better. It does not become Mistress Patience and you to be intimate with such as we are, especially now that Mistress Patience is a great heiress; for her father has obtained the large property of Arnwood, and it will be hers after his death. It is not fit that the heiress of Arnwood should mix herself up with forester's daughters; and as we had friends who offered to assist us, and take our sisters under their charge, we thought it better that they should go; for what would become of them, if any accident was to happen to Edward or to me? Now they will be provided for. After they have been taught, they will make very nice maids to some lady of quality," added Humphrey. "Don't you think they will, my pretty Clara?"

Clara burst into tears.

"You are very unkind, Humphrey," sobbed she. "You had no right to send away your sisters. I don't believe you—what's more!" and Clara ran away into the house.

CHAPTER 25

OUR READERS may think that Humphrey was very unkind; but it was to avoid being questioned by Clara, who was evidently sent for the purpose, that he was so harsh. At the same time, it must be admitted that Mr. Heatherstone having obtained possession of Arnwood rankled no doubt in the minds of both the brothers, and every act now, on the part of him or his family, was viewed in a false medium. But our feelings are not always at our control, and Edward was naturally impetuous, and Humphrey so much attached, and so much alarmed at his brother's danger, that he was even more excited. The blow fell doubly heavy, as it appeared that at the very same time Patience had rejected his brother, and taken possession of their property, which had been held by the family for centuries. What made the case more annoying was, that explanation, if there was any to offer on either side, was, under present circumstances, almost impossible.

Soon after Clara left him Humphrey returned to his brother's room. He found him awake, and talking to Oswald. Ardently pressing his brother's hand, Edward said:

"My dear Humphrey, I shall soon be well now, and able, I trust, to quit this house. What I fear is, that some explanation will be asked for by the intendant, not only relative to my sisters having left us, but also upon other points. This is what I wish to avoid, without giving offence. I do not think that the intendant is so much to blame in having obtained my property, as he does not know that a Beverley existed; but I cannot bear to have any further intimacy with him, especially after what has taken place between me and his daughter. What I have to request is, that you will never quit this room while I am still here unless you are relieved by Oswald; so that the intendant or anybody else may have no opportunity of having any private communication with me or forcing me to listen to what they may have to say. I made this known to Oswald before you came in."

"Depend upon it, it shall be so, Edward; for I am of your opinion. Clara came to me just now, and I had much trouble and was compelled to be harsh, to get rid of her importunity."

When the surgeon called he pronounced Edward out of danger, and that his attendance would be no longer necessary. Edward felt the truth of this. All that he required was strength; and that he trusted in a few days to obtain.

Oswald was sent over to the cottage, to ascertain how Pablo was going on by himself. He found that everything was correct, and that Pablo, although he felt proud of his responsibility, was very anxious for Humphrey's return, as he found himself very lonely. During Oswald's absence on this day Humphrey never quitted the room; and although the intendant came up several times, he never could find an opportunity of speaking to Edward, which he evidently wished to do.

To enquiries made as to how he was, Edward always complained of great weakness, for a reason which will soon be understood. Several days elapsed, and Edward had often been out of bed during the night, when not likely to be intruded upon, and he now felt himself strong enough to be removed; and his object was to leave the intendant's house without his knowledge, so as to avoid any explanation.

One evening Pablo came over with the horses after it was dark. Oswald put them into the stable, and the morning proving fine and clear, a little before break of day, Edward came softly downstairs with Humphrey, and, mounting the horses, set off for the cottage, without anyone in the intendant's house being aware of their departure.

It must not be supposed, however, that Edward took this step without some degree of consideration as to the feelings of the intendant. On the contrary, he left a letter with Oswald, to be delivered after his departure, in which he thanked the intendant sincerely for all the kindness and compassion he had shown towards him; assured him of his gratitude and kind feelings towards him and his daughter, but said that circumstances had occurred, of which no explanation could be given without great pain to all parties, which rendered it advisable that he should take such an apparently unkind step as to leave without bidding them farewell in person; that he was about to embark immediately for the Continent, to seek his fortune in the wars; and that he wished all prosperity to the family, which would ever have his kindest wishes and remembrances.

"Humphrey," said Edward, after they had ridden about two miles across the forest, and the sun had risen in an unclouded sky, "I feel like an emancipated slave. Thank God! my sickness has cured me of all my complaints, and all I want now is active employment. And now, Humphrey, Chaloner and Grenville are not a little tired of being cooped up in the cottage, and I am anxious as they are to be off. What will you do? Will you join us, or will you remain at the cottage?"

"I have reflected upon it, Edward, and I have come to the determination of remaining at the cottage. You will find it expensive enough to support one where you are going, and you must appear as a Beverley should do. We have plenty of money saved to equip you and maintain you well for a year or so; but after that you may require more. Leave me here. I can make money, now that the farm is well stocked; and I have no doubt I shall be able to send over a trifle every year to support the honour of the family. I also do not wish to leave the country until I know how my sisters get on with the Ladies Conynghame; it is my duty to watch over them. I have made up my mind, so do not attempt to dissuade me."

"I shall not, my dear Humphrey, as I think you have decided properly; but I beg you will not think of laying by money for me—a very little will suffice for my wants."

"Not so, good brother; you must and shall, if I can help you, ruffle it with the best. You know that I require no money, and therefore you must and shall, if you love me, take it all."

"As you will, my dear Humphrey. Now then, let us put our horses to speed, for, if possible, we will tomorrow morning leave the forest."

By this time all search for the fugitives from Worcester had long been over, and there was no difficulty in obtaining the means of embarkation. Early the next morning everything was ready and Edward, Humphrey, Chaloner, Grenville, and Pablo set off for Southampton, one of the horses carrying the little baggage which they had with them. Edward, as we have before mentioned, with the money he had saved, and the store at the cottage, which had been greatly increased, was well supplied with cash; and that evening they embarked, with their horses, in a small sailing vessel, and, with a favourable light wind, arrived at a small port of France on the following day. Humphrey and Pablo returned to the cottage very much out of spirits at the separation.

132

"Oh, Massa Humphrey," said Pablo, as they rode along, "Missey Alice and Missey Edith go away! I wish go with them. Massa Edward go away. I wish go with him. You stay at cottage. I wish stay with you. Pablo cannot be in three places."

"No, Pablo; all you can do is to stay where you can be most useful."

"Yes, I know that. You want me at cottage very much, so I stay at cottage."

"Yes, Pablo, we will stay at the cottage, but we can't do everything now. I think we must give up the dairy, now that my sisters are gone. We will make a large enclosed place, to coax the ponies into during the winter, pick out as many as we think are good, and sell them at Lymington. That will be better than churning butter."

"Yes, I see; plenty of work for Pablo."

"And plenty for me, too, Pablo; but, you know, when the enclosure is once made, it will last for a long while; and we will get the wild cattle into it if we can."

"Yes, I see," said Pablo. "I like that very much; only not like trouble to build place."

"We shan't have much trouble, Pablo; if we fell the trees inside the wood at each side, and let them lie one upon the other, the animals will never break through them."

"That very good idea—save trouble," said Pablo. "And what you do with cows, suppose no make butter?"

"Keep them, and sell their calves; keep them, to entice the wild cattle into the pen."

We must now return to the intendant's house. Oswald delivered the letter to the intendant, who read it with much astonishment.

"Gone! is he actually gone?" said Mr. Heatherstone.

"Yes, sir, before daylight this morning."

"And why was I not informed of it?" said Mr. Heatherstone. "Why have you been a party to this proceeding, being my servant? May I enquire that?"

"I knew Master Edward before I knew you, sir," replied Oswald.

"Then you had better follow him," rejoined the intendant in an angry tone.

"Very well, sir," replied Oswald, who quitted the room.

"Good Heavens! how all my plans have been frustrated!" exclaimed the intendant, when he was alone. He then read the letter over more carefully than he had done at first. " 'Circumstances had occurred of which no explanation could be given by him'. I do not comprehend that—I must see Patience."

Mr. Heatherstone opened the door, and called to his daughter.

"Patience," said Mr. Heatherstone, "Edward has left the house this morning; here is a letter which he has written to me. Read it, and let me know if you can explain some portion of it, which to me is incomprehensible. Sit down and read it attentively."

Patience, who was much agitated, gladly took the seat and perused Edward's letter. When she had done so, she let it drop in her lap, and covered all her face, the tears trickling through her fingers. After a time the intendant said:

"Patience, has anything passed between you and Edward?"

Patience made no reply, but sobbed aloud. She might not have shown so much emotion, but it must be remembered that for the last three weeks since Edward had spoken to her, and during his subsequent illness, she had been very unhappy. The reserve of Humphrey, the expressions he had made use of, his repulse of Clara, and her not having seen anything of Edward during his illness, added to his sudden and unexpected departure without a word to her, had broken her spirits, and she sank beneath the load of sorrow.

The intendant left her to recover herself before he again addressed her. When she had ceased sobbing, her father spoke to her in a very kind voice, begging her that she would not conceal anything from him, as it was most important to him that the real facts should be known.

"Now tell me, my child, what passed between Edward and you?"

"He told me, just before you came up to us that evening, that he loved me."

"And what was your reply?"

"I hardly know, my dear father, what it was that I said. I did not like to be unkind to one who saved my life, and I did not choose to say what I thought, because, because—because he was of low birth; and how could I give encouragement to the son of a forester without your permission?"

"Then you rejected him?"

"I suppose I did, or that he considered that I did so. He had a secret of importance that he would have confided to me, had you not interrupted us."

"And now, Patience, I must request you to answer me one question candidly. I do not blame you for your conduct, which was correct under the circumstances. I also had a secret which I perhaps ought to have confided; but I did consider that the confidence and paternal kindness with which I treated Edward would have been sufficient to point out to you that I could not have been very averse to a union—indeed, the freedom of communication which I allowed between you must have told you so; but your sense of duty and propriety has made you act as you ought to have done, I grant, although contrary to my real wishes."

"Your wishes, my father?" said Patience.

"Yes, my wishes; there is nothing that I so ardently desired as a union between you and Edward; but I wished you to love him for his own merits."

"I have done so, father," replied Patience, sobbing again, "although I did not tell him so."

The intendant remained silent for some time, and then said:

"There is no cause for further concealment, Patience; I have only to regret that I was not more explicit sooner. I have long suspected, and have since been satisfied, that Edward Armitage is Edward Beverley, who, with his brother and sisters, was supposed to have been burnt to death at Arnwood."

Patience removed her handkerchief from her face, and looked at her father with astonishment.

"I tell you that I had a strong suspicion of it, my dear child, first from the noble appearance, which no forest garb could disguise; but what gave me further conviction was, that when at Lymington I happened to fall in with one Benjamin, who had been a servant at Arnwood, and interrogated him closely. He really believed that the children were burnt; it is true that I asked him particularly relative to the appearance of the children—how many were boys and how many were girls, their ages, etc.; but the strongest proof was, that the names of the four children corresponded with the names of the children of the Forest, as well as their ages, and I went to the church register and extracted them. Now this was almost amounting to proof; for it was not likely that four children in the forest cottage should have the same ages and names as those of Arnwood. After I had ascertained this point, I engaged Edward, as you know, wishing to secure him; for I was once acquainted with his father, and at all events well acquainted with the Colonel's merits. You remained in the house together, and it was with pleasure that I watched the intimacy between you; and then I exerted myself to get Arnwood restored to him. I could not ask it for him, but I prevented it being given to any other by laying claim to it myself. Had Edward remained with us, all might have succeeded as I wished; but he would join in the unfortunate insurrection, and I knew it was useless to prevent him, so I let him go. I found that he took the name of Beverley during the time he was with the king's army, and when I was last in town I was told so by the commissioners, who wondered where he had come from; but the effect was that it was now useless for me to request the estate for him, as I had wished to do—his having served in the royal army rendered it impossible. I therefore claimed it for myself, and succeeded. I had made up my mind that he was attached to you, and you were equally so to him; and as soon as I had the grant sent down, which was on the evening he addressed you, I made known to him that the property was given to me; and I added, on some dry questions being put to me by him relative to the possibility of there being still existing an heir to the estate, that there was no chance of that, and that you would be the mistress of Arnwood. I threw it out as a hint to him, fancying that, as far as you were concerned, all would go well, and that I would explain to him my knowledge of who he was after he had made known his regard for you."

"Yes, I see it all now," replied Patience; "in one hour he is rejected by me, and in the next he is told that I have obtained possession of his property. No wonder that he is indignant, and looks upon us with scorn. And now he has left us: we have driven him into danger, and may never see him again. Oh, father! I am very, very miserable!"

"We must hope for the best, Patience. It is true that he has gone to the wars, but it does not therefore follow that he is to be killed. You are both very young—much too young to marry—and all may be explained. I must see Humphrey, and be candid with him.".

"But Alice and Edith, where are they gone, father?"

"That I can inform you. I have a letter from Langton on the subject, for I begged him to find out. He says that there are two young ladies of the name of Beverley, who have been placed under the charge of his friends, the Ladies Conynghame, who are aunts to Major Chaloner, who has been for some time concealed in the forest. But I have letters to write, my dear Patience. Tomorrow I will ride over to the cottage to see Humphrey Beverley."

The intendant kissed his daughter, and she left the room.

Poor Patience! she was glad to be left to herself, and think over this strange communication. For many days she had felt how fond she had been of Edward, much more so than she had believed to be. "And now," she thought, "if he really loves me and hears my father's explanation, he will come back again." By degrees she recovered her serenity, and employed herself in her quiet domestic duties.

Mr. Heatherstone rode over to the cottage the next day, where he found Humphrey busily employed as usual; and, what was very unusual, extremely grave. It was not a pleasant task for Mr. Heatherstone to have to explain his conduct to so very young a man as Humphrey; but he felt that he could not be comfortable until the evil impression against him was removed, and he knew that Humphrey had a great deal of sterling good sense. His reception was cool; but when the explanation was made, Humphrey was more than satisfied, as it showed that the intendant had been their best friend, and that it was from a delicacy on the part of Patience, rather than from any other cause, that the misunderstanding had occurred. Humphrey enquired if he had permission to communicate the substance of their conversation to his brother, and Mr. Heatherstone stated that such was his wish and intention when he confided it to Humphrey. It is hardly necessary to say that Humphrey took the earliest opportunity of writing to Edward at the direction which Chaloner had left him.

CHAPTER 26

BUT WE must follow Edward for a time. On his arrival at Paris he was kindly received by King Charles, who promised to assist his views in joining the army.

"You have to choose between two generals, both great in the art of war—Condé and Turenne; I have no doubt that they will be opposed to each other soon—that will be the better for you, as you will learn tactics from such great players."

"Which would your Majesty recommend me to follow?" enquired Edward.

"Condé is my favourite, and he will soon be opposed to this truculent and dishonest court. I will give you letters to Condé and recollect that whatever general you take service under, you will follow him without pretending to calculate how far his movements may be right or wrong—that is not your affair. Condé is now just released from Vincennes; but, depend upon it, he will be in arms very soon."

As soon as he was furnished with the necessary credentials from the king, Edward presented himself at the leveé of the Prince of Condé.

"You are here highly spoken of," said the prince, "for so young a man. So you were at the affair at Worcester? We will retain you, for your services will be wanted by and by. Can you procure any of your countrymen?"

"I know but of two that I can recommend from personal knowledge; but those two I can venture to pledge myself for."

"Bring me the officers tomorrow at this hour, Monsieur Beverley—*au revoir.*"

Edward went to Chaloner and Grenville, who were delighted with the intelligence which he brought them. The next day they were at the prince's leveé, and introduced by Edward.

"I am fortunate, gentlemen," said the prince, "in securing the services of such fine young men. You will oblige me by enlisting as many of your countrymen as you may consider likely to do good service, and then follow me to Guienne, to which province I am now about to depart. Be pleased to put yourself into communication with the parties named in this paper, and after my absence you will receive from them every assistance and necessary supplies which may be required."

A month after this interview Condé, who had been joined by a great number of nobles, and had been reinforced by troops from Spain, set up the standard of revolt. Edward and his friends joined them, with about three hundred English and Scotchmen, whom they had enlisted; and very soon afterwards Condé obtained the victory at Blenan, and in April, 1652, advanced to Paris.

Turenne, who had taken the command of the French army, followed him, and a severe action was fought in the streets of the suburb D'Antoine, in which neither party had the advantage. But eventually Condé was beaten back by the superior forces of Turenne; and not receiving the assistance he expected from the Spaniards, he fell back to the frontiers of Champagne.

Previous to his departure from Paris. Edward had received Humphrey's letter, explaining away the intendant's conduct; and the contents removed a heavy load from Edward's mind; but he now thought of nothing but war, and although he cherished the idea of Patience Heatherstone, he was resolved to follow the fortunes of the prince as long as he could. He wrote a letter to the intendant, thanking him for his kind feelings and intentions towards him, and he trusted that he might one day have the pleasure of seeing him again. He did not, however, think it advisable to mention the name of his daughter, except in enquiring after her health, and sending his respects. "It may be years before I see her again," thought Edward, "and who knows what may happen?"

The Prince of Condé now had the command of the Spanish forces in the Netherlands; and Edward, with his friends, followed his fortunes and gained his good will.

Time flew on, and in the year 1654 the court of France concluded an alliance with Cromwell, and expelled King Charles from the French frontiers. The war was still carried on in the Netherlands. Turenne bore down Condé who had gained every campaign; and the court of Spain, wearied with reverses, made overtures of peace, which were gladly accepted by the French.

During these wars Cromwell had been named Protector, and had shortly afterwards died.

Edward, who but rarely heard from Humphrey, was now anxious to quit the army and go to the king, who was in Spain.

After the peace and the pardon of Condé by the French king the armies were disbanded, and the three adventurers were free. They took their leave of the prince, and then hastened to King Charles, who had left Spain and come to the Low Countries. At the time of their joining the king, Richard, the son of Cromwell, who had been nominated Protector, had resigned, and everything was ready for the Restoration.

On the 15th May, 1660, the news arrived that Charles had been proclaimed king on the 8th, and a large body of gentlemen went to invite him over. The king sailed from Scheveling, was met at Dover by General Monk, and conducted to London, which he entered, amidst the acclamations of the people, on the 29th of the same month.

We may leave the reader to suppose that Edward, Chaloner, and Grenville were among the most favoured of those in his train. As the procession moved slowly along the Strand, through a countless multitude, the windows of all the houses were filled with well-dressed ladies. Chaloner, Edward, and Grenville, who rode side by side, as gentlemen-in-waiting, were certainly the most distinguished among the king's retinue.

"Look, Edward," said Chaloner, "at those two lovely girls at yon window. Do you recognize them?"

"Indeed, I do not."

"Why, thou insensible and unnatural animal! they are thy sisters, Alice and Edith: and do you not recognize behind them my good aunts Conynghame?"

"It is so, I believe," replied Edward. "Yes, now that Edith smiles I'm sure it is they."

"Yes," replied Grenville, "there can be no doubt of that; but will they, think you, recognize us?"

"We shall see," replied Edward, as they now approached within a few yards of the window.

"Is it possible," thought Edward, "that these can be the two girls in russet gowns that I left at the cottage? And yet it must be. Well, Chaloner, to all appearance, your good aunts have done justice to their charge."

"Nature has done more, Edward. I never thought that they would have grown into such lovely girls as they have, although I always thought that they were handsome."

As they passed, Edward caught the eye of Edith, and smiled.

"Alice, that's Edward!" said Edith, so loud as to be heard by the king, and all near him.

Alice and Edith rose and waved their handkerchiefs, but they were obliged to cease, and put them to their eyes.

"Are those your sisters, Edward?" said the king.

"They are, your Majesty."

The king rose in his stirrups, and made a low obeisance to the window where they were standing.

"We shall have some court beauties, Beverley," said the king, looking at him over his shoulder.

As soon as the ceremonies were over, Edward and his two friends went to the house in which resided the Ladies Conynghame and his sisters.

We pass over the joy of this meeting after so many years' absence, and the pleasure which it gave to Edward to find his sisters grown such accomplished and elegant young women. That his two friends were warmly received we hardly need say.

"Now, Edward, who do you think was here today—the reigning belle, and the toast of all the gentlemen?"

"Indeed! I must be careful of my heart. Dear Edith who is she?"

"No less than one with whom you were formerly well acquainted, Edward—Patience Heatherstone."

"Patience Heatherstone," cried Edward, "the toast of all London?"

"Yes; and deservedly so, I can assure you; but she is as good as she is handsome, and, moreover, treats all the gay gallants with perfect indifference. She is staying with her uncle, Sir Ashley Cooper; and her father is also in town, for he called here with her today."

"When did you hear from Humphrey, Edith?"

"A few days back. He has left the cottage now, altogether."

"Indeed! Where does he reside then?"

"At Arnwood. The house has been rebuilt, and I understand is a very princely mansion. Humphrey has charge of it until it is ascertained to whom it is to belong."

"It belongs to Mr. Heatherstone, does it not?" replied Edward.

"How can you say so, Edward! You received Humphrey's letters a long while ago."

"Yes, I did; but let us not talk about it any more, my dear Edith. I am in great perplexity."

"Nay, dear brother, let us talk about it," said Alice, who had come up and overheard the latter portion of the conversation. "What is your perplexity?"

"Well," replied Edward, "since it is to be so, let us sit down and talk over the matter. I acknowledge the kindness of Mr. Heatherstone, and feel that all he asserted to Humphrey is true; still I do not like that I should be indebted to him for a property which is mine, and that he has no right to give. Nay, much as I admire, and I may say, fond as I am (for time had not effaced the feeling) of his daughter, it still appears to me that, although not said, it is expected that she is to be included in the transfer; and I will accept no wife on such conditions."

"That is to say, because all you wish for, your property and a woman you love, are offered you in one lot, you will not accept them; they must be divided, and handed over to you in two!" said Alice, smiling.

"You mistake, dearest; I am not so foolish; but I have a certain pride, which you cannot blame. Accepting the property from Mr. Heatherstone is receiving a favour, were it given as a marriage portion with his daughter. Now, why should I accept as a favour what I can claim as a right? It is my intention to appeal to the king and demand the restoration of my property. He cannot refuse it."

"Put not your trust in princes, brother," replied Alice. "I doubt if the king, or his council, will consider it advisable to make so many discontented as to restore property which has been so long held by others, and by so doing create a host of enemies. Recollect also that Mr. Heatherstone and his brother-in-law, Sir Ashley Cooper, have done the king much more service than you ever have, or can do. Besides, merely for what may be called a point of honour, for it is no more, in what an unpleasant situation will you put his Majesty! At all events, Edward, recollect you do not know what are the intentions of Mr. Heatherstone; wait and see what he proffers first."

"But, my dear sister, it appears to me that his intentions are evident. Why has he built Arnwood? He is not going to surrender my property, and make me a present of the house."

"The reason for rebuilding the mansion was good. You were at the wars; it was possible that you might, or that you might not return. He said this to Humphrey, who has all along been acting as his factotum in the business; and recollect, at the time that Mr. Heatherstone commenced the rebuilding of the mansion, what prospect was there of the restoration of the king, or of your ever being in a position to apply for the restoration of your property? I believe, however, that Humphrey knows more of Mr. Heatherstone's intentions than he has made known to us; and I therefore say again, my dear Edward, make no application till you ascertain what Mr. Heatherstone's intentions may be."

"Your advice is good, my dear Alice, and I will be guided by it," replied Edward.

"And now let me give you some advice for your friends, Masters Chaloner and Grenville. That much of their property has been taken away and put into other hands I know; and probably they expect it will be restored, upon their application to the king. Those who hold the property think so too, and so far it is fortunate. Now, from wiser heads than mine, I have been told that these applications will not be acceded to, as is supposed; but, at the same time, if they were to meet the parties, and close with them at once, before the king's intentions are known, they would recover their property at a third or a quarter of the value. Now is their time: even a few day's delay may make a difference. Impress that upon them, my dear Edward, and let them, if possible, be off to their estates tomorrow and make the arrangements."

"That is advice which must be followed," replied Edward. "We must go now, and I will not fail to communicate it to them this very night."

We may as well here inform the reader that the advice was immediately acted upon, and that Chaloner and Grenville recovered all their estates at about five years' purchase.

Edward remained at court several days. He had written to Humphrey, and had dispatched a messenger with the letter, but the messenger had not yet returned. On the following day a drawing-room was to be held, and Edward's sisters were to be presented. Edward was standing, with many others of the suite, behind the chair of the king, amusing himself with the presentations as they took place, and waiting for the arrival of his sisters, when his eyes caught, advancing towards the king, Mr. Heatherstone, who led his daughter Patience. That they had not perceived him was evident; indeed her eyes were not raised once, from the natural timidity felt by a young woman in the presence of royalty. Edward half concealed himself behind one of his companions that he might gaze upon her without reserve. She was indeed a lovely young person, but little altered, except having grown taller and more rounded and perfect in her figure. There was the same pensive, sweet expression in her face, which had altered little; but the beautiful rounded arms, the symmetrical fall of the shoulders, and the proportion of the whole figure, was a surprise to him; and Edward in his own mind, agreed that she might well be the reigning toast of the day.

Mr. Heatherstone advanced and made his obeisance, and then his daughter was led forward, and introduced by a lady unknown to Edward. After he had saluted her, the king said, loud enough for Edward to hear:

"My obligations to your father are great. I trust that the daughter will often grace our court."

Patience made no reply, but passed on; and, soon afterwards, Edward lost sight of her in the crowd.

If there ever had been any check to Edward's feelings towards Patience, the sight of her so resplendent in beauty acted upon him like magic; and he was uneasy till the ceremony was over, and he was enabled to go to his sisters.

When he entered the room, he found himself in the arms of Humphrey, who had arrived with the messenger. After the greetings were over, Edward said:

"Alice, I have seen Patience, and I fear I must surrender at discretion. Mr. Heatherstone may make his own terms; I must waive all pride rather than lose her. I thought that I had more control over myself; but I have seen her, and feel that my future happiness depends upon obtaining her as a wife. Let her father but give me her, and Arnwood will be but a trifle in addition!"

"With respect to the conditions upon which you are to possess Arnwood," said Humphrey, "I can inform you what they are. They are wholly unshackled, further than that you are to repay by instalments the money expended in the building of the house. This I am empowered to state to you, and I think you will allow that Mr. Heatherstone has fully acted up to what he stated were his views when he first obtained a grant of the property."

"He has indeed," replied Edward.

"As for his daughter, Edward, you have yet to 'win her and wear her', as the saying is. Her father will resign the property to you as yours by right; but you have no property in his daughter, and I suspect that she will not be quite so easily handed over to you."

"But why should you say so, Humphrey? Have we not been attached from our youth?"

"Yes, it was a youthful passion, I grant; but recollect nothing came of it, and years have passed away. It is now seven years since you quitted the forest, and in your letters to Mr. Heatherstone you made no remark upon what has passed between you and Patience. Since that, you have never corresponded or sent any messages; and you can hardly expect that a girl, from the age of seventeen to twenty-four, will cherish the image of one who had treated her with indifference. That is my view of the matter, Edward."

"And it may be true," replied Edward mournfully.

"Well, my view is different," replied Edith. "You know, Humphrey, how many offers Patience Heatherstone has had, and has every day, I may say. Why has she refused them all? In my opinion, because she has been constant to a proud brother of mine, who does not deserve her."

"It may be so, Edith," replied Humphrey. "Women are riddles; I only argued upon the common sense of the thing."

"Much you know about women," replied Edith. "You do not meet many in the New Forest."

"Very true, my dear sister; perhaps that is the reason that the New Forest has had such charms for me."

"After that speech, sir, the sooner you get back again the better!"

retorted Edith. But Edward made a sign to Humphrey and they beat a retreat.

"Have you seen the intendant, Humphrey?"

"No; I was about to call on him, but wanted to see you first."

"I will go with you. I have not done him justice," replied Edward, "and yet I hardly know how to explain to him——"

"Say nothing, but meet him cordially; that will be explanation sufficient."

"I shall meet him as one whom I shall always revere, and feel that I owe a deep debt of gratitude. What must he think of my not having called upon him?"

"Nothing. You hold a place at court. You may not have known that he was in London, as you have never met him. Tell him that I have just made known to you his noble and disinterested conduct."

"You are right—I will. I fear, however, Humphrey, that you are right, and Edith wrong, as regards his daughter."

"Nay, Edward, recollect that I have, as Edith observed, passed my life in the woods."

Edward was most kindly received by Mr. Heatherstone. Edward, on Mr. Heatherstone repeating to him his intentions relative to Arnwood, expressed his sense of that gentleman's conduct, simply adding:

"You may think me impetuous, sir; but I trust you will believe me grateful."

Patience coloured up and trembled when Edward first saw her. Edward did not refer to the past for some time after they had renewed their acquaintance. He wooed her again, and won her. Then all was explained.

About a year after the Restoration there was a fete at Hampton Court, given in honour of three marriages taking place—Edward Beverley to Patience Heatherstone, Chaloner to Alice, and Grenville to Edith; and, as his Majesty himself said as he gave away the brides, "Could loyalty be better rewarded?"

But our young readers will not be content if they do not hear some particulars about the other personages who have appeared in our little history. Humphrey must take the first place. His love of farming continued. Edward gave him a large farm, rent free; and in a few years Humphrey saved up sufficient to purchase a property for himself. He then married Clara Ratcliffe, who about two years before the Restoration, was claimed by an elderly relation, whose infirm state of health did not permit him to quit the house. He left his property to Clara, about a year after her marriage to Humphrey. The cottage in the New Forest was held by and eventually made over to Pablo, who became a very steady character, and in the course of time married a young girl from Arnwood. Oswald, so soon as Edward came down to Arnwood, gave up his place in the New Forest, and lived entirely with Edward as his steward.

Printed in Germany